SKIN REBELLION

Skin Hunter Book 2

TANIA HUTLEY

S tuck in a worker's shelter in the buried city of Old Triton, Milla dreamed of escaping her dangerous life.

Devastated by the news her best friend Tori was being transferred to another shelter, she stole a stranger's identity band and became Rayne, a participant in the Skin Hunter contest.

A chip was embedded in the base of her skull so she could transfer her consciousness into the body of a biologically engineered clouded leopard. In her Leopard Skin, Milla's senses and abilities were heightened. But when her Skin was wounded, those injuries also appeared on her human body.

One of her competitors, pro gamer Cale, offered to help Milla train for the contest. As they trained together, their feelings for each other grew. So when Cale was kicked out of the contest, Milla was heartbroken.

On the day of the contest, Milla battled her way to the top of the tower. But another competitor, Sentin, threw her off the tower and claimed the winner's prize.

Milla lost both the contest, and her Leopard Skin.

Devastated and badly injured, Milla learned Director Morelle planned to experiment on her. Then Milla made another discovery. Her human body had grown stronger and faster, mimicking the speed and strength of her Leopard Skin. Using her newfound strength, she was able to break out of the Morelle Corporation and flee back to the darkness of Old Triton.

Now all she wants is to save her mother and Tori from Director Morelle, and get her beloved Leopard Skin back...

Chapter One

I was ready to smash a window to get inside the house. Instead, I find one that's unlatched. It's small, high up, and awkward, but I think I can climb up to it.

Digging my fingertips and toes into the rough brick exterior, I scramble up the side of the house. Climbing would be a lot easier if I still had a leopard's body instead of a human one.

At least my human body is stronger and faster than it used to be. The old Milla would never have been able to scale the vertical outside wall of a house, rough brick or not. But even the new, enhanced me is weaker and slower than my leopard was.

In my Leopard Skin, I would have bounded up in an instant. I wouldn't have had to struggle and curse.

Pushing the window open, I squeeze through and drop soundlessly inside. I stifle an exclamation as I land on bare feet that are bruised and cut.

My heart is pounding. I'm not certain the house I've broken into is the right one. In fact, the only thing I *am* sure of is that I have stompers after me, and if they catch

3

me, they'll probably hand me back to Director Morelle so her scientists can cut me open. I need to stay silent and undetected while I figure out who's in the house.

Whoever's here, they must be asleep. The house is quiet.

It's dark in here, but my night vision is a lot better than it used to be. I limp forward, trying to figure out what kind of room I'm in. In Old Triton, people live in shelters or small apartments, so I've never been inside a house like this one. The room I've landed in is huge. There's a couch in the corner facing a switched-off holo, which means this could be a living room. But there are also tables cluttered with electronic equipment. Tangles of wires snake around monitors and into exposed circuit boards. Delicate-looking tools lie among the mess. And is that a robotic head?

Easing forward to see the head better, I accidentally bump my hip against the table. A metal pipe falls off it, striking the floor with a deafening crash.

Shit.

My cat burglar skills could do with a little work.

I wait, breath held and body tense, listening for sounds of anyone waking or moving. All I can hear is the drumming of my own heart. Could the house be empty? Is its owner away somewhere?

I should search the place, and I'd kill for a drink of water after a day spent running and hiding. But I can't walk past the robotic head on the table, because it's facing me, making me feel like I'm being watched. Letting my breath out slowly, I pick it up and study it in the moonlight that comes from the window. Its face is smooth, made from some kind of flexible polymer. Its cybernetic eyes glint, like my old one used to. It gives me the creeps.

But I'm being paranoid. There's no way it could really be watching me. Unless… could those eyes hide a camera?

A harsh voice comes from behind me, making me jump and drop the robot head.

"The police will be here in a minute. Leave now, and you might get away."

The room floods with light. A woman stands in the doorway, her expression grim. Her face looks more lined and care-worn than the last time I saw her, though perhaps that's because I've woken her. I can smell both her fear, and her determination to defend her house and protect what's hers.

My face is still mostly hidden by the T-shirt I tied around my nose and mouth. Moving slowly so as not to scare her any more than I already have, I reach up and tug it off.

"Doctor Gregory," I say. "It's me."

"Rayne?"

Doctor Gregory is dressed in pyjamas and soft slippers, which helps explain why I didn't hear her approach, though my enhanced hearing should still have caught the shushing of slippers on her hard floors. Problem was, I let myself get distracted.

"What are you doing here?" she demands.

Not exactly the welcome I was hoping for.

"You said…" I falter, aware of how badly I've been counting on the doctor's help. "You gave me your address. You said if I needed you, I could come."

If Doctor Gregory's called the police, I need to leave. But I have nowhere else to go.

"What happened to you?" She frowns. "Are you okay? How did you get in? The front door is locked."

I take a step toward her without thinking about my injured feet, and wince. After escaping from the Morelle Corporation wearing only a hospital smock, I found some clothes on a washing line. I'm wearing baggy jeans and a giant T-shirt, and I stole a second one to tie around my face. But I couldn't find any shoes, and running on bare feet has left them raw.

"I came in through the window."

"The window? Why?" Her gaze drops to my feet, and her frown deepens. "You're bleeding. Sit down and tell me what's going on."

"The police are coming?"

She waves me to the couch. "Sit. I'll call them off."

If stompers could burst in at any moment, the last thing I want to do is sit down. But the doctor still looks jumpy, and I can hardly blame her. Obediently, I sink onto the couch in the corner, though I'm coiled like a spring, ready to run if I need to. Even on wounded feet.

She taps the band around her wrist, frowns at its control panel, then looks up at me. "I've cancelled the call and logged it as a false alarm. They were still a few minutes away, so I don't think they'll bother coming to check."

She's too casual about it for my liking, but she has no idea I'm being hunted. She still thinks I'm Rayne.

I have so much to tell her, I don't know where to start. And I'm dreading having to confess I've been lying to her about who I really am.

"Thank you," I say. "And sorry to wake you. I know it's late."

She shakes her head, brushing off my apology. "Before all this madness started, I would have checked what the disruption was before placing an emergency call. But now…" She runs her hand over her face. "I've been on edge. Of course, we all have."

"Madness? What madness has started?"

"You know. The war."

"The *war*?" My throat is dry, and the word comes out

so hoarsely, it makes me cough.

"You don't know?" She looks as shocked by my ignorance as I am. "We're at war with Deiterra." She crosses to a door and goes into her kitchen. "You sound like you need something to drink."

When she comes back with a glass of water, I gulp it down gratefully, then wipe my mouth with the back of my hand. "When did the war start?" I ask. "Have many people been hurt? Any Old Tritoners?"

If war's broken out, Ma and Lily could be in danger. And what about Cale?

"How can you not know about the war?" she asks.

"I was unconscious, and maybe I was out for longer than I thought. How much time has passed since the contest?"

"The Skin Hunter contest? That was, let's see, ten days ago. Saturday before last."

"I was unconscious for *ten days*?" I gape at her, shocked. I had no idea the doctor who tried to run experiments on me had kept me unconscious for that long. No wonder my body has healed after I was so badly injured in the Skin Hunter contest. The doctor must have wanted me whole so she could monitor exactly what was happening when she used my Leopard Skin to wound me again.

"What happened, Rayne?" Doctor Gregory sits next to me on the couch. Her eyes are soft and she's back to being the kind woman I remember. Taking the empty glass from my hand, she sets it on the low table next to the couch.

I swallow. The first thing I should tell her is that I'm not Rayne. But how can I explain the truth without sounding like a criminal? Until I find Cale, Doctor Gregory is the only person who can help me. If she turns her back on me after learning the truth, I'll have nowhere to turn.

"I'll tell you everything," I say, stalling. "But first, will you tell me about the war? I'm worried about my family and friends."

"Before we talk, I should get some healing spray and bandages for your feet." She starts to rise again, but I put a hand on her arm to stop her.

"My feet can wait. Please. I need to know."

She sinks back down. "Well, shortly after the contest, there was a series of explosions. Deiterran terrorists hit police stations and military targets. A co-ordinated attack. They killed thousands of soldiers, and destroyed almost our entire stockpile of weapons."

"What?" It comes out as a breathless gasp. Could there really have been so much chaos and death while I slept?

"I'm sorry. I know what a shock—"

"Did civilians die?" I interrupt. "My mother and my best friend are both in Old Triton, and my brother's in an academy."

"It was mostly policemen and soldiers killed. But they also blew up a portion of the wall, and collapsed a section of New Triton. An office building came down." She picks at the seam of her trousers, her hands restless. "People are saying the war started because the Deiterrans think Skin technology violates the peace treaty. If that's true, the researchers working on the project are at least partly responsible for the attacks. I share that blame." She looks stricken at the idea. No wonder her hair is grayer than last time I saw her, and the lines around her eyes are more deeply scored.

"I'm sure it's not your fault. But don't we know why the Deiterrans attacked? Haven't they told us?"

She shakes her head. "Deiterra denied responsibility. The Deiterran ambassador swore it wasn't them. For the first few days, everyone thought The Fist had done it. But

President Trask found proof the ambassador was lying, and a few days ago, he officially declared war. Here, I'll show you what the Deiterrans did to the wall."

She taps her band, and the holo in the corner of the room flicks into life. This is the first time I've watched a hologram since my cybernetic eye was replaced with a real one, and I'm amazed at how easy it is to focus on it. It's showing footage of smoking rubble, the 3-D projection so real I can almost smell the smoke.

"That's the hole in the wall," says Doctor Gregory. "The few soldiers we have left are guarding it. They're expecting the Deiterran army to come through and attack us."

At first I can't tell how big the rocks are, then I spot a man in army fatigues standing at the base of one of them. He looks like a fly guarding an apartment complex. The wall is immense, at least a hundred stories tall, and a mountain of rock has spilled from it. There's so much rubble it looks like it's blocked any gap in the structure. Did the collapsed office building fall on top of it? I can see some rubble with sharp angles through the smoke, like destroyed rooms.

"The Deiterrans managed to blast all the way through," says the doctor. "Can you imagine how much explosive material that would take? The earth shook all the way to the other end of Triton."

The wall was built almost five decades ago, after the ecological collapse and food wars. Since then, there have only been rumors and speculation as to what Deiterra might be like. As far as I know, the Deiterran ambassador and Sentin are the only ones who've been to the other side, and they've always refused to talk about it.

"What about the automated attack systems built into the wall?" I ask. The wall is supposed to be able to destroy anything that's a threat. Drones can't go anywhere near it, for fear of getting shot down by the old anti-aircraft weapons installed when we still had planes and places to fly to.

She shakes her head. "I don't know."

I peer through the dust and debris, trying to get a glimpse through the gap in the wall, to see into Deiterra. All I see is fallen rock.

The doctor touches her band again, and the holo changes to show Director Morelle. She's standing in what I recognize as the lobby of the Morelle Corporation scraper, with the Triton flag hanging behind her. The sight gives me the chills. Not just because the director looks real enough to step out of the holo, but because I'm looking inside the building I escaped from only hours ago. In that building, a red-haired doctor was about to cut my Leopard Skin to pieces, just to see the effect it would have on my human body.

And somewhere in that building, my leopard is still waiting for me.

"No more Triton lives need be lost," Morelle is saying. "My gift to Triton is the means to safely defend our great cities. To end this war swiftly and decisively, ensuring no innocents suffer any more harm."

The camera pulls back a little to show President Trask standing by the director's side, nodding as she speaks.

"In a series of cowardly attacks, the Deiterrans have brutally and callously slaughtered thousands of brave soldiers. But President Trask has accepted my offer to use Skins to protect Triton. Manufacturing has begun and the first Skins have already rolled off the production line. Soon, we'll be defended by an unstoppable force."

I draw in a sharp breath. "She's going to fight Deiterra with Skins?" When I turn to Doctor Gregory, she nods.

"I'm worried too," she says, pinching the skin on her throat. "I don't know if they've determined the cause of the somatoform injuries you displayed on your human body when your Skin was injured. They must prevent it from happening again, but I'm not sure the Skins have had enough testing…"

My attention switches back to the director, and I tune out the doctor's concerns, which sound like the same ones that got her kicked out of the Morelle Corporation.

"We're training volunteers to use the Skins," Director Morelle says. "They'll operate them from a secret location, where they can come to no harm." The view changes, panning across a giant, windowless room. Pods are arranged in rows across the floor. The pods are smaller and less elaborate-looking than the one I used when I transferred into my leopard, and when the camera zooms back I can't believe how many of them there are.

The director's building an army. Hundreds of pods means hundreds of Skins.

The camera focuses on a small group in army fatigues marching into the room. They're all young, in their mid-teens, and must be Old Tritoners because they obviously haven't been tweaked. Some have acne, most are pale, and one girl has a large mole on her cheek that would have been removed from any New Tritoner at birth.

Surely they're too young to be soldiers? They're marching in perfect formation, their arms all swing to exactly the same height, and their steps are precisely the same. They must have been training for some time.

When I picture hundreds of them transferring into Leopard Skins and padding out to war in perfect unison, my stomach churns. Is it smart to give so many kids that much strength and power?

The young soldiers each lie down on a pod. The

camera zooms in on one of the boys closing his eyes. Then it cuts back to the director giving her speech in the lobby of the Morelle scraper.

"On Thursday, our president will join me for a public event in Central Square," she says. "You'll get to see the new Skins the soldiers will use to defend our glorious city."

Morelle nods at President Trask, and the President nods back, his expression serious. He has shiny black hair that's full on top and cut short on the sides. He's wearing a cream jacket in contrast to the director's severe navy one, but they both have bronzed skin that's as smooth as glass, and they both look ageless.

"With Director Morelle's help, Triton has nothing to fear," President Trask gazes out from the holo with his brow slightly creased in a well-practised, fatherly way. "And with the protection our new Skin Soldiers will provide, we'll quickly repel any and all Deiterran forces, and ensure they never threaten us again." His job seemingly done, he looks back at the director.

"Finally, I'd like to make a comment about the winner of the Skin Hunter contest," says Morelle.

The camera pulls back a little more to show the Reptile Skin standing upright on the director's other side, with its knees bent. Its jewel-green scales glow in the lobby's bright light, and though it's impossible to read any emotion on its regal face, its large eyes gleam with intelligence.

Sentin.

I lean forward, wishing I could talk to him. He warned me about the director and said he wanted to stop her. What's he doing by the director's side?

Is he friend or foe?

"Sentin is half Deiterran, but has lived in Triton most of his life," says Morelle. "He has become an invaluable source of intelligence, and proven his loyalty. Further questions about his allegiance will not be tolerated."

"Have you seen enough?" Doctor Gregory switches off the holo. "Things have been quiet since this clip aired. Deiterra hasn't responded. I'm not sure if that's a good sign or a bad one, but I think we're all on edge, waiting for something to happen."

I frown, still disturbed by that huge room with hundreds of pods. "Why is the president accepting hundreds of Skin Soldiers from Director Morelle? He didn't want her to manufacture the Skins at all."

"He changed his mind, now we need them for protection." She sighs, still pinching worriedly at her throat. "Perhaps it's the right thing to do. Director Morelle is the only one who can defend Triton, even if I still have concerns about the Skin technology. There's no doubt it needs more testing, but in the face of the threat we face from Deiterra, Skins could be the only viable solution."

I stare at her. Can't she tell that everything Director Morelle says is a bare-faced lie?

While I was unconscious, the director went from only reluctantly being allowed to run a contest with five prototype Skins, to manufacturing an entire *Skin Army*? And the president is standing by while she announces her army. No, more than standing by. He's thanking her for it.

Seems like Sentin was right, because the vague hints he let slip are coming true in the worst possible way. What did he tell me? That the contest was just a diversion?

"Sentin warned me the director would start a war," I say.

Doctor Gregory blinks at me for a moment, then frowns. "That's absurd. The director didn't start the war."

"But what if she did?"

Chapter Two

Bless her, Doctor Gregory fixes me something to eat when I tell her how hungry I am. I fall on the food, trying not to shovel it in too fast. It's good food, too. Much better than the tasteless gunk the machines spit out in the shelters.

The doctor obviously wants to ask more questions. She impatiently watches me eat, sitting opposite me and sipping a cup of hot tea. She cleared the clutter off one of her worktables, moving all her electronic gadgets to the other table so we could use it as a dining table. I guess just because Director Morelle kicked her out, she hasn't stopped being a scientist.

I've barely swallowed my last mouthful before she asks, "Are you ready to tell me why you're here in the middle of the night, and why you knew nothing about the war?"

I wipe my palms down the legs of my jeans and drag in a breath. It's time to start revealing my secrets.

"I need to show you something first," I say, mostly to delay the moment I have to confess to lying. "Using the Leopard Skin has changed me."

"Changed you how?"

"My eyesight and my sense of smell are sharper. And I'm stronger and faster than I used to be."

She frowns, her gaze flicking down to my hands and back up again. "Improved eyesight is to be expected when you have a new eye implanted. Your vision must have previously been sub-par, thanks to your old cybernetic eye. And the cybernetics could have been affecting your olfactory system."

I get up, and walk carefully on my damaged feet to pick up a long metal bar that's lying on her other cluttered worktable amongst the mess of electronic equipment. The bar is only a little thicker than one of my fingers, but whatever metal it's made of is strong. I show it to Doctor Gregory. "Do you mind if I bend this?"

"Bend it? I suppose not, but how do you propose to…?" She gapes as I grip the ends of the bar and force them together, my muscles straining as I slowly lever the bar into a U shape. I remember Brugan doing the same thing to a weight lifting bar when he was in his Devil Bear Skin.

"How did you do that?" Doctor Gregory stands to take the bar from my hands. The muscles in her neck stand out as she struggles with it, testing whether she can get it to bend. Finally she gives up and puts it back on the table.

"You believe your strength increased as a direct result of using the Leopard Skin?" she asks.

"That's right."

"The Skin transferral technology was in development for many years, and no test subject has ever displayed symptoms like yours."

I shrug. "And nobody else had their human body injured when their Skin was hurt, but you watched it happen to me."

"That's true." She frowns, rubbing her chin. "The director must be told about this. The changes to your physiology are far more extreme than we ever considered and transferrals must be stopped until we know more. Considering the circumstances, perhaps she'll allow me to help with the study. I'll need to contact her, to let her know—"

"Director Morelle already knows," I interrupt. And it must be true. By now Morelle must have seen the restraints I tore free from when I escaped from her lab.

"She knows?" The doctor paces across the room, clearly upset. "I developed significant parts of the transferral technology. If a subject's physiology is affected, *I'm* responsible. Perhaps the director doesn't understand the implications—"

"You're not responsible. The director's the one in charge." I hobble back to the chair and sink down, glad to be off my feet again. "Besides, I'm grateful for the change. Without the extra strength my Skin gave me, I'd probably be dead by now. Experimented on and dissected in the director's lab."

"*Dissected?*" She spins to face me, her brow furrowed. She's probably wondering if I'm a liar or just plain crazy.

My heart sinks. I've barely begun to tell her what's really been going on. And if she doesn't believe me now, how's she going to feel when I tell her I'm not Rayne?

"The director's not the person you think she is." I say. "She's been scheming and lying the entire time. Sentin said he only entered the contest to keep an eye on her. He seems to know what she's up to."

"In that case, I'd like to speak with Sentin."

"So would I. But he's with the director, and she might be monitoring his calls. We should talk to Cale instead."

"Cale? Why?"

I hesitate, trying to think of a good reason. I can't

exactly admit it's because I miss him, and need to tell him how sorry I am for pushing him away.

"He's affected by this too," I say instead. "He should know what's happening. Would you call him for me?"

"You can't call him yourself?"

"My band doesn't work." When she looks puzzled, I add, "There's a lot more I need to explain, but it'll be easier if I tell you both at once."

"But we can't call him now. It's the middle of the night."

I think of all the midnight training sessions Cale and I had, and manage a twisted smile. "Believe it or not, that's our best time."

She still looks uncertain. And tired. She's in rumpled pyjamas, and her wispy gray hair floats in a halo around her face rather than being tied back in her normal bun. My heart goes out to her. She never asked for any of this, yet she's taken me in and fed me when I had nowhere else to go. I want to tell her how bad I feel for waking her, but she's already calling Cale.

It takes a while for Cale to answer, and when his hologram appears above the doctor's band, he's tousle-haired and rubbing his eyes. His hair looks a little longer than last time I saw him, and his square jaw is dark with stubble.

I hadn't forgotten how handsome he is, but it hits me all over again, like I'm seeing him for the first time. Even half asleep, he's handsome enough to suck the air from my lungs.

He's wearing a faded gray T-shirt that looks like the one he had on when I last saw him. What wouldn't I give to be able to go back to that day, to tell him how much he means to me instead of letting him walk away?

"Hello?" Cale's voice is gruff with sleep.

My heart is thudding, but at the same time, my throat

constricts. I was afraid I'd never get to see him or speak to him again, and there are so many things I want to say that I'm not sure where to start.

"I'm sorry to wake you," Doctor Gregory says. "I'm with Rayne. She thought it would be okay to call this late, considering everything that's been going on." Then she glances at me. "I'm going to expand the range so Cale can see you, okay?"

Cale's soft brown eyes turn suddenly hard. "That's not Rayne," he says in a flat, hostile tone.

I drag in a loud breath, my gaze flicking between him and the doctor.

She gives him a puzzled frown. "What do you mean?"

"Her face and name were broadcast on b-Net. She's Milla Scully, and she's wanted for murder. She killed the real Rayne and took her place. You shouldn't believe anything she tells you."

Chapter Three

The doctor eyes widen and she gets slowly up from the table, staring at me as though I'm about to bite her.

I stand up too, meeting the doctor's gaze as my stomach turns itself inside out. "I didn't kill Rayne. I swear I didn't."

"Why should we believe you?" Cale's tone gets even harsher. "You've already proven you're a liar."

"Please, just hear me out. It's true, my name's Milla and I took Rayne's place. But I didn't hurt her, and I hated lying to you both. I wanted to tell you the truth, but I was afraid of being kicked out of the contest."

"Why would you take Rayne's place?" Doctor Gregory asks in a breathy voice. She isn't moving, but the muscles in her legs are tense, and her scent gives her away. She's preparing to move quickly. Maybe to shut herself in the bathroom, to lock herself away so she can call the police again.

I put my hand out to her, speaking fast. "Rayne and her boyfriend came into my shelter one night. I had no idea who she was, I never even spoke to her. But I saw they were being targeted. You can't just walk in to a shelter wearing clothes like they were and expect to walk out again." The words tumble out quickly. Though I'm terrified they won't believe me, it's a relief to finally admit the truth. "Two men attacked Rayne. They stabbed her. I couldn't do anything to stop it, though I tried. I swear I tried. Somehow, I was left holding Rayne up while she died. Her blood was on my hands and the announcement of her being chosen for the contest was on the holo."

Doctor Gregory still looks wary, and Cale is silent, his lips pressed into a line so hard that looking at him breaks my heart.

"I stole her band," I admit. "It was a split second decision, a crazy thing to do. I regretted it as soon as I'd done it, but it got me into the contest."

"If you didn't kill Rayne, it would be easy to prove." Cale's tone hasn't softened. "The security cameras must have shown who really did it."

"The place was crowded. If the cameras even worked, chances are they wouldn't show anything. That's if anyone cared enough to watch the feed."

"Convenient," he mutters.

"I was arrested. The stompers let me go because there wasn't any evidence. Because I didn't kill anyone." When he doesn't say anything, I add, "You know me, Cale. You've come to know me better than anyone. Do you really think I could kill someone?"

He stares at me in silence, his eyes narrowed. Perhaps he's trying to decide whether to call the stompers and turn me in.

"Listen," I say desperately. "There's more going on than you know. Director Morelle knew I wasn't really Rayne. She called me by my real name, then told me she was keeping my secret because she wanted me to compete."

"I was wondering how you could have deceived the director," says the doctor. "None of this makes sense, but I find it hard to believe she wouldn't have known your real identity. She was strict on security. I doubt anyone could fool her for long." She sounds thoughtful rather than afraid, and her muscles have relaxed a little. Hopefully I'm making progress.

"Director Morelle wanted to study me, to use me as a human guinea pig. She let Cale and I train at night, then tried to run tests to figure out why my human body was wounded when my Leopard Skin was hurt. After the contest, my body was a mess. Her doctor injected me with something to keep me knocked out for days, so I could heal before she started her experiments. That's where I've been all this time. Lying unconscious in a laboratory, waiting for her to cut me up into little pieces."

"You've been in a coma?" Cale asks. Am I just being hopeful, or has a tinge of worry crept into his eyes, softening his anger a little?

"I didn't know the war had started, but I'm sure the director is behind it, pulling the strings. And there's something else." I catch the doctor's gaze. "I think Director Morelle's using a Skin herself. She must have made one in secret. I don't know whether she's using it all the time, but if she is, who knows what she really looks like?"

The doctor frowns, shaking her head. "That's not possible. Realistic humanoid avatars are illegal."

I say nothing, keeping my eyes on hers. After a moment, she sinks back into her chair.

"It's possible," she admits. "I was the lead scientist on the project for years, until she started edging me aside. I couldn't understand why she was pulling me away from my work for other, less important assignments. Like taking care of the contestants. I'm the last person she should have given that job to."

"You must be too honest," I tell her. "Maybe she has other scientists who aren't."

"We shouldn't be talking so openly over the network," says Cale. "It's not secure."

"Will you come over here?" I ask. "We could talk in person."

"How can either of us trust you now?" His anger flares again, his eyes so cold they sear though my chest and deep into my heart. "And what makes you think Doctor Gregory will let you stay in her house when she's just found out you're wanted for murder?"

The doctor blinks several times, her hand resting against her cheek. "Well, I don't know."

I let out a breath, trying not to let my dismay show. Cale's right. Of course the doctor won't want me here after Cale's revelations. "I can find somewhere else to sleep. But would it be okay for me to come back tomorrow so we can talk some more? We're the only people who know what's really going on, and nobody else would understand what I'm talking about."

"What about your injured feet?" asks the doctor. "Do you have anywhere else to go?"

"I'll be fine. Plenty of dark corners in Old Triton I can hole up in." The idea makes my stomach flutter with nerves, but I give her a reassuring smile. Before my Skin changed me, it would have been too dangerous for me to consider sleeping outside. But I'm a lot stronger now, and anyone who decides to bother me will find I'm tougher than I look.

Cale makes a sound like clicking his tongue on the back of his teeth. "You can't sleep rough."

"That's right," agrees the doctor. "If you've nowhere else, you'll have to stay here. May I have your word that you're telling the truth now?"

"I promise I am. In fact, why don't you test my blood?" I offer her my arm, sweeping my gaze over the equipment on her cluttered workbench. "I probably still have the drugs the director gave me in my system. It'll prove I've been knocked out and that part of my story is true."

She shakes her head. "That's not necessary. And I suppose if you intended to murder me, you would have done it by now."

"I've never killed anybody." Why is it that when I say it out loud, it always sounds like a lie?

"I'll drop by first thing in the morning to make sure you're okay," says Cale. For a moment I think he's talking to me, then I realize he means to check on the doctor, probably to make sure I haven't killed her in her sleep. Does he really think so little of me now?

I might deserve his suspicion, but it still makes my heart ache so badly, I have to turn my face away to hide the tears that prickle the backs of my eyes. When we trained together, it was the way Cale trusted me that brought down my barriers. I hate that I've lost that trust.

Since moving to the shelter, there's only been one other person I could really depend on. Tori's my best friend, and means as much to me as Cale does. But she was moved to another factory, and I may never see her again.

Now I've lost Cale too, and it was my own fault for not telling him the truth a lot earlier.

"We'll see you in the morning," agrees Doctor Gregory. She disconnects the call and turns back to me, her expression troubled. "It's late and we could both use some rest," she says. "I'll show you where you can sleep."

I swallow hard, trying to shift the lump in my throat.

"Wait. I know I have no right to ask you for any more favors. You've already done a lot more than most people would. But if I don't speak to Ma, I won't be able to close my eyes. Would you please call her for me? I need to know she's okay."

"Now?" she asks with a sigh. "In the middle of the night?"

"I put my band onto Rayne's body, so the stompers will have told Ma I was dead. It's been weeks, but I'd like to let her know I'm alive."

The doctor blinks. "Of course. She shouldn't continue to believe the worst. But I have no way to give you any privacy."

"That's okay."

When Ma answers, she sounds hoarse and weary. Her hologram forms above the doctor's band, and the image is far clearer than when I used to speak to Ma using my old glitchy band. It's almost like seeing her in person. My chest tightens. She looks every bit as ancient and exhausted as she sounds.

"Ma. It's me." The tears that stung my eyes earlier force their way free and leak down my cheeks.

"Milla? That's you?" Her voice cracks. "Love, is it really you?"

The raw emotion in her face makes my chest feel impossibly tight, like it's going to crush my heart into pieces.

"I'm here, Ma. I'm okay."

"They told me…"

"I know. I can't explain what happened to me, but I want you to know I'm okay."

"Where are you, love?"

"With a friend. How are you? Are you still at the same shelter?"

She's crying too hard to answer for a while, but finally chokes out something that sounds like, "You're really alive?"

"I'm alive." I wipe my eyes on my sleeve. My throat feels raw, like the tears I'm trying to swallow are made of acid. "Everything's fine," I lie.

"What happened? Why did they tell me you were dead?"

"It's a long story, Ma. I'm sorry, I can't tell you right now." I glance at the doctor's tired face. "I can't talk for long, but I wanted to hear your voice and check you were okay."

"I'm okay. I'm working."

"No double shifts?"

"Don't worry about me, love." Another burst of tears, then she sniffs hard. "You're sure you're not hurt? Do you have a job? Which shelter are you in?"

"I'll tell you everything later, Ma."

"I wish I could see you, but my holo app is barely working." She tugs a scrap of fabric out of her pocket and presses it against her nose. "When I got the message about William, I thought I'd lost you both. I was afraid—"

"What message? Did you talk to him?" We haven't been able to contact my little brother for a couple of years, since we accepted an offer to transfer him from the rundown orphanage he hated, to a military academy where he was supposed to be given free schooling.

"It was a recorded message to tell me he's a soldier now. In one of those Skin things."

"He's *what*?" The image of the teenaged soldiers I saw on the holo flashes in front of me, and my stomach turns over. "But he can't be. He's too young."

"Too many of the regular soldiers died in those bomb attacks. The message said he'd volunteered and was now part of the army, but as many times as I call, his band still won't connect. I don't know if they've blocked my number, or if he doesn't want to talk to me." She sobs again. "They'd let him *talk* to me, wouldn't they?"

"I don't know, Ma." My mind is racing. "William went to an academy owned by Director Morelle. That must be where all her volunteers for her army have come from. We thought the academy was some kind of charity, helping get kids out of orphanages. But all this time, she's been training soldiers."

I feel sick. My little brother was always so sweet, it's impossible to imagine him as a soldier forced to kill people. And what kind of Skin will they make him wear? What if he gets hurt in his Skin, and his real body gets wounded too, like me?

"Have you seen the new Skins?" I ask Doctor Gregory. "Do you know what they're like?"

The doctor shakes her head, but Ma answers. "I've been moved to the factory that's making them. Horrible things. And that technology's not safe. I don't want them sucking out his thoughts, putting his brain into one of those things. They didn't even ask me, and I'm his mother. They won't take my calls. Nobody will talk to me, or tell me anything. They won't even say if he's alive or dead."

"I'll see what I can find out, Ma."

"Will you, love?" She sucks in an audible, shuddering breath. "When I thought I'd lost both of you, it just about drove me mad."

"I won't let anything happen to William. I promise, Ma. I'll make sure he's safe. And if Director Morelle's taken him against his will, I'll get him back."

Chapter Four

After having been asleep—unconscious—for so long, I don't know how I could be so exhausted. But incredibly enough, the doctor has an entire second bedroom she doesn't even use, and it's quiet and comfortable. I sleep so soundly that I'm barely up and showered before Cale arrives the next morning.

Doctor Gregory found some clean clothes for me to wear, and I manage to ease a pair of borrowed sneakers over my battered feet. I've been hoping Cale might have forgiven me for lying to him about who I was, but I can tell by the way he barely glances at me that he hasn't.

I want to tell him how much I missed him, but the words die on my lips when I see his expression. His easy smile is gone and his eyes hold a wariness that makes a lump form in my throat.

He doesn't waste any time asking how I am, or making small talk. The doctor invites him to sit and he pulls out one of the chairs around the doctor's cluttered work table and perches on its edge, as though he's ready to spring up and leave at any moment.

"Would you like a drink?" the doctor asks him, going into the kitchen. "Juice? Coffee?"

"Nothing, thanks." And to me, "What makes you think Director Morelle is using a Skin?"

I take one of the other chairs at the table, picking the one closest to him in spite of his hostility, because of the bitter-sweet longing his scent stirs in me. He still smells fresh, like the air in New Triton after it's rained. It reminds me of training with him, and how amazing it felt to race him up the never-wall, and to rest with him after we finally managed to exhaust ourselves. We used to talk about everything.

If only I'd trusted him enough to tell him my secret.

"She was stronger than a person should be. Much stronger than me." I study his hands, resting on the table. He has such long, graceful fingers. They're the hands of a floater, smooth and unscarred.

He snorts. "That doesn't mean anything. She's fine-tuned her muscles with nano technology."

"Her scent is wrong. I didn't notice when we were in the training room, because there were so many other smells. But when she touched me, I knew. I could tell."

The doctor comes out of the kitchen with a glass of juice. She exchanges a glance with Cale, and their doubt is obvious.

"We need to contact Sentin," I say. "He knows what her plans are. He won the contest so he could fight her from the inside."

Doctor Gregory puts the juice down in front of Cale and sits opposite us, shooting him another doubtful look as she settles on her seat. My heart sinks. They seem to agree that I can't be trusted.

I need to get William out of Morelle's army, and get my Leopard Skin back. It'll be more difficult going up against the director without their help, but if I have to do it by myself, I will.

"Director Morelle is showing off the new Skin Soldiers in the city square today, right?" I ask. "Sentin will be there. If I can figure out a way to get close enough, maybe I can talk to him."

"I'm going to the square." Cale still isn't meeting my eyes. "I need to make contact with some friends from the Fist."

"You're still with the Fist?" I blink at him. "Didn't people think they were behind the bombings? Isn't it dangerous to be out in public with them?"

"If anyone knew we were Fist members, we'd already have been arrested. Besides, the Fist had nothing to do with the bombings."

I shake my head. "You should still be careful."

"The president accused the Fist because he wants to silence us. If we let him scare us into backing down, who'll speak up for Old Triton?"

"If you stick your head up, it'll get kicked off your shoulders."

It's one of Tori's favorite sayings, but I already know I'm wasting my breath. There's no reason for Cale to be so passionate about how unfair things are for sinkers. He's a floater who could live a life of privilege. But he has such an inflated sense of right and wrong, it's practically a birth defect. He's willing to risk his life for a city he doesn't live in, and I can't help but admire him for it.

"Speak for yourself. You're not going to the square today." He finally lets his gaze meet mine, but his expression is tight and there's no trace of warmth in his face.

"I need to talk to Sentin."

"Not in public. You'll never get close to him. And you'll be arrested on sight."

"I'll tie some cloth over my face to hide my scars, and keep my head down."

"You can't risk it." Cale's tone is hard, as though he's giving me an order.

I resist the urge to tell him I don't need him to protect me. It's not like I haven't told him that before.

"I have to." I keep my voice even. "My brother's one of the director's soldiers. I promised my mother I'd get him back, and I can't do that by hiding here."

The doctor leans forward, her expression turning sympathetic at the mention of my promise to Ma. "I can help with your disguise," she says.

"You don't get it." Cale runs his finger over the condensation on the outside of his glass of juice. "The people I'm meeting are planning something."

"Planning what?"

He hesitates, looking from Doctor Gregory to me, and back again. "To disrupt the announcement," he says reluctantly, using his jeans to wipe the moisture off his finger. "That's all I can tell you. It's better if you don't know."

Doctor Gregory folds her arms. "They're not going to hurt anyone?"

"No, not really."

"Not *really*?"

Cale's bronzed cheeks are reddening. He lifts his hands. "Okay, look. My understanding is they've planted a couple of poppers under the stage. They'll make a big bang, but won't do much damage, just force an evacuation of the square. The president will be there, and they want to embarrass him and interrupt Director Morelle's speech. That's all."

"I'm going anyway," I insist.

Cale shakes his head. "Don't you get it? The place will be swarming with police. Not to mention the new Skins the director wants to show off. If you're recognized, you won't get away."

"This might be the only chance I get to contact Sentin." I set my jaw.

"I don't like what your friends are doing," Doctor Gregory interrupts. She frowns at Cale, uncrossing her arms so she can punctuate her words by tapping the table with her forefinger. "They could hurt innocent people. Besides, there's a war on, and now, more than ever, we need to pull together. It's not the time for political statements or terrorist attacks."

"Did you know the president shut down Sub Zero?" Cale stabs at his band. "Now the only feed we get is the official news on b-Net."

I stare down at Rayne's band, which is still fastened uselessly around my wrist. If Sub Zero's gone, it's a huge blow to the Fist, who rely on the indie feed for their broadcasts. And not just the Fist. Pretty much everyone in Old Triton connected to Sub Zero for real, uncensored information.

"They've cut off our only way to get the truth out, and Director Morelle's using the war as an excuse to make conditions even more miserable for workers," Cale runs his hand through his hair in a gesture of frustration. "She's converted her biggest factory for Skin production, and moved the manufacturing of all her other products to other factories. She's not producing less, she's just crammed more equipment into the spaces she has. And she's forcing her workers to work a lot of extra hours."

I catch my breath, remembering the hoarse, exhausted way Ma answered her band when the doctor called her for me. I'd thought it was because we'd woken her. Before all this happened, she was already working so many hours I worried about her all the time.

"All the more reason for me to talk to Sentin." My tone is so harsh, both Cale and the doctor look a little startled. "Ma works in the Skin factory, and the way she sounds, she's not far away from dropping dead on the job, just like my father did. If Director Morelle really started this war, then she's killing my mother, and she's stolen my brother to fight for her." I narrow my eyes at Cale. "I don't care what your friends are planning. I know what I need to do, and nobody's going to stop me."

"You think Sentin will tell you the truth about what's going on?" Cale asks doubtfully.

"It's a place to start."

Maybe I'm pinning too many hopes on Sentin, but I can't stop thinking of the confident way he told me Director Morelle was planning to start a war. The Deiterran war is dragging my family further into misery, and if Sentin's trying to end it, I'm on board.

Doctor Gregory sighs. "I still don't like it. But I can make sure you're not identified. I have a magnetic wrap you can tie around your band that'll stop it being read in case they sweep the crowd. And I can alter the way you look." She gets up to open a drawer under one of her worktables, and rummages around in it before pulling out a couple of jars. "This is a two-part silicone modelling compound. It's a little old, but should work fine. And I have some makeup to go over it."

"You're going to paint my face?" I ask.

"I used to be good at this kind of thing. Come on, I'll give it a try." She carries a chair into the bathroom and makes me sit in front of the mirror, a place I normally avoid. She spoons out a little of the gel from both jars, mixing them together on a small board. "Good, the compounds haven't hardened. They look fine."

She uses a small, flat spatula to dab the goo into the

hollow place in my cheek, where drops of super-heated polymer ate the flesh away. The stuff feels cold, but not unpleasant. In fact, it's soothing. It stops my scars from itching.

When she's done smoothing goo over my face, she steps back to examine me. My skin is tightening as the silicone dries. I don't like anybody looking at me so closely, but her look of concentration is so intense it's almost funny.

"Now for some makeup," she says in the distracted tone she uses when she's concentrating. "I'll darken your skin. It'll even you out and you won't stand out so much. I doubt there'll be many Old Tritoners at the square."

"They're too busy working themselves to death," I mutter.

When she's finished with my face, the doctor rubs dark makeup onto my hands. Finally she stands back with a nod. "All done. Your scars are less obvious, but still faintly visible from close up. I'm sure I've got bandages somewhere. I'll put one across your nose and cheeks and it'll look like you've just been tweaked and are waiting for the surgery to heal."

Opening my eyes, I stare at the woman in the mirror. That can't be me. My face is smooth, and a healthy shade of tawny brown. Both cheeks are full and even. I look like a New Tritoner.

I look like I'd never been burned.

My heart constricts, and I jerk my eyes away. There's no use wishing for things I can't have. I'd never have survived all these years if I let myself do that.

"Are you okay?" The doctor's face falls. "You don't like it?"

I take a deep breath, getting myself under control. Then, without looking back at the mirror, I reach for her hand. It feels fragile in mine, her skin loose. "You did a good job. Thank you." I squeeze her hand gently before letting it go. I'm grateful that Doctor Gregory was the one the director assigned to look after us. If Director Morelle only gave her the job to sideline her, she made a mistake. Without the doctor, I'd probably be dead by now.

"No need to thank me. I enjoyed it."

"Not just for the makeup. For everything. For letting me stay. For taking me in and helping me."

She shakes her head, puffing her cheeks out, but she looks pleased. "It's nothing. Anyway, there's one more thing you need if you want to go unnoticed. And believe me, I've wanted to do this since the first time I saw you." She pulls a pair of scissors out of her bathroom cupboard and reaches for my hair. "Just a trim to neaten things up. I don't know who cut it for you, but they should get their eyesight checked. It's crooked on that side."

Tori was the last person to cut my hair, and that was months ago. I like to keep a long fringe to cover as much of my face as possible, and usually get someone to crop the rest to shoulder-length so I can easily tie it up while I'm working. But I've neglected it for a while, so it's way past that. The doctor's right, it badly needs a trim.

She takes it above my shoulders so it swings, and layers my fringe so it feels lighter. I don't know where she learned how to cut hair, but she's much better at it than Tori. I look like I've stepped out of a New Triton salon, though I don't let myself study the mirror for more than a second or two. I don't want to get too attached to my new look, or forget it's just an illusion.

When I walk into the living room, I'm both eager and afraid of seeing Cale's reaction.

Sure enough, his eyes widen and his mouth drops open. I feel my face go warm. Unexpectedly, my eyes prickle.

Dammit, I don't even know why I'm getting emotional. It's just some stupid makeup, and what does it matter if he sees what I could have looked like if my life had been different? It's not real. Underneath the makeup, my scars are as ugly as ever.

"Let's go." The words come out sounding rough.

"Sure." He scrambles to his feet, then checks himself, like he's trying too hard to be casual.

"Wait a minute. First, let me take a look at your feet." The doctor sits me down, kneeling in front of me, which means I can focus on her and not have to look at Cale. She changes the bandages she applied earlier, spraying on a liquid that cleans the wounds and numbs the pain. "You're healing much faster than I would have expected," she says as she helps me ease the sneakers back on. "I wonder if that's part of it?"

"Part of what?" asks Cale.

I hesitate. Though I don't want to keep any more secrets from Cale, if I tell him about how my Skin changed me, will he see me as even more of a freak? If I'm not quite human anymore, I'm not sure I want him to know.

"I'll tell you on the way to the square," I promise.

As a final touch, the doctor presses a wide bandage across the bridge of my nose, and gives me a cap to pull down over my eyes. The bandage starts itching right away, but I resist the urge to scratch in case my makeup comes off.

"Time to go." I start for the door.

"Please be careful, both of you." Doctor Gregory crams her hands into the pockets of her trousers, then perches restlessly on the arm of her couch. "Don't go close to the stage. I'll watch the announcement on the holo, but I wish you hadn't told me what your friends were planning,

Cale. Now I'm going to be on edge the entire time, waiting for it to happen."

"We'll be careful," I promise. But the exploding stage is the least of my worries. If Sentin's there, I'll somehow have to get close to him without letting Director Morelle see me, and Cale's right, the square will be crawling with stompers. This could be a huge mistake. Still, I have to try.

Chapter Five

Cale and I get in a cab, and the streets are quiet at first. But it doesn't take long before our cab connects to another in front, then more latch on behind. Soon we're part of an endless string of cabs, and as we near the square, the sidewalks become full of people walking the same way we're going.

Reluctantly, I tell Cale about how the Leopard Skin changed me. Even as I'm determined not to lie, I can't help playing it down. Still, he looks shocked. And he's too quiet, listening to my explanation without asking questions like he normally does. The way he stares out the cab's window without saying a word makes me feel desperate. All I want is to grab him and tell him again how sorry I am.

Instead, I turn my own face away and gaze sightlessly out at the crowd. My throat feels so tight, it's aching. Any chance of Cale forgiving me is getting more and more unlikely. As if my scars weren't bad enough, and the way I couldn't let him kiss me without freaking out, now he's discovering how far from normal I really am.

We get out of the cab a block or so from the square,

and mingle with the throng of people streaming in. For such a big crowd, it's strangely quiet. All the faces around me are grim, without a smile to be seen.

My feet still hurt, though not so much that I couldn't run if I need to. I stick close to Cale, but in spite of the New Triton sun, I feel cold and empty inside. I'm losing everyone I love, and the tighter I try to hold on, the more they slip away.

A pair of stompers stand on every street corner with their hands on their weapons, scanning the crowd. I'm not as afraid of them now as I used to be, but I keep my head down and use Cale's tall body and wide shoulders for cover. It's not difficult to slip past the stompers when the crowd is so large, we're being jostled on either side.

At the far end of the square is the Presidential Office, a tall, solid-looking building about twenty-five stories high, with impressive decorative columns and arches. A stage has been set up in front of it, with a podium and microphone for the director's speech. She's not here yet, but a large group of reporters have set up their cameras next to the podium and are getting shots of the crowd arriving.

A surveillance drone flies overhead, and I fiddle with the magnetic wrap tied around my band, checking it's still fastened tightly under my sleeve. So many New Tritoners get themselves tweaked, the drones usually scan bands rather than trying to recognise peoples' changing faces. Still, I keep my cap pulled over my eyes, just in case. Drones used to be common in Old Triton, but the Fist got so good at bringing them down, these days we hardly see any. Now they're mainly used to police crowds.

Cale stops dead, and I almost run into him. He stares toward a statue of Edward Morelle, the director's grandfather and founder of the Morelle Corporation. It's on the other side of the square, some distance from the stage.

"I'm supposed to be meeting my friends by the statue," he says. "But they're not there."

I swallow the lump that's been blocking my throat since his silence on the cab ride, and try to sound as normal as I can. "You want to go over there and wait for them?"

He shakes his head. "Better not. I'll just keep an eye out."

I motion toward the stage. "Let's get closer."

"Not too close."

"But that's where Sentin will be." I turn to push my way through the crowd.

"Wait." He grabs my arm and a shock of awareness jolts through me. It's not like the last time he put his arms around me, when his grip made me feel trapped. This time, I only feel glad for his touch. If he cares enough to take my arm, maybe I can hope he might forgive me.

"It's too dangerous," he says. When he frowns I only see worry in his expression, not anger or disgust. More reason to hope.

"You said your friends weren't going to hurt anyone," I remind him.

"There's always a risk. If they made the poppers too big, they could injure some bystanders by mistake."

He still cares about my safety. The realization eases the iron bands crushing my heart and makes me want to throw my arms around him. Instead I gently tug my arm from his grip. "I'm sorry, Cale, but I have to get close to have any chance of talking to Sentin. You stay here and look for your friends. I'll meet up with you later."

"No, we'll stick together."

He lets me lead him forward, and we mingle with a group that's crowding the stage. If people notice me for the bandage I'm wearing across my nose, it's not unusual enough for them to look twice. I'm no threat, just a skinny

—no, a *slim* girl who's just been tweaked, wearing floater's clothing, with a floater's bronzed skin. Maybe my features aren't perfectly even, my lips aren't as full as they could be, and my eyes don't turn up in just the right way, but the difference isn't enough for me to stand out.

I'm one of *them*.

It's a weird feeling. I keep thinking about the night I saw Rayne walk into the shelter. In Old Triton, she stood out like a beacon, her beauty as extreme as my own ugliness. Even with a bandage on my face, I never imagined I could walk unnoticed among people like her.

A sudden blast of music from the stage makes me jump. The people around us focus on the stage, then move forward, cramming more closely together as everyone tries to see what's happening.

Cale twists around, peering through the moving people, still hunting for his friends. He's looking more and more worried.

"Something must have happened to them," he mutters. "I don't like it."

"Come on." I lead him closer to the stage, wedging us into the tightly packed rows near the front.

Somebody jostles me from behind, pushing me into the man in front of me. He grunts, but stays focused on the stage. "Deiterran," he says in a contemptuous tone, and his friend spits on the ground. A few others mutter slurs, but nobody seems to want to say the insult too loudly.

Craning my neck, peering between people's heads, I already know what I'm going to see before I catch a jewel-green flash of scales.

It's Sentin's Reptile Skin. He must have come out of the Presidential Office, and he's climbing onto the stage, flanked by a line of stompers.

Cale moves up beside me and we exchange a look. I

can tell he's wondering the same thing I am. How are we going to attract Sentin's attention? The stompers arrange themselves in a row at the back of the stage, and Sentin stands in front of them. If Cale or I try to coax Sentin off the stage to talk to us, the stompers are sure to see.

In his giant Reptile Skin, Sentin stands still, his body upright and his head not moving, though his silver eyes are restless. His pupils are black, vertical slits, and they slide back and forth, examining the crowd.

Before I can come up with a plan to make him notice me, Triton's President strides out of the Presidential Office and onto the stage. He's even more handsome in real life than he looks on the holo, almost like a superhero from a cartoon. Was he rich enough to afford his expensive body and face before he was elected to run the city? He's been in charge for so long, I can't remember what he used to look like.

The crowd greets his appearance with claps and cheers. They edge forward, packing in tighter, and the din of everyone talking at once quietens down.

President Trask steps up to the microphone and clears his throat. He used to be against the whole idea of Skins, but now he makes a long speech about how proud he is that Triton technology has created such a brilliant new tool, and how he and Director Morelle are working in partnership to defend our great city.

He finishes his speech by introducing Director Morelle in such a fawning way, I have to wonder what could have happened to make him Morelle's biggest fan. I imagine the Deiterran attacks were a shock, but I can't help but wonder if that's the only thing that triggered the change.

When Director Morelle steps out of the Presidential Office, the crowd around me erupts with claps and cheers. They surge forward, pushing and shoving in a polite, New

Triton way. In his excitement, the floater next to me jabs his elbow in my face and almost rips the bandage off my nose.

"Watch it," snarls Cale, and the guy gives him a startled look before shuffling over to give me a little more room.

Director Morelle gets on the stage slowly, ambling up to the microphone so the applause goes on for what seems like forever. Eventually, she holds up both hands in an 'aww shucks, that's enough' gesture, and the huge crowd falls silent on command.

A chill runs over me. I touch Cale's arm to get his attention, and he bends his head so I can speak quietly into his ear.

"I don't remember her ever being this popular."

He nods, his expression grim. "Nobody's ever been this popular. Director Morelle's made herself the saviour of Triton."

"Thank you." Director Morelle's voice booms over the microphone. "I appreciate your warm welcome. But I know I'm not who you've come to see today. You're here to see your new soldiers. And although the Skins will be operated by the sons and daughters of Triton, you can rest assured our volunteers will be in no danger. While the Skins fight on the front line, their operators will be in a secure location, safe from harm. Watching the Skin Hunter Contest, you all saw for yourselves how impressively the Skins fought, yet the competitors remained completely unscathed." She turns to Sentin for confirmation and he nods and steps forward.

"That is correct," he says into the microphone, before stepping back. I guess that's his main job, to lie for the director. His human body might not have been hurt in the contest, but mine sure was.

"Our new Skin Soldiers will ensure there will be no more deaths," the director declares. "No more wounded." She pauses for dramatic effect. "No more war!"

The crowd erupts on cue, but instead of waiting for the cheers to die down, she turns and looks behind her.

As one, the crowd falls silent.

That's when I see them. Two lines of armoured creatures are marching in formation out of the Presidential Office.

An excited murmur starts from behind me. It builds as the Skins march toward us. Then unseen trumpets blast a fanfare I'm sure I've heard before, probably on a holo show set in medieval times.

Through the drawn-out, triumphant notes of the trumpets, I hear a sound that makes me shiver with dread. It's a sound that's hated by every sinker, yet the clueless floaters around me still cheer.

It's the stomping of heavy boots.

The director is beaming. "Here are the knights of Triton, ready to stride into battle."

Sunlight glints off the black armour of the creatures marching toward us. Though the Skins sound like stompers, I can see why the director called them knights. Their armor makes them look a little like medieval knights.

But I'm willing to bet that nobody wearing armor ever marched as smoothly as these knights. Their armor doesn't seem to have any joints, but looks like part of the knight's body, like Aza's Wasp Skin, only less organic and more like metal. The armor covers their entire body, including their head.

The murmurs around me grow louder, the crowd starting to cheer. The lines of Skins are probably an exhilarating sight to them. But my chest feels tight with a horrible foreboding.

The knights pour out of the Presidential Office. There are dozens of them. Maybe a hundred or more. And every one is identical.

"Though the knight's skeleton is humanoid, its DNA mix gives it enhanced senses. For example, we've used eagle DNA to make its vision eight times better than that of a human. And its body is constructed from a bullet-proof ceramic composite."

The knights are completely black, except for their yellow eyes. Their heads are animal shaped rather than human, with pointed ears like a bat, and a short snout. As they march closer, their size gets more threatening. They're much taller and wider than a regular person, and their long arms hang to mid-thigh, like Brugan's Devil Bear Skin. Everything about them is big and hulking. To me, they look like an armored version of the devil bear, but with a sleeker bat-like face.

Every soldier is exactly the same. They have no distinguishing features or marks to identify them. Even if they've never learned to fear the chilling sound of a stomper's boots, why can't this crowd of floaters see what a dangerous idea it is to have anonymous, identical soldiers?

"There are a lot more Skins than I thought," mutters Cale. His expression tells me he doesn't like the knights any more than I do.

I edge closer so my shoulder is touching him and our arms are pressed together. He doesn't pull away. Maybe because he hasn't noticed what I'm doing, but I'm hoping it's because he wants to feel my touch right now as much as I need to feel his.

Instead of climbing the steps onto the stage like the president and director did, the Skins march around it, toward the front row of the crowd. Now I can see that their armor is made up of plates that slide over each other to allow their joints to move, but the edges of the plates slide so smoothly, they're all but invisible.

The knights each have guns nestled in hollows on the outside of each thigh, set inside their legs as though the weapons are growing organically from their bodies. The sight makes me even more uneasy. It's always been illegal for anyone but stompers to have guns, and that was bad enough.

I'd thought the director's new Skins might be beautiful, like my clouded leopard, but there's nothing beautiful about these soldiers. Maybe some of my revulsion is because of their resemblance to the devil bear, and my memories of Brugan's bloody ruthlessness. But even if I hadn't known Brugan, the knights are obviously killing machines, and their menacing size and lack of expression would probably still give me chills. Though the Skins march like a human would, I can't see a trace of humanity in them.

They're monsters.

But it seems like the only one who might agree with me on that is Cale. The rest of the crowd are cheering as though these creatures have really been designed to save them.

As though in response to a silent command, the knights stop in unison. They stand at attention beside the stage, staring straight ahead.

"The knights are strong, fast, and agile," says Director Morelle. "Super human, well armed, and deadly. The knights are *your* soldiers. Here to protect you."

The crowd cheers even louder.

"The knights will prevent any more terrorist attacks," she announces. "There will be no more injured children. No reason for fear." She lifts both arms, her chin tilted up, her perfect face addressing the heavens. "The knights will strike terror in the hearts of our enemies. They're New Triton's heroes. Our instruments of peace stand before you."

Everyone around us is clapping, hooting, and stomping their feet. The noise is deafening.

Amongst the din, I cup my hands around my mouth and bellow. "SENTIN."

My lone voice is all but lost in the noise of the crowd, but the Reptile jerks his eyes in my direction. I push my way out from behind the tall guy with the elbows, so Sentin can see me. For a moment I'm exposed to the stompers, the director, or whoever might be watching. Then I duck back behind the tall man.

I've taken a huge risk. Now it's up to Sentin to seek me out, if he decides to.

My heart beats hard and I'm ready to run if stompers approach. As I try to see as much as I can while keeping hidden, the wild applause slowly dies down.

"These are the first of the knights, but my factory will produce hundreds more." The director's voice cuts through what's left of the noise, killing it completely. "It's not enough for us to simply defend ourselves. We must prevent such a devastating attack from ever happening again. We will cross the border wall and take control of Deiterra, subduing the enemy's forces and bringing them under Triton's leadership."

The crowd cheers again, while the news reporters get close-up shots of the Skins.

When Morelle lifts a hand for silence once more, her expression has hardened.

"But now I must tell you about something shocking. Something that proves how much we need our new soldiers." She stops to scan the crowd, a frown creasing her brow, and I shrink a little smaller.

"We have uncovered a serious plot, and captured four Old Triton traitors who planned to blow up this very stage. They intended to kill your elected president, and they didn't care how many they murdered in the process."

Cale makes a noise in the back of his throat, like he's struggling to breathe. The blood drains from his face.

Chapter Six

E ight more of the Skin Soldiers march out of the Presidential Office. Each pair of knights is dragging someone between them. The first is a pale-skinned man in his mid-twenties who's bleeding from a deep cut below his eye.

Cale sways a little, like he's about to pass out. "That's them," he mutters. "The friends I was supposed to meet."

My legs feel weak too, but it's not with fear for his captured friends so much as an overwhelming sense of relief that Cale wasn't with them when they were arrested. I don't know what I would have done if he were being dragged onto the stage with them.

The next pair of knights is hauling along an Old Triton woman, who's obviously been beaten. Her dirt-covered clothes are ripped and bloody with fresh wounds, and bruises are forming on her arms and face. She's struggling against the knights, her face twisted with rage. As the knights pull her closer to the stage, she turns her head and spits on one of them. The knight seemingly ignores the saliva dribbling down its black metal cheek, but I see its armoured fingers become claws. They dig so viciously into her arm that blood trickles to her elbow.

Behind them, the other two sinkers are both young men. All four are about Cale's age. One has had his nose broken and blood is smeared over his cheeks. The other looks only half conscious. His eyes are unfocused and the tops of his shoes scrape across the ground.

The knights line their four prisoners up at the front of the stage. Around us, the crowd is booing the sinkers, shouting their anger at the four battered prisoners. Their faces are so twisted with spite and outrage, my heart sinks for Cale's friends. I doubt they'll be shown any mercy.

Director Morelle steps aside to let President Trask take over the microphone.

"All four of you are guilty of treason," announces the president. "You plotted to kill me, and you conspired with the enemy. You're Deiterran agents, terrorists, and traitors to your country."

"We have nothing to do with Deiterr—" The woman's shouted denial becomes a scream of pain as the knight holding her arm digs its claws even harder into her flesh.

The man with the broken nose lifts his head. "The president deserves to die," he yells. "For the crimes he's committed against Old Triton." Though the knights have him by the upper arms, he manages to force one hand up enough to rip the front of his shirt, revealing a tattooed hologram of a fist on his chest. "What's buried will rise!" His shout rises over the booing of the crowd.

At a gesture from President Trask, one of the knights holding the tattooed man grabs his face, wrapping his big, armored hand over the man's mouth. Even over the noise the crowd are making, I can hear the crunching of broken bones as the knight's hand presses into his nose. The people around me shift from foot to foot, cheering the knights, and jeering at the sinkers.

The president holds up one hand up for silence. "The Fist are a criminal organisation of vandals and terrorists. And now they've aligned themselves with Deiterra, they will be swiftly dealt with. The first duty of our new Skin Soldiers will be to arrest all Fist members and hold them accountable for their crimes."

I choke back a horrified gasp and clench my fists to keep from grabbing Cale and dragging him forcibly away from here. He's a Fist member. So was Tori, last time I saw her. Could the stompers already know that? Have they been keeping tabs on who belongs?

President Trask motions to the four prisoners on the stage. "In times of war, justice must be dealt swiftly, and traitors must be made an example of. Their guilt has been proven. The sentence is execution."

The woman prisoner's face jerks up, her eyes wide with shock. She gulps for breath for a moment, then yanks her arm, trying to free it from the knight's grip. She may as well be trying to bend steel. But she's not trying to get away. She has her hand clenched and she's trying desperately to give the Fist's salute. "What's buried will rise!" she screams.

My heart feels like it's being crushed. Her defiance and courage reminds me of Tori. It's all too easy to imagine Tori up there, on that stage, captured while fighting for what she believes in.

Bile burns up my throat. Though I didn't want the Fist to blow up the stage or put innocent lives in danger, I can't believe nobody's speaking up against this madness. The crowd around me *want* to see the sinkers killed. They're baying for blood, cheering and shouting as four knights line up in front of the prisoners.

Even Sentin's just standing there, not speaking up or making a move to stop what's about to happen. His scales have turned such a dark green they're almost black, but he's motionless, staring at the prisoners without blinking.

Each knight pulls a gun from the hollow in its thigh, and trains it on the sinkers. Their guns have longer barrels than the ones the stompers use, and maybe it's my imagination, but they look even nastier and more lethal.

I grab Cale's hand and grip it tightly. He's trembling, and I can feel his fear, rage, and shock, even stronger than my own. As terrible as it is for me to watch this, how much worse is it for him?

At a signal from the president, the knights fire their weapons. The loud retort of gunfire echoes through the square as the four Fist members drop to the ground.

There's a moment of absolute silence as the entire crowd takes in the unprecedented sight of four bloody corpses lying on the stage. Then the crowd erupts into cheers so loud, the sound swells to fill the square.

I close my eyes, struggling to catch my breath, but I can still see the four dead sinkers as though the terrible image of their bodies has been permanently imprinted on my retinas.

I tug on Cale's hand. "Let's go." The words burn their way up through a throat that feels raw.

Cale ignores me. I'm not sure he heard me, or has registered that I'm gripping his hand. He's staring wide-eyed at the stage, his Adam's apple bobbing as he swallows.

President Trask speaks up again and the crowd's cheers die down. "The Fist are a destructive force aligned against Triton, but we will stamp them out. Effective immediately, the knights will start patrolling the streets of Old Triton. A curfew is now in place. All law-abiding Old Triton citizens must remain off the streets from sunset to sunrise, so our new Skin Soldiers can identify and deal with terrorists."

I draw in a sharp breath, waiting for somebody to speak up, to say this isn't fair, that they can't do this. If we were in Old Triton, the crowd would shout a thousand objections. If there's a curfew, where will the rough sleepers go? Anybody who can't find work isn't allowed to sleep in a shelter. And what about the night shift workers who walk to their jobs just before dawn, or the day workers who finish as night is falling? What about the food stalls, and the app sellers, and all the people struggling to make enough money to feed their families?

"The curfew is a temporary measure," says President Trask. "It will remain in force until we've wiped out the Fist, won the war with Deiterra, and made our great dual cities of Triton safe for good."

Somebody starts clapping and the sound grows quickly as more people join in.

I gape in disbelief at the people around me. Don't they understand what this means? It's impossible to stay off the streets when you have to go to work, which means no sinker will be safe from the knights. Every Old Tritoner will have to break this new curfew, including Ma and Tori.

Are they trying to stamp us out?

President Trask steps away from the microphone, giving control back to Director Morelle. She motions the knights forward and they advance to parade in front of the crowd, their boots as loud on the ground as any line of stompers. The crowd cheers louder.

I feel sick.

The feeling only gets worse when the director and president head back inside the Presidential Office, and Sentin goes with them. I need to talk to him more than ever, but there's no way to make contact. I might have taken a chance and followed him toward the Presidential Office, but some of the knights are standing to attention in front of it.

Instead I stumble away, dragging a pale and silent Cale with me. We push our way out through the tightly packed crowd without speaking. We don't need words. He looks as shocked and helpless as I feel.

Chapter Seven

That night, my nightmares are interrupted by a loud bang that jerks me awake. The doctor's house is shaking, and I jump out of bed, breathing hard, listening for more noise or any hint of where the danger is coming from.

Doctor Gregory calls from her bedroom. "Are you all right, Rayne?"

The shaking stops. Everything falls quiet.

"What was that noise?" I shout back, not bothering to remind her that she called me by the wrong name.

"Could have been another attack."

The light clicks on in the living room, sending a bright sliver under the door of Doctor Gregory's spare bedroom where I've been sleeping. A moment later, I hear the holo in the living room come to life, and join the doctor in front of the screen.

A news announcer is speaking, and she looks agitated, glancing from side to side. "...a loud explosion," she says. "It's too early to know what caused it, but as you saw a few minutes ago, the studio shook. We'll give you a full report as soon as we know more."

"It had to be another bomb." The doctor sinks into a chair. "I thought the director's new soldiers were going to stop this kind of thing…" She trails off, glancing at me. The doctor watched yesterday's ceremony on the holo. She was shocked by the public execution of the four sinkers, but doesn't understand why I think the director's new Knight Skins are so terrible.

A sharp rapping comes from the front door, making us both jump.

Doctor Gregory taps her band to switch off the holo, then turns to me, wide-eyed. "It's almost three o'clock in the—"

I put my finger against my lips, warning her to silence, though it's a little late for that. The lights are on and we weren't being quiet. Whoever—or whatever—is at the door must already know we're here.

Logic tells me it can't be the director's Soldier Skins at the door. They wouldn't knock. But I was having a nightmare about them when the explosion woke me, and now I can't shake the feeling they've come for me.

"I'll see who it is," whispers the doctor, getting up and padding toward the door in her bare feet and pyjamas.

My scarred face is too recognisable to take any chances, so I slip into the kitchen where I can't be seen from the door. Poised to run, I listen to the click of the lock and the creak of the door opening.

The doctor exclaims with surprise. "What are you doing here?" she asks.

"I believe we need to talk." The male voice is familiar.

I let out a relieved breath and step back into the living room.

The last time I saw Sentin out of his Reptile Skin was when we travelled to the arena for the Skin Hunter contest. He's tall, a little lean, and his expression is as serious as ever. His angular face is not as perfectly regular as most tweaked floaters. His mouth is a little higher on one side and his nose is slightly too long. But he has a floater's bronzed skin and unmarked hands. His dark hair is razored shorter than last time I saw him, in a defiantly severe style. A military style, I guess, that isn't designed to be flattering. Still, in a city of perfect people, he somehow manages to be handsome. Maybe it's the intelligence in his eyes.

But I wish he wouldn't wear those high-tech glasses, the ones that let him see when people are lying. Those glasses make me uncomfortable.

He nods at me. "You wanted to see me?"

"How'd you know I'd be here?" I resist the urge to tug self-consciously at the T-shirt and leggings I was sleeping in.

"Where else would you be, Milla?" His gaze goes to Rayne's band that's still on my wrist. "With that band, you couldn't sleep in a shelter even if you weren't wanted for murder."

His matter-of-fact tone takes the sting out of his words. I'm not surprised he called me by my real name. He probably knows everything about me.

"Come and sit down." The doctor waves him toward the couches in front of the holo. "You're out late. Did you hear the explosion?"

Sentin sits stiffly on one of the couches. He's wearing all black, like he has every time I've seen him out of his colorful Reptile Skin. His fitted black trousers and shirt accentuate his angular body. "A bomb was planted in a police station in Old Triton. The blast was strong enough to bring down the New Triton street above the police station, and destroy at least one residential building."

Doctor Gregory puts her hands to her mouth and sinks onto the other couch. "Oh my Lord."

"Did you see the explosion?" I ask. For him to have seen it and be here so soon afterward means it must have been a lot closer than it sounded.

He shakes his head, his sharp gaze on me as I pull out one of the chairs from the table and sit facing him. "I didn't see it. But I knew it would happen."

"How did you know?" I ask, at the same time as the doctor demands, "You knew and didn't warn anyone?"

"I learned she was planning another attack, but I couldn't discover where." His gaze turns to Doctor Gregory. "I had no way to stop it, so I decided to use it. While her eyes are elsewhere, on the carnage she's created, I could come here."

"Who do you mean?" The doctor's voice wavers as though she's afraid of the answer. "Do you know who's responsible for the explosion?"

Sentin blinks at her without answering. There's only one person he could be talking about, but I understand why the doctor is struggling to believe it. After all, she worked for Director Morelle for years.

"The director wouldn't be involved in terrorist activity," insists Doctor Gregory when he doesn't reply. "Are you implying she blew up a building? Why would she do that? It makes no sense."

"She needs the war," says Sentin. "Having an active enemy is helping her achieve her goals."

"I can't believe she's attacking her own city to perpetuate the war." The doctor shakes her head. "That's impossible."

"I don't get it either," I say, though I have no trouble

believing the director would blow up buildings and kill innocent people. "She's already rich and powerful. Why start a war? What's she going to get out of it?"

He gives me a disappointed look, like he expected better from me. "You need to ask? Look at what she's already achieved."

"She's made herself insanely popular with floaters," I say. "But at the expense of sinkers, who are even worse off than before."

"It's enabled her to create an army," he says. "One that's completely loyal to her. And President Trask's placed himself in her debt. Without her help, he would have been swept out of power on a wave of fear and panic. He's becoming her puppet, though even as a figurehead he won't last much longer. The director's plan for a coup is well underway. It will happen when she announces she's taken control of Deiterra."

"She wants to take over Triton *and* Deiterra?" I lean back, looking up the ceiling, and let the full significance of the director's actions wash over me. "Is she really that power hungry?"

Sentin cocks his head. "Let me ask you something, Milla. When you were in your Leopard Skin, how did you feel?"

"Alive," I say at once.

"Powerful?"

"And strong."

He nods. "As did I. And I believe Director Morelle has been using a Skin for many years."

"Rayne… I mean, Milla said the same thing." Doctor Gregory absentmindedly fiddles with a strand of her wispy gray hair. "The director could have made a Skin in her own likeness, but why would she bother? What's the point of having a Skin that's just like your real body?"

"You've been working on the Skin technology for some time?" he asks.

"I helped develop the technology, right from the early days, when Edward Morelle first conceived of the program. Believe it or not, I've been working on it for a little over thirty years."

Edward Morelle is the director's grandfather. I had no idea he was the one who started working on the Skin technology. He died before I was born, but I learned about him in school, and there are statues of him everywhere. His picture hangs in every Morelle factory and shelter.

"Have the Skins you transferred into made you feel more powerful?" Sentin asks her.

The doctor shakes her head. "Not that I noticed. But I worked on the transferral technology, not the Skins themselves. My chip was coded to a specific Skin that was utilitarian. A testing device." She walks over to the creepy robot head that still lying on her workbench, and picks it up. "A biological version of this, because we can only transfer consciousness into organic tissue. But the device I used was little more than a basic vessel with sensors that could be changed out. I could easily replace its eyes, for example, to test different sensory inputs."

"Using a Skin has the ability to alter brain chemistry," Sentin says. "If the director has used one for a significant period, I suspect she feels superior to others. More than human. And therefore, entitled to rule."

His words rock me back in my seat. Is that why I'm stronger now? Because I've convinced myself I'm more than human?

Sentin's sharp gaze is on me. With those damn glasses on, I bet he knows exactly what I'm thinking. Feeling my face heat, I look away, down at my hands. What if I can't trust my own thoughts? Did my beautiful Leopard Skin give me delusions? I don't think I'm superior to everyone else, but I do feel like a better version of myself. Maybe that's how it starts.

"I've felt it, too." His tone is unexpectedly gentle. "Wearing my Skin heightens my confidence. I must be careful to temper my thoughts, to ensure I don't become reckless."

"Great," I mutter. "So we're both crazy."

I don't think I've ever seen Sentin smile before. It's a sight to behold. Without the serious expression he wears like a mask, he looks like a different person.

"It's what I was trying to study when Director Morelle fired me." Doctor Gregory leaps to her feet and paces across the room. "When I saw your somatoform injuries, I tried to tell the director how important it was to determine the extent of the effect. She wouldn't listen. But is it an expansion of the mind's frame of reference that causes it? New neural pathways being created? Is it physiological, or psychosomatic?"

I'm not sure whether she's talking to us, or herself. I don't understand a word she's saying.

"The director doesn't need you to study it," says Sentin. "She's already researched the effect, and is using it in the new Skins."

I frown at Sentin. He's so certain about everything. "How do you know so much?" I demand. "And why does the director seem to think you're on her side?"

He doesn't look upset by my question, but Sentin never lets much emotion register on his face. "I've made myself invaluable to her. I needed to, in order to get close."

"How'd you do that?"

He considers me for several long moments, and I have no idea whether he's going to answer. Before he can, Doctor Gregory speaks up.

"I don't have the equipment here to manufacture a Skin's components." She taps her cheek with one finger, absorbed in thought. "I could examine your brains, but there's only so much we'll be able to measure without the means to stimulate the same neural centers. Could you bring your Reptile Skin here, perhaps, Sentin? It's a shame we don't have your Leopard Skin, Rayne. I wonder if there's a way to get hold of it? I could devise some tests to study what might be causing the effect."

She called me Rayne again, but she hasn't noticed. She's too focused on the impossible idea that she could get hold of my Leopard Skin.

Sentin runs his gaze across the doctor's cluttered work-benches. "If we can obtain one of the new Skins, do you have the equipment here to enable us to transfer into it?"

She makes a dismissive gesture. "That would be simple. The difficult part will be getting access to imaging equipment to track your neural processes."

I shake my head impatiently. "What are you both talking about? We need to stop the war, not waste time with scientific tests. And why would we want to transfer into one of the new Skins? We should be working out ways to sabotage the director's plans. Maybe we should report the director for using an illegal humanoid Skin. Or get the Fist to broadcast what she's up to, so it can't be covered up."

"I'm afraid President Trask has no power over the director any more." Sentin pushes his glasses further up his nose. "And with Sub Zero shut down, the Fist have lost their voice. Besides, we can't accuse Director Morelle of crimes without proof."

"Then what do we do? If you're right, and she's the one blowing up Triton, we can't let her get away with it."

Sentin nods. "If the director achieves her goal of absolute control over Triton and Deiterra, things will only get worse. We'll suffer hardships we can't currently conceive of. Hardships even Old Tritoners can't imagine."

The intense look is back on his face. Sentin has a slow, thoughtful way of speaking that makes me believe every word he says.

"How do we stop her?" I lean forward on my chair, hoping he has an answer. Things are already becoming unbearable for sinkers. We can't let her go on like this.

"We need to confront Director Morelle—the real director—in her private apartment. That's where her human body will be."

Doctor Gregory frowns. "She's never allowed anyone access to her apartment. Her elevator is the only way up, and she'll have security protocols in place. Besides, even if you could find a way in, how would you convince her to change her plans?"

Sentin turns his gaze on the doctor. "Getting into her apartment is the only course of action which ensures—"

"Shhh." I jerk my head toward the door, my stomach clenching as I catch a familiar sound. "Turn off the lights. I hear something."

"What—?" the doctor starts to say, but I jump up and grab her arm.

"Turn off the lights," I hiss. "Quick. It's stompers. They're coming this way."

She taps her band and the living room plunges into darkness. The sound of boots on the sidewalk is getting louder, so she and Sentin must be able to hear it now too. Stompers are marching in unison, and it sounds like there's at least a dozen of them. Are they coming here to arrest me?

"I'll take a look." The doctor starts toward the front door.

"Stop," I lunge to grab her.

"Don't open the door." Sentin pitches his voice just as low.

She frowns at me, pulling away from my hand. "I'm just activating the window." She touches the controller next to a section of wall by the front door, and it becomes transparent.

The figures outside aren't stompers, but a squad of knights. They're marching down the sidewalk directly across from the house, and their boots have a metallic sound.

I shrink back, ducking behind a table. If they come up the doctor's front steps, where will I go? The house shares its back wall and one side wall with another property, and the living room windows look out onto a small strip of grass that's visible from the street. If I jumped out the window, they'd easily spot me.

"Don't worry," whispers the doctor. "It's one-way glass. We can see out, but they can't see in."

"The Skins' senses are exceptional," Sentin murmurs from behind me. "They may be able to see and hear us in spite of the nature of the glass." When I glance back, I see he's hiding too. It's only because my vision is so good that I can make him out in the darkness.

I turn back to the soldiers in time to see one of them turn its head and stare toward us, as though it can make us out. Its eyes are bright yellow with small black pupils. They're closer together than human eyes would be.

A chill of fear runs over me. The sound of the knights' marching is a metallic version of the noise stompers' boots make, but at least stompers are human. These things? They've been designed to hunt and kill.

"They're going past," mutters the doctor.

I stay hidden until the last of them has marched past.

Then I slowly straighten, wiping my sweaty hands on my leggings and breathing a silent sigh of relief that they don't seem to be looking for me or Sentin. Maybe they're just patrolling the neighborhood. Perhaps the director is tightening the noose for all the citizens of Triton, not just sinkers.

Stepping forward to watch them go, I can't help but notice that as the soldiers' feet pound the sidewalk in perfect time with each other. They must have trained hard to be so in sync. Or maybe the director made the Skins to communicate silently with each other, like ants that use chemicals so they can all work together.

"My brother's in one of those Skins." I turn to Sentin. "He was in one of the director's academies and now he's one of her so-called volunteers, using a Knight Skin."

Sentin steps closer. "The director has been planning this for a long time. She started funding her private schools six years ago, specifically to train her soldiers." His voice is pitched low, as though he's afraid the knights might still be able to make out what he's saying.

"You said the Skins change people's brains. What's it doing to my brother?"

"Imparting an increased sense of strength and power, just as our Skins gave us. And the director's been experimenting with influencing and enhancing certain other emotions. Loyalty is the one she's primarily focused on."

"Loyalty to her?" I draw in my breath when he nods. "I need to find William before he can use a Skin for too long. I have to get him out."

Sentin blinks slowly, pushing his glasses up his nose. Then he shakes his head. "I'm sorry, Milla. This is far bigger than saving one person. I need your help to get to the director's real body and prevent this war from reaching its conclusion."

"He's my brother. I can't just let her do what she wants to his brain."

The doctor activates the light, and the room is suddenly bright again. "If I can get my hands on one of those Skins, I might find a way to reverse the effect," she says.

"We need one of those Skins," agrees Sentin. "But not to study. We can use it to get access to Director Morelle's private apartment."

I drag in a deep breath. I failed William when I let him be sent to the director's school. At the time, it seemed too good to be true. I should have known there'd be a price to pay, but no matter what, I won't let William be the one to pay it.

"When I find my brother, you can have his Skin." My voice is firm, and I stare them both in the eyes, daring them to object. "Study it or use it, I don't care which. But first, I'm going to break William out of the director's army."

Chapter Eight

There's a knock on the door the next morning, and this time our visitor is Cale. He obviously didn't sleep much either, because he looks almost as grim and exhausted as I am. Sentin's revelations left me with a tight feeling constricting my chest, and I've been pacing ever since, trying to figure out how I'm going to find William.

"You'd better sit down," I say to Cale. "Sentin dropped by a few hours ago, and you're not going to like what he had to say."

The doctor exchanges a greeting with Cale, but she's busy at her workbench, concentrating on something she's doing with her equipment.

"Devising tests," she explains when I ask. "When sensory inputs are enhanced, new neural pathways are formed. To understand the changes, we need to be able to map those pathways."

I nod as though I understand, and sit with Cale on the couches in the corner. We speak quietly so as not to disturb the doctor, though I'm not sure she'd notice if the house was rocked with another bomb blast.

Cale asks the same thing I did. How does Sentin know so much?

The answer Sentin gave me doesn't satisfy him. He shakes his head, frowning. "He's been helping Director Morelle so he gets access to what she's planning? Did he say how he's helping her?"

I shrug. "He won the contest. He has to stick around, doesn't he? Wasn't that part of the deal with him keeping his Skin?"

"There's got to be more to it than that." Cale leans back, frowning. "I don't trust him."

I think of Sentin's inscrutable face, and the way I can never tell what he's thinking when he studies me from behind his x-ray specs. "I'm not sure whether I trust him either, but he has access to the director. He can give us information."

"Did he say anything about the president's vendetta against the Fist?"

I shake my head. "Have you heard anything? Have any more Fist members been arrested?"

"There have been some raids, but not many members caught. Most safe houses are still operating."

"You have to promise me you'll be careful, okay?"

"Of course."

I narrow my eyes at him, because we both know he won't be. If Cale sees somebody in trouble, he'll rush to help them without a thought for his own safety. That's just the way he is.

"My friend Tori joined the Fist a few years ago," I say. "I'm worried about her, but I can't call her with this." I hold up my wrist, showing him Rayne's band.

"She's your friend from the shelter?"

I nod. "I need to know whether she's okay. Can you look her up on b-Net and see if her profile's listed? Her online handle is Torinado." It's a long shot, because she was active on Sub Zero rather than the official feed, but I lost her number when I gave my band away and I can't think of any other way to get hold of her.

While he's searching b-Net, Doctor Gregory makes a sound of frustration. "I'm stuck on a problem that I should be able to solve. Having my sleep interrupted has made me sluggish." She stands up. "I need to rest for an hour or two. That should help me concentrate."

"We'll keep our voices down," I tell her.

When she's gone, Cale looks up from his band and shakes his head. "Tori's not listed." He frowns at my expression. "Hey, I'm sure she's okay. You said she was smart, right? I bet she's keeping away from the knights."

I swallow hard. He's right. I should try not to worry.

"I'm sorry." His tone is gentle, and his eyes have lost the coldness that's been breaking my heart for the last couple of days. Their soft warmth makes me want to reach out and touch him. Could he have forgiven me?

"I'm the one who's sorry," I say. "I should have told you I wasn't Rayne."

His eyes shutter and he glances away.

My heart sinks. Not forgiven, then.

Cale lets out a slow, regretful sigh. "I want to trust you again, but how can I? I still don't get how you could keep lying about who you were after everything we went through together."

"I know. I messed up."

"Was everything a lie?"

"Of course not." Jumping to my feet, I keep my face turned from him so he doesn't see how much his question hurt me. I'm going to break down if we keep talking like this, and that's the last thing I want to do. "Anyway, we have more important things to worry about right now. I need to find where the director's recruits are, and figure out how get my brother William out of there." My tone brisk, I pace to the edge of the closest workbench. "Any idea where the kids she's turned into soldiers are transferring into the Skins? On the holo it looked like a big warehouse with hundreds of pods."

He hesitates, and I can tell he's still thinking about how I lied to him. I'm afraid he's going to say something that'll make me feel worse.

"You know the place I mean?" I demand. "It must be somewhere in Old Triton. One of her factories she's repurposed, maybe?"

Thankfully, he lets go of whatever he was going to say, and nods. "She's had more than one interview in that place, and she's answered questions about it." He uses his band to switch on the doctor's holo and search for the clip he wants.

Projected in 3-D is the same giant, windowless warehouse I saw before, with rows and rows of pods. Some pods are empty. Many aren't. Boys and girls lie inside them, and a monitor is above each one, displaying health data for the people in the occupied pods.

Director Morelle stands next to a pod where a teenaged boy is lying. A Knight Skin stands next to her, dwarfing her. Next to the knight is a woman in a suit, holding a microphone.

"How many Skins have you manufactured?" the woman asks Director Morelle.

"Hundreds. And there are many more on the production line."

"This warehouse will house the soldiers? All the young

men and women who'll transfer into the Skins will do it here, is that correct?"

"Until we run out of room. An overflow facility is being prepared."

The camera pans around the enormous space. It's hard not to be awed by the number of pods inside it. The 3-D holo image is so sharp, it looks like I could reach into it and pick up a pod and it would fit into the palm of my hand.

"Here's one of the soldiers." The interviewer motions to the pod where the boy is lying motionless with his eyes closed. "I'm told his mind is inside this Knight Skin." She looks up at the tall knight standing next to her.

The knight inclines its head.

"Can you speak?" she asks.

"Yes, ma'am." The boy in the pod doesn't move, but it's presumably his voice that comes from the knight's mouth.

"What's it like being in there? You're very tall." The interviewer gives a little laugh, like she's made a joke.

"It's our job to defend Triton, ma'am." The knight sounds like he's reading a line, like what he's saying has been scripted. "We'll fight Deiterra, and we'll win."

"How strong are you?"

The knight hesitates. Surprised by the question, perhaps? Maybe the interviewer has gone off script.

"Stronger than you can imagine," it says. Though it's a young man speaking, the Skin looks so alien I can't think of it as anything other than an 'it'. "We are far more powerful than any human."

Is that contempt in its voice?

The interviewer must hear it too, because her eyes widen. She turns to Director Morelle. "What happens if one of the knights gets out of control? Couldn't they be dangerous?"

"Each Skin has a failsafe built into it. In the base of its skull is the chip that controls it, and wiping that chip cuts the connection between the Skin and its operator."

"Have you just given away a secret vulnerability?" The interviewer smiles, clearly still trying to keep the interview light hearted.

"Not at all." The director's expression stays serious. "For an enemy to wipe a knight's chip would be all but impossible." She raps her knuckles against the knight's arm, presumably to demonstrate the toughness of its armor.

"And if a Knight Skin tries to hurt a Triton citizen you can trigger the failsafe?"

"That's right." The director steps forward and the camera zooms in on her, enlarging her image and making fewer of the pods visible. "If that ever happened, the consequences would be immediate. I'll show you." She reaches above the pod to push a button on the side of its monitor.

The button makes no sound, but the giant Knight Skin next to the interviewer immediately slumps.

In the pod, the boy flicks his eyes open. The color drains from his face and his mouth open and closes as though he can't believe what just happened. "My Skin," he gasps.

The director puts a hand on his arm, presumably to comfort him. Or to stop him from saying anything else in front of the camera.

"The knights belong to Triton," says Morelle in a firm tone, her 3-D image staring so intently out of the holo, it's as though she's looking right at us. "They're here to save us."

Cale switches off the clip. "That's not what I've heard." His mouth twists. "Word is, the knights have already killed dozens of Old Tritoners. They're out of control, doing whatever they want. The curfew is just an excuse they're using to get rid of rough sleepers and sinkers without jobs."

I squeeze my eyes shut, fear for Ma flooding through me. One way or another, everyone I love is in danger. Ma asked me to save William, and if I can find him, he can help me protect her.

"How do we find the place with all the pods?" I ask.

He shoots a frown at me. "Why do you want to know? All the director's soldiers are there. It's the last place you'd be able to get into, if that's what you're thinking."

"That's where William will be."

"There's no way you'll be able to get to him. Anyway, I have no idea where that building is."

"Can you ask your friends in the Fist? They're all over Old Triton. A big place like that, one of them has to know where it is."

He presses his lips together. "I'll ask them on one condition. I need you to promise you won't do anything reckless like trying to break in."

"If we find it, maybe I can figure something out." When he hesitates, I add, "This is important. If you won't help me, I'll find another way."

He studies me a moment longer. Finally he shakes his head with a huff of breath and taps his band. No holo-gram appears, but Cale starts moving his mouth, talking silently. His implant is transmitting his unspoken words to the Fist member he's talking to.

Watching his silent conversation is just as weird as when I saw Aza doing the same thing. Nobody in Old Triton has implants for silent conversations, though if they did, it would make the shelters much quieter.

When he eventually disconnects, I blink at him. "What did your friend say?"

"He'll only talk face-to-face. I need to meet him at a safe house."

"Then let's go."

He shakes his head. "I'm going alone. The safe house is close to the breach in the Deiterran wall, and that area's the most dangerous place in the city right now."

"I'm still coming."

"No way." He gets up from the couch. "Those streets will be crawling with police and knights. You're wanted for murder, remember?"

"And you're a Fist member, which means they'll be targeting you too."

He gestures to his face. "I'm a New Tritoner. You know how many Fist members are from New Triton?"

His tweaked features and bronzed skin might make him a little safer, because nobody expects floaters to belong to an Old Triton resistance movement. But in Old Triton, he'll stand out.

"Where you come from won't matter if they find you in a Fist safe house," I tell him.

"I'll be careful."

"I can't stay behind." I get to my feet. "It'd kill me to have to sit around and do nothing while you put yourself in danger. I'll tie something around my face to hide it."

"Yeah, because a strip of cloth is sure to keep hundreds of super-advanced, deadly soldiers from shooting you on sight." He looks up at the ceiling, lifting both hands and giving an exaggerated shrug. "But there's no point asking you to stay where it's safe, is there? You'll come anyway, no matter what I say."

"William's my baby brother. I promised Ma I'd find him."

"You're risking your life for nothing. Even if my friend knows where the pods are, there's no way to get your brother out."

"One problem at a time. I'll leave a note for Doctor Gregory, then let's go."

Chapter Nine

The wall that separates Triton from Deiterra is at Triton's northern edge. It's solid concrete, meters thick, and it towers above Old Triton and most of New Triton.

It's been there all my life, along with plenty of speculation about what Deiterra might be like, so seeing an entire section of the wall has been turned to rubble feels like the weirdest kind of dream. When we peek around the corner of a building, I freeze, staring at the damage.

The breach is even more enormous in real life than it looked on the holo. Concrete boulders have torn through the closest Old Triton buildings, and the New Triton walkway overhead has a jagged, dangling edge. So much of New Triton has been torn away, I can see a wide swathe of the sky. Although I'm standing in Old Triton, the sun's filtering all the way down to my face and it's bright enough to make me squint.

But the most surreal part? Through the mountain of rubble and all the dust that still drifts around the crumbling wall, I catch a glimpse of green. My first ever view of Deiterra is of a dizzyingly tall tree covered with leaves. There are trees in New Triton, but none even close to that size, and nothing grows in Old Triton.

It's like looking through a portal to another world.

"Soldiers," hisses Cale, tugging me back behind the building.

As if I needed telling. The director's knights are stationed all around the rubble, alert for signs of Deiterrans forcing their way through the breach. The knights are wielding weapons so close to the wall, I wonder why its automated weapons system hasn't targeted them. I guess it must have been destroyed with this part of the wall.

"This way," Cale whispers in my ear, jerking his head toward an alley.

I follow him back into darkness, down a long, narrow Old Triton back street to an anonymous wooden door set into a graffiti-covered brick wall. Judging from the paint peeling away from the wood, the door used to be painted slime green. Or maybe the wood's moldy—in the darkness of the alley, under a New Triton overpass that's blocking any sunlight, it's hard to tell.

Cale knocks softly on the door. "What's buried will rise," he murmurs with his mouth close to the door. "It's Cale. Open up."

There's a small window next to the door, but it's covered with a thick curtain so I can't see into it. The door creaks open no more than a crack. Suspicious eyes peer out of the gloom, first examining Cale, then jerking to me.

"Who are you?" the man inside demands.

"We're friends of Gareth," Cale says. "Let us in."

The man's eyes flick back to me. "Show me your face."

Cale shakes his head. "Not out here. They're looking for her."

The man grudgingly steps back and we follow him into

a gloomy room that stinks like a toilet. It's so dark, it takes a moment for my eyes to adjust.

Five small metal-and-canvas beds take up one side of the room. In the corner, three people are sitting around a table on broken-down old chairs. An old-fashioned paper map of the city is pinned to the wall. It's tattered and torn, but pins have been stuck into it, though I'm not sure what they mark.

A small table against the wall serves as a kitchen, and a water faucet has been jury-rigged onto a pipe that runs haphazardly along the wall. Through an open door, the bathroom is where the stench is coming from.

As the door shuts behind us, Cale coughs as though he's trying not to gag, then lifts his sleeve to cover his nose. I've lived in Old Triton so long, the stench shouldn't bother me, but my stomach still turns over. Probably because my sense of smell is a lot more sensitive than it used to be.

"Where's Gareth?" asks Cale, his voice muffled by the jacket.

"Show me your face," repeats the man, gesturing at me. He's a sallow-skinned sinker, probably in his thirties, wearing a lumpy, stained woollen hat that looks like it was knitted by hand by someone who didn't really know how. Judging from his wiry frame, he's as used to hard work and basic rations as I am. Several of his teeth are missing, and when he talks, my gaze lingers on the dark gaps.

I tug down my bandanna and his eyes widen when he sees my scars. Then he gives me a nod. I guess a sinker with a face like mine is unlikely to be an enemy.

One of the people at the table gasps. "Milla?" She flies at me, grabbing my shoulders. "What are you doing here?"

I gape at her, my heart expanding to fill my chest. Then I wrap my arms around her. "Tori." Her name gets stuck in my throat, so it comes out as a mangled croak.

"What are you doing here?" she asks again, hugging me with a grip so fierce, I'm all but crushed. "I can't believe it's you."

"I can't believe it either. I was afraid I'd never see you again."

"Can't get rid of me that easily." She gives me a last squeeze and lets me go. "But look at you with two eyes. How did that happen? Does the new one work? It matches your other one perfectly."

"They grew it from my DNA, especially for me."

She raises her eyebrows. "No kidding? Leave you alone for a few weeks, and what do you get up to?" She grabs my arm and lifts it. "What are you doing with this fancy band? That isn't gold, is it? And who cut your hair?"

I snort out a breathless laugh. "Who cut my *hair*? I haven't seen you in weeks, so much has happened, I'm not sure where to start, and that's what you want to know?"

My heart feels so light I could float away. After the terrible events of the last few days, finding Tori gives me hope that things could get better. She looks exactly the same as when I saw her last. Her long, dark hair is pulled back into a ponytail that explodes into a mass of curls, and her crooked smile always looks like she's cooking up trouble.

"Sit down and tell me everything." She strides over to the table and hooks her thumb at the two people sitting there, staring curiously at us. Cards are scattered on the table and it looks like they must have been playing a game. "These two will make room. That's Keren and Franco." Then she nods to the toothless man who opened the door for us. "The rude one is Spade."

Keren has a broad face, and a nose that's wider than it is long. She's bundled in so many layers, she reminds me of when I worked in the part of the factory where we packaged goods up for shipping. She's like a well-wrapped parcel.

Franco is her opposite, so thin that he looks like he's in training to be able to slip through prison bars. He's chewing on the end of a small plastic stick, and I get the feeling he's never still for long.

They both give me friendly nods and move their game over to one of the beds without complaint. It seems like Tori's in charge and they answer to her. But that can't be right, can it? Sure, she used to go to Fist meetings sometimes, but she didn't mention giving anyone orders.

"Where's Gareth?" asks Cale.

Tori cocks her head. "Who are you, pretty-boy?"

His jaw tightens at the nickname, but the friendliness of his tone doesn't change. "I'm Cale. Gareth said he'd meet me here."

"He'll be back soon. Sit down." She turns back to me. "Tell me everything."

I sit down and fill her in on all the things that have happened since I last saw her, keeping my voice low so the other three Fist members can't hear. I'm just glad Cale's there to back me up so Tori doesn't think I've gone completely insane, or that I'm making it all up.

When we lived in the shelter together, Tori could always top anything bad that happened. *This is nothing*, she'd say, before coming up with a far-fetched story about something terrible she'd had to suffer, to make whatever hardships we were going through seem minor in comparison.

Not this time.

I would have sworn she could never be lost for words, but her mouth drops open soon after I start talking, and her eyes keep getting wider and wider. To be fair, I can hardly believe my own story. Swapping bands with a dead girl, competing in the Skin Hunter contest, and escaping from Director Morelle? It all sounds way too crazy to be true.

"What happened to you?" I ask when I've finished. "You were transferred to a new job and a new shelter. How'd you end up here?"

She shakes her head as though breaking out of the spell my story cast on her. Then she snorts. "My new job turned out to be looking after the boss, if you get what I mean. He decided I was going to warm his bed for him."

"What?" My stomach turns over. If I'd known, I would never have let her walk out of the shelter that night. I've no idea what I could have done to help her, but together we'd have come up with *something*.

Cale's expression has gone dark. "Can he get away with that?"

"Asshole thought he could, until I stabbed him in the knee with a fork. He chased me, but he was bleeding buckets and limping pretty badly. I got away and spent the next couple of nights on the street."

"Alone?" My voice rises.

She gives a dismissive shrug, but her gaze flicks down so quickly, most people would miss it. "I'm too punchy for anyone to mess with. You should know that by now, slugger."

It's only because I know her so well that I can tell things must have happened that she doesn't want to talk about. While I was settling into my own private bedroom at the Morelle Corporation, she probably went through hell.

I turn my face away for a moment, willing myself not to let my anguish show. Even if I'd known what she was going through, what could I have done to help her?

"Anyway," she says. "I couldn't find work and couldn't

bluff my way into any of the shelters. So I went looking for a Fist safe house I'd heard about. I knew Gareth from the meetings, but we'd only spoken a few times, so I wasn't sure whether he'd take me in. Long story short, he turned out to be one of the good ones. Gareth made room for me right away, no questions asked. I've been here ever since."

Her voice is warm when she talks about Gareth, and her eyes sparkle. Could there be something between them? If so, I hope I get to meet him. Any man Tori falls for must be one of a kind.

"You're running things here?" I ask.

"Gareth is. But he's been busy tracking the knights, collecting proof of how many sinkers they're killing. We were broadcasting the footage on Sub Zero, until they shut it down. Now, the only way we'll be able to get it out is if we can hack b-Net."

"You think you can do that?" asks Cale.

"Gareth will find a way."

Yeah, there's definitely something between her and Gareth. Her lips twitch up a little when she says his name, as though thinking about him makes her happy.

"Gareth's been spending a lot of time on the street," she adds. "So I've been helping out here." She glances at Keren, Franco, and Spade, who've gone back to their card game, and raises her voice so they can hear her. "These fools need someone to tell them what to do, or they'll likely get themselves killed." Judging from the grins they shoot her, they're used to her sharp tongue.

"I didn't know you were so involved with the Fist."

She wrinkles her nose at me. "They're the only ones trying to make this hell-hole a little less shitty."

Her words send a pang of guilt through me. She's right. Now I feel selfish because I never joined.

"Why are you staying so close to the breach in the wall?" asks Cale. "Isn't that risky?"

"We're trying to get people through to the other side. Into Deiterra."

"What?" Cale goes slack-jawed, and I must look just as shocked.

"Across the breach?" I ask. "Through all that rubble, with soldiers guarding both sides?"

She nods. "It's a challenge, that's for sure."

"But why would you risk it?" demands Cale.

"The Fist has been trying to help sinkers for a long time, but things are only getting worse. Now, with the wall down, there's another chance for us. Conditions must be better in Deiterra, because they have more land and less people. If we can find a way through the breach, we can send people to a whole new life." She gets up and goes to the map to tap one of the pins sticking into it. "We've lost three people so far, but each time we get closer to finding a way through."

I stare at the map, at the thick black line that marks the wall. On the other side is empty space, because if any map maker knows what's over there, they aren't saying. Our peace treaty forbids any Tritoner from setting foot on Deiterran soil, so President Trask has always pretended Deiterra doesn't exist. All anybody knows about it is based on rumours that are decades old.

But on Tori's map, someone has drawn in the tree I saw, and put in a few more around it as well. Have they seen more trees, or are they just speculating?

The idea of going through the wall makes me feel a little like the first time I transferred into a Skin. Like there's an entirely different life in reach, one I never dreamed of. The possibilities make my head spin. Could someone really get to the other side?

"How can anyone get past the knights?" asks Cale.

"That's the tricky part. But all the rubble in front of the breach actually helps. It's like a giant maze. We're mapping it at night, looking for a way that's not obvious, so we can sneak our people through."

"What happens if someone makes it to the other side?" Cale gets up to stand in front of the map, peering at it like it holds the answers. "You really think the Deiterrans will let them stay?"

"Why not?" Her chin lifts in a stubborn tilt. "We can give them information and help them fight against Triton. We have skills. And why should we be loyal to Triton after the way we've been treated all these years?"

All those hours in the factory and the shelter when I allowed myself to dream about a better life, it would never have occurred to me to consider trying to get to Deiterra. I learned about the food wars at school, when Deiterra fought to stop Triton from expanding onto any more of their land. When the wall was built, Deiterra was less populated than Triton, but that was decades ago. Who knows what's happened since then?

"So you've given up trying to make things better for the workers here in Old Triton?" Cale asks.

"Of course not," she snaps. "We've taken out a few knights. But there are over a thousand of them, and they're a lot worse than the stompers ever were. We've lost good people. More than ever before." She waves one hand around the small room, her eyes flashing. "And I'm trapped in this stinking hovel, fighting a battle I know we can't win, sending kids to their death. So don't lecture me on giving up, okay? What are you doing to help, *floater*?"

He raises both hands, glancing at the card players who are openly staring. "Hey, I didn't mean anything. I was with Gareth at fifty-third when it was raided. It's thanks to him I got away."

"You were there, pretty-boy?" Her tone softens, and she gives Cale an up-and-down look, as though assessing him with fresh eyes.

I blink at him. I had no idea he'd actually been caught up in a raid.

"We lost some good people at fifty-third." He lets out a loud breath. "And I knew the four executed in the square."

"That shocked us all." Tori shakes her head. "Did you see whether—?"

A loud bang interrupts her. Then there are a series of cracks that sound like gunshots.

"What's that?" Cale demands, as the card players jump to their feet.

"Sounds like fighting." Striding to the window, I move the thick curtain aside so I can peek out. The alley is clear, but the sound of gunfire is loud.

Cale moves beside me. "See anything?"

"Nothing."

The door creaks open, and I spin around. Tori is easing outside.

"What are you doing?" I hiss.

"Gareth is due back." She sounds worried. "The soldiers could be shooting at him. He might need help."

Before I can tell her it's too dangerous, she disappears into the alley.

Chapter Ten

I take off into the alley after Tori.

"Don't, Milla," Cale calls after me. But his footsteps are just behind me, following me out.

Just as I catch up with Tori, she lifts her baggy shirt and tugs a gun out of the waistband of her jeans.

I stare at it, shocked. "Where'd you get that?"

"Stole it from a stomper."

"If you get caught with it—"

"Yeah, I know. But they can only kill me once, right? Gun or no gun, I'm already on their hit list."

She moves quickly down the alley, hugging the walls. I stare after her for a moment, wanting to tell her to get rid of the gun, that it's too dangerous to have one. But she's right. Having an illegal weapon won't make her any more of a target.

Cale and I follow her down the alley to its entrance, and peek around the corner. All I see at first is dust kicked up from all the rubble around the breach in the wall. As more guns fire, flashes of light reflect off the dust.

Then figures emerge. Men and women are pouring

through the hole in the wall, scrambling over and around the boulders.

Deiterrans.

They're wearing combat gear and firing guns.

A line of knights in front of us are firing back at them, mowing the Deiterran invaders down. Their bullets tear through the line of enemy soldiers, while the Deiterrans' bullets slow the knights down, but don't drop them.

Some knights don't even bother to pull their weapons. They leap at the Deiterrans, moving faster than any human could. Their armored hands transform into claws. With vicious swipes they slice through flesh and sever limbs.

I flinch backward as blood sprays across the rocks.

The Deiterrans are being carved to pieces. The knights march forward, relentless and seemingly invulnerable. Mowing them down.

Tori says something into my ear, but the deafening cracks of gunfire drown her out.

Then I spot someone sprinting out of the darkness of a New Triton street. A man is running toward our alley, skirting the sunlit area near the breach. A knight is on his heels, thundering behind him, catching up fast.

"Gareth!" gasps Tori. She jumps out from the cover of the alley into full view of the oncoming knight and aims the gun at Gareth, sighting down its barrel like she knows how to use it. With her other hand, she makes frantic 'get down' motions.

Gareth dives forward and Tori fires. The bullet hits the knight, making it flinch. Tori fires again and again. The bullets don't seem to hurt it, but Gareth manages to sprint away from it, gaining a slight lead.

The sound of Tori's gunfire is lost in the noise from the battle that's still raging. But as soon as she runs out of bullets, the knight will take Gareth down. Both he and the knight are almost on us. We need to get back to the safe house and barricade ourselves in. Even then, it'll probably just punch its way through the door.

I'm turning to run when somebody comes up beside me. The others from the safe house have followed us out. Franco is next to me, and he tenses as though he's ready to spring. He can't mean to attack it? The Skin will tear him to pieces.

Gareth rounds the corner into the alley and charges past us, heading for the safe house. The knight is right behind him. As it thunders around the corner, all the Fist members leap on it, trying to bowl it over. With one sweep of its arm, it sends Franco flying. Tori and Spade cling to its other arm, struggling to hang on. Keren leaps on its back. Gareth skids to a halt, turns back, and tackles its feet. Cale rushes to grab its free arm before it can tear the others off.

When I realize what's happening, I throw myself squarely at its middle, using all my strength to overbalance the knight. It goes down with a grunt of surprise, landing heavily. I keep hold, but even with all of us pinning it, the knight still thrashes around, impossibly strong. We won't be able to hold it for long.

Tori scrambles up, jams her gun into one of the pointed ears on the top of the knight's head, and pulls the trigger. The knight goes limp.

The Fist members pull themselves off it, Keren extracting herself from underneath its shoulders with a grimace of pain. I get to my feet. Tori's face is pale and her hands are shaking. The knight is still intact, but its eyes have gone dull. Blood and brain matter leak out of its ear.

"Come on," says Gareth in a low voice, peering back

out of the alley. "Let's get out of here before any more knights see us."

We run silently back to the safe house, the sounds of battle still loud behind us. Good thing their gunfire is deafening. If the Knights hadn't been so busy slaughtering all those Deiterrans, they'd have heard us for sure.

When we get inside, Gareth puts his arms around Tori. "You okay?" he asks.

She frowns. "Am *I* okay? You're the one who decided to race a knight."

He laughs and kisses her forehead. "Not on purpose, believe me." Releasing her, he turns to us. "Thanks for jumping in." He gives a nod that includes everyone in the room. "That knight didn't know who he was messing with." His gaze goes to me and he sticks his hand out, flicking his shaggy fringe out of his eyes. "I'm Gareth. And what you did was impressive."

I shake his hand, letting my small hand be swallowed up in his huge one. He's a big guy, the tallest in the room, and I can see why Tori likes him. His unruly beard is bushier than Tori's exploding ponytail, his smile is large and even, and his eyes crinkle like he's thinking about something funny. He already seems to have brushed off the fact he was seconds from death.

"Milla," I say.

"Welcome." He turns to Cale and slaps his back. "Good to see you both."

Keren is at the window with the curtain pulled aside so she can see out. "It was a slaughter out there. The Deiterrans didn't stand a chance." Over the top of all her other clothing layers is a threadbare brown coat, which she tugs further around her as though she's cold. She's short and wide, and if I hadn't seen her charge at the knight and leap fearlessly onto its back, I wouldn't have believed it.

Tori sinks into one of the chairs at the table. "Inside those Skins, they're just kids." She shakes her head. "How could they do that? How could children rip those people apart?"

I swallow, remembering the carnage. I've seen more than my share of violence, and Rayne bled to death in my arms. But I've never seen killing on that scale.

The stick of plastic Franco was chewing on has miraculously survived the fight, and he talks with it clenched between his teeth. "The knights have been doing worse things to us."

I meet Cale's gaze. "Could the Skins be making the kids more ruthless? Changing their brains, like Sentin said?"

"Maybe." He sounds grim.

The others look questioningly at me, but I can't explain. My chest feels too tight to breathe. Is William in one of the Skins that are still out there tearing the Deiterrans to pieces? Has the director already turned him into one of her killing machines?

"Show them the clip of the pods." I nod at Cale's wrist. "Do any of you know where this room is, the one where the soldiers transfer into the Skins?"

Cale activates his holo and shows them the news clip of the windowless warehouse with its rows and rows of pods.

As soon as the image appears, Tori nods. "We've already talked about it. Spade thinks he knows where it is." She looks at the toothless man.

Spade pushes up his knitted hat to scratch his greasy hair. "Could be the Meat Locker on one-fifty-seventh in the Packing District. That's where they used to store the crappy protein that goes to the shelters. I worked there for a while, loading the so-called meat onto trucks."

I let out a relieved breath. Finally I'm making some

progress. "My brother's body will be there. He's one of the director's soldiers." I ignore Spade's shocked grunt. "Now all I need is to get in. I'll take a look at the factory from the outside, figure out if there's a way."

The sound of gunshots seems to be tapering off. Perhaps the slaughter is over.

Cale shakes his head. "The whole area will be crawling with knights."

"That building could be a good target for the Fist." Gareth raises his eyebrows at Tori as though asking her opinion.

"A target?" I shake my head. "No way. Not with my brother there."

"Hey, don't worry." He holds up both hands. "I'm not in the business of killing kids. But if we can find a way to evacuate it and blow up the pods, I'm on board with that." He strides to the table and sits down next to Tori. The smile he shoots her warms my heart, and it gets even warmer when Tori smiles back. If a squad of knights walked in, I'm not sure either of them would notice. They're too busy glowing at each other.

But after a moment, Tori manages to drag her gaze to me. "Milla, you have to tell Gareth the story you told me. What's been happening to you, and how you got here."

I press my lips together. Stealing a dead girl's band isn't something I'm proud of. I don't want to share it with a bunch of strangers.

"You know I was the saber-toothed tiger in the Skin Hunter contest?" Cale says after a moment. "Well, Milla was the leopard. And we're pretty sure Director Morelle started the war herself, blaming Deiterra for the stuff she blew up. She built a Skin army and brainwashed a bunch of teenagers so she could invade Deiterra and rule the world." When I catch his eye, he gives me a little shrug and a hint of a grin. "Long story short," he adds. "There's more, but that's the highlight reel."

I nod gratefully. "That pretty much covers it."

They're all gaping at us. The stick Franco was chewing is hanging motionless from his bottom lip. Karen's wide nostrils are flared, making then look enormous. And I can count how few lower teeth Spade has left.

Gareth sits back in his chair and makes a whistling sound. "Highlight reel," he repeats with a laugh, his eyes crinkling.

"Told you it was a good story." Tori looks smug. "Anyone else but Milla telling it, I'd say they'd been drinking too much street brew."

"Director Morelle's brainwashing kids?" Gareth's smile fades, but I get the feeling it's just under the surface, waiting for any chance to reappear. He has no frown lines, but plenty around his eyes. I wouldn't have thought the leader of the Fist would have much to smile about, but his wide grin seems as much an identifying feature as his bushy beard, or the enormous, calloused hands he's resting on the table.

"Her soldiers," I say. "Including my brother."

"We think she can influence their thoughts," explains Cale. "Something to do with transferring into the Skins."

"That's why I have to get him away from the director. Break him out of the Meat Locker."

"I understand." Gareth gives me a sympathetic look. "And I wish I knew a way to do that. But a factory full of soldiers will be the hardest place in Triton to walk into, let alone get out of." He seems genuinely sorry, like he really cares. I can see why his entire team were ready to throw themselves at a knight to save him.

Franco pulls the plastic stick out of his mouth. He and

Spade are sitting on the beds, while Keren is still by the window.

"If the Skins change people's thoughts, tonight's target was a good choice," says Franco.

"We're blowing up the factory tonight," explains Tori. "The one where they make the Skins."

I draw in a sharp breath. "You can't. That's where my mother works."

Gareth leans back in his chair. "Don't worry, all the workers have been briefed. With the number of sinkers the knights have been killing, everyone wants to get them off the streets. The grunts at the factory are the ones who told us that inside their ears is the one place the knights don't have armor. Gave us the means to finally be able to take them down."

Keren's nostrils flare, and she folds her arms, leaning back against the wall. "Soon as the director realizes that's how we're killing them, she'll change that."

I cross to the table, still focused on Gareth. "I don't get it. How can you blow up the factory without killing anyone?"

"Most night shifters aren't going to turn up to work at all. A few minutes before the bomb goes off, the fire alarm will be triggered and the few who show up will evacuate. They know it's going to happen and to get out fast."

"What if not everyone gets out in time? Or the bomb explodes early?"

"Hey, it'll be okay." Gareth gets up from his seat to put his large hand on my arm. His voice is soothing. "Sure there's a little risk. But we need to stop the knights from being manufactured. Then we might stand a chance of reducing their numbers."

I pull away from his hand, stepping back. "Ma's the one you're putting at risk."

"Why don't you call her? Make sure she's not going to turn up for work tonight. Then she'll be safe."

"Even if you manage not to kill people, destroying the factory will leave Ma without a job. She'll starve."

"We'll look after her." Tori motions around the room. "This isn't much, but we're surviving."

I blink at her. She was the one who called it a stinking hovel, and with seven people in it, the tiny room feels impossibly crowded. The air in here is so pungent I can barely breathe. And it already has five beds crammed into it. Adding more will mean there's barely room to walk.

"What about the hundreds of other workers?" I ask. "You going to squeeze them all into safe houses? How do you plan to feed them?"

Her eyes narrow. "Would you rather the streets were overrun with knights?"

"Better than putting hundreds of people out of work. You know they won't all survive."

"People are dying already, Milla. You haven't been on the streets the last couple of weeks. You don't know how bad it is."

"I don't like this. There has to be a better way" I fold my arms and glower at her. Tori's parents died years ago, so she's used to being on her own. Besides, it's not *her* mother she's putting in danger.

"I understand how worried you are." Gareth's eyes are creased with sympathy. "I wish we didn't have to take such drastic action. But this will make things better, I promise."

Cale moves over to me. He doesn't try to touch me, but stands next to me, shoulder to shoulder. "I don't like it either," he says. "Too much can go wrong."

"I hear you." Gareth spreads his hands. "But it's already set up. The explosion's scheduled to go off half an hour after night shift starts, and there's no turning back."

It's early afternoon, and night shift doesn't start until eight. That's several hours I'll spend worrying.

I can't hear gunshots any more, so perhaps the fighting's over and all the Deiterrans are dead. Hopefully the coast is clear, because if I stay in this stinking room, I'm going to suffocate.

"I'm going to take a look at the Meat Locker," I say, turning for the door. "Scope the place out and see how hard it might be to get inside."

Tori stands up. "Milla, please don't—"

"I need to do something, or I'll go crazy."

"Be careful," says Gareth.

To my relief, Cale doesn't object or tell me how insanely dangerous it is, or how reckless I'm being. He just follows me outside. "I'm coming with you," he says.

Chapter Eleven

C ale and I head away from the wall, taking a wide circle around where the knights were fighting, and keeping to the darkest, most narrow alley-ways. The packing district is two hours away on foot, and if Cale weren't with me I'd have to walk. Instead, he uses his band to call us a cab.

Safely inside, we drive silently along streets that used to teem with people. The food stalls, the app sellers, the racks of cheap, colourful clothing are all gone. A few sinkers walk briskly with their heads down, hurrying to wherever they have to be, and occasional groups of rough sleepers are tucked into dark corners. But compared to what it used to be like, the streets are eerily quiet. They look darker than ever without the bright signage of stalls, and the portable, blue-flamed burners the noodle sellers use to cook their offerings.

But we haven't gone far before our cab passes a squad of black-armored knights out patrolling. Then another squad. In fact, the number of knights on the streets almost outnumber the people.

We circle the block and make sure the coast is clear before getting out of the cab.

At the farthest end of the street from the Meat Locker are the remains of some street stalls that once sold food and drinks. Their owners built them on the sidewalk, attaching them to the brick wall of the building behind them. The structures were ramshackle to start with, and now they're empty shells with splintered walls and smashed counters.

We stop behind one so we can peer around it at the Meat Locker. The building is only just visible at the other end of the street. Like all the big factories, the old food manufacturing center is housed in the base of a giant scraper that soars up into New Triton. In New Triton, it's probably a fancy apartment building, or filled with expensive stores and plush offices. The Old Triton base that supports it is made of thick concrete reinforced with steel, and has no windows at all.

There's only one entrance into the factory, a door with two knights guarding it. I bet more knights will be inside the building, keeping watch over the hundreds of pods that hold all the director's soldiers.

Just because it looks like there's no way to get inside, doesn't mean I'm going to give up.

Though this street is darker than most, there's only one group of five rough sleepers anywhere near it, and they're huddled in an alcove just past the ruined stalls, a little closer to the Meat Locker than we are.

There are a lot of rough sleepers in Old Triton, and the ones without jobs mostly survive by hustling for credits, selling sex, or beating people and robbing them. They hang out in the darkest corners, and their eyes adapt so they can see better than their marks.

Before my leopard changed me, I would have steered

well clear of them. But I'm stronger now, and a lot less afraid. If I lie down with them, I'll be able to watch the Meat Locker's door and work out if there's any way to do the impossible and break into the place.

I can tell by Cale's expression that he doesn't like the idea. He has his jacket hood tugged over his head and his sleeves pulled down to hide his hands. Not many floaters visit the darkest parts of Old Triton, and even in the gloom, a knight's enhanced eyesight would pick out his bronzed skin and tweaked face.

"These streets are crawling with knights," he whispers. "Haven't you seen enough?"

I have my own hood pulled low, and a bandanna tied over my nose and mouth. When I speak, my voice is muffled. "I need you to hide in here." I motion to the remains of the fallen-down stall we're sheltering behind. It looks like there's enough space to duck under what's left of the shelves and not be seen. "I want to watch for a while to see if anyone goes in or out of the Meat Locker."

"Milla, you can't stay out here, in full view. It's not safe."

"I'm stronger and faster than I used to be, remember?"

"You're still no match for a knight."

"Trust me. Please." As the words leave my mouth, I'm all too aware of what I'm asking. The one thing he said he couldn't do was trust me.

But to my relief, he steps into the ruined stall and crouches behind what's left of the counter. "I don't like this," he mutters.

"Thank you." I head further down the street toward the Meat Locker to where the group are sleeping. Without a word, I fit myself into the alcove with them.

"Who're you?" slurs one of the rough sleepers. She's an old woman with a red face that's pockmarked and sagging. She's propped against the wall, holding a tin cup that's got to be full of street brew. Judging from her sunken, bloodshot eyes and sagging cheeks, she's been drunk for more years than I've been alive.

"Nobody," I mumble. With my face mostly covered, I doubt she can even tell if I'm a man or woman.

The old woman cackles as though I've said something hilarious. "Nobody," she repeats. "Nobody's here."

Sitting next to her, a large, bearded man spits on the sidewalk. "Shut it, Gama," he growls. Gama is Old Triton slang for grandmother, but he doesn't use it in an affectionate way, and there's no way these two are related.

It takes several seconds for Gama's bleary eyes to focus on him, and when she manages it, she raises her cup as though he's asked her to propose a toast. "I'll talk 'til I die, then I'll talk more once I'm dead." she slurs. "Big men try to shut me up. Where those men now? In a worse hell than this, if there is one."

My body tenses. Is the old woman asking for violence? If there's anything my years in the shelter taught me, it's to be wary around men like him.

But the bearded man just grunts and spits again. The movement extends his neck, and I catch a glimpse of a tattoo under his shirt. It's the Fist's closed fist symbol, and these days I'm guessing that's a dangerous thing to have. He has a bottle of his own and is clearly trying to drink himself into unconsciousness.

The other three—two men and a woman—are curled up together on the concrete, probably already asleep. Maybe I lucked out and found a group who're just here to rest. They might be night shifters at a factory who either couldn't find a place in a shelter, or decided to take their chances outside. Sleeping in a shelter is a lot less danger-ous, especially these days, but the air's a lot fresher out here. I wonder if they realize they picked a place that's so close to the knights' base.

I hear footsteps. Metallic boots on concrete, marching in unison. It's coming from around the corner, and getting closer.

Knights are coming.

I slump down further until I'm lying on the sidewalk with the sleepers. Holding my breath, I make my breathing slow and even, pretending to be asleep too.

When the knights come around the corner, all I can see from under my hood is their shiny black boots. I watch the boots march past the fallen-down stall where Cale's hiding, letting out a small breath of relief as they move away from it without looking inside. As the knights get closer to me, it feels like their shadows fall over me, chilling me, though there's no sun for them to cast a shadow.

Maybe it's because I'm lying down that they seem so big, but the monsters look enormous.

Four have marched past us, heading toward the Meat Locker, and the last two have drawn level with us, when the old woman speaks up.

"Knights," she says, and cackles. "You want a dragon to kill or princess to kiss? Drink with me, eh? I'll start a dragon, become a princess. Just like magic."

The four who've gone past, stop and turn. The last two also stop, but they're so close they tower over us.

"What are you talking about?" The question comes from one of the knights. The tone is contemptuous, but the voice is young and reedy. The boy using the Skin can't be much older than sixteen.

Gama laughs even harder, slopping her drink onto her hand. "Knights not have balls?" She snorts. "You sound like you don't have—"

She makes a strangled sound. All I can see is her body

lifting. The knight must have picked her up by the front of her jacket. It lifts her right up until her feet are kicking above the ground.

"What did you say?" the knight demands in its reedy voice.

I force myself not to move. There's nothing I can do to help the old woman. I doubt I'd stand a chance against a single knight, let alone six of them.

"Hurt her," demands the second knight in what's definitely a girl's voice. "Make her sorry."

There's a soft cracking noise, then the old woman lands on the sidewalk, her head smacking hard against the concrete. The sound makes me flinch, but Gama must have been dead before she hit the ground, because her head is twisted too far around.

The girl-knight laughs. It's a delighted sound, a joyful giggle. It chills me more than anything else. Even more than seeing the Deiterrans slaughtered, or hearing the soft cracking sound of Gama's neck snapping.

"I get to kill one too," crows the girl-knight. She steps up to the bearded man and reaches down to grab his neck.

"No time," calls one of the four knights that have gone ahead. "We have orders. We're going to be late."

The girl lets out a disappointed sound, but lets the man go. The two of them join their friends before all six knights march away in a pack.

I stay still, just twitching my head to ease my hood up a little so I can see where the knights go. None of the other rough sleepers move a muscle, though I know they're all awake. I can hear their fast, shallow breaths, and smell their fear.

The knights march into the Meat Locker, nodding at the guards as they enter. When the last one has disappeared inside, I let out a long breath and push myself up to sitting.

"Bastards," snarls the bearded man, wiping his hand over his neck as though the knight's fingers left something nasty behind. "You see the director on the holo? She said the knights were going to kill the Deiterrans, not us."

"You believed that?" One of the other men lifts his head and makes a sound of disgust. "They're worse than the stompers. Moment I saw them I knew they would be."

Getting to my feet, I look down at Gama's body. Though I didn't know her, I can't stand to see her lying there like discarded trash. A cold anger burns in the pit of my stomach. She didn't deserve to die like that.

Cale emerges from the stall and motions for me to join him behind it. When I do, he grabs me by the arms with a worried frown. "Are you okay? They didn't hurt you?"

"I'm fine." I nod toward Gama's body. "I don't want to leave her on the sidewalk. You think we can carry her to a street further away, then call a cab and take her to the morgue?"

He nods. My own horror at the way she died is reflected back in his eyes. "I'll call one."

While he taps his band, I cast another long look at the Meat Locker. It's clearly the knights' base of operations, where they leave to go on their patrols and where they return afterward. Old Triton is twenty-eight stories high, and the scraper looks big enough to house hundreds, maybe thousands, of pods.

Cale was right when he said there was no way to get into the building.

No way, except one.

If I transferred into a Knight Skin, I might be able to walk right in.

Chapter Twelve

Cale calls Ma to arrange for her to meet us outside her factory that evening, just after seven o'clock when her day shift ends. While we wait for her to finish work, I study the factory. It's where the Skins are being made, and the Fist's explosives are already planted inside. There's a main entrance where the grunts go in and out, and a roller door for deliveries. Both doors are guarded by stompers rather than knights, which is one good thing. Still, what I've decided to do isn't going to be easy.

When Ma sees me, she grabs me in a bear hug with a cry of relief. "You're okay, love?" Her voice is thick with tears and she hugs me so tightly I can feel her bones poking out under her thick layers of clothing. "You have a new eye? I thought so, but my holo app's barely working, so I couldn't tell for sure. Oh it's good to see you. Are you safe? Are they still looking for you? You're much too thin."

"I'm too thin?" I protest. "You feel like you haven't eaten in a year."

Her arms might be skinny, but hard work has made her

strong. It takes me a while to prise free from her grip so I can introduce her to Cale. Then we head to a dark side alley where we can talk without attracting attention.

"You're okay, Milla?" she demands again. "You're not hurt, are you?"

"I'm fine. See?" In spite of the threat of being identified by any street cameras the Fist might not have knocked out, I tug my bandanna down so she can see my face. I can't get over how old Ma looks. Her hair is gray and lank, and her face is etched with lines of worry and strain.

"What happened to you? Why did they tell me you were dead? And now they're saying you killed someone?"

I hitch the bandanna back into place. "I didn't kill anyone. But I'll have to explain when we have more time. Ma, I came to ask you for something."

"Anything, love."

"You know The Fist are going to blow up your factory tonight?"

"I heard. That's why I'm not working the night shift." Then she frowns. "You haven't joined the Fist, have you? Not that I don't appreciate what they're trying to do, but you're in enough danger already."

"I'm not working with them. Not really." I glance guiltily at Cale, because as it turns out, that's exactly what I'm doing. "I'm just trying to find William."

Her brow smooths, and she gives me a smile so filled with hope that it makes my heart ache. "I know you will. You'll find him. You'll keep him safe."

I exchange another glance with Cale. His lips are tight and his expression pained. I dragged him into my plan while we were waiting for Ma to finish her shift, and just as I expected, he didn't like it one bit. He agreed to call Gareth and Tori for me so I could talk through what I wanted to do, but he also spent a lot of time trying to convince me my plan sucks.

"I figured out where William is," I tell Ma. "But to get him out of the director's army, I'm going to need one of the Knight Skins. Is there any way to get one out of the factory?"

"One of the Skins?" She sucks in a whistling breath through the gaps in her teeth. "They're always guarded. There are stompers on the line, more than ever before. And the Skins are big and heavy. You can't exactly tuck one under your arm."

"That's the door where trucks pick up the finished Skins and take them to the Meat Locker, right?" I point to the roller door, and when Ma nods, I ask, "Are there any Skins waiting to be picked up?"

"A couple. The truck doesn't come until there are six Skins ready for collection."

"Are the two that are ready near the roller door?"

She nods again, and I let myself feel a sliver of hope. Maybe my crazy plan could actually work.

"One more question, Ma. Where's the button to open the roller door from the inside?"

Next to me, Cale looks stony faced. I can tell he's biting his tongue, not wanting to tell me again how dangerous my plan is, because he doesn't want to worry my mother.

She frowns. "I suppose it's on the wall next to the door. I couldn't say for sure."

I can't help glancing again at Cale. When I catch his eye, he opens his mouth as though his objections are about to pour out, and I turn quickly back to Ma.

"One last question. I can't get into the factory without clearance. Would you lend me your band so I can pretend I'm you?"

Ma's eyes widen. It's a lot to ask. The punishment for

wearing somebody else's band is suffering a miserable death in an overcrowded jail. I've been risking it for so long, I'd almost forgotten how shocking the idea of breaking that law is to everyone else.

"But you can't go into the factory now." Ma shakes her head. "Not when they're about to blow it up."

"I still have more than thirty minutes. I just need to open the roller door before the bomb goes off, then I'll get out of there. Piece of cake."

"Milla—"

"It's the only way to get William out, and it's not as dangerous as it sounds." I wave a hand at the night shifters who are turning up to work, shuffling in through the factory's entrance. There are far less than normal, but a dozen men and women are heading inside. "They're all going in, and they know about the bomb. The fire alarm will go off, then everyone will have a good ten minutes to get out. Plenty of time."

Her eyes search my face, then go to Cale. "What do you think?" she demands. "Should I let her do it?"

He lifts his eyes to the heavens, like he's wishing she hadn't asked him. Then he lets out a long sigh. "Maybe you can stop her, but I can't. It's dangerous and I wish she weren't doing it. But she's convinced this is the only way."

Ma nods slowly and looks a little less worried, though I don't think Cale said anything reassuring. Her fingers go to the catch on her plain worker's band, and she presses the release. It springs open, and without it, her wrist looks naked. I've never seen her without a band before. Come to think of it, I've never seen anyone without a band.

"You'd better take off the one you're wearing first, love." She motions to my arm. "Lovely band, that one. Where'd you get it?"

"From a floater." I stare down at Rayne's delicate gold

band. It took me out of the shelter and gave me my Leopard Skin, but it's useless to me now, especially in Old Triton. Still, I find myself strangely reluctant to take it off. I've been Rayne for what feels like forever, and without a band, I'm nobody at all. Without a band, I don't officially exist, and the penalty for that is the same as stealing somebody else's identity.

What am I doing putting Ma in that kind of danger?

"You don't have to do this," murmurs Cale. "We can come up with another way."

I shake my head. "This is the best chance we're going to get." Closing my eyes, I take a deep breath and remember what it felt like to be the leopard, drawing on every bit of the leopard's strength. Then I force my fingers under the band and wrench it as hard as I can.

The lock snaps open and the band clatters onto the sidewalk.

Rayne is officially gone. She's dead now. It feels like I'm giving up my identity all over again.

Ma's mouth slackens and her eyes go wide. "How'd you do that?" She bends to pick up the band, frowning at the latch that's supposed to be all but unbreakable.

Cale is gaping too. Though I filled him in on all the details on how I'm stronger than before, seeing it for himself must be a shock.

"I'll tell you later, okay Ma? The clock is ticking."

She wraps her own band around my wrist and fastens it shut. "There. Promise you won't let them catch you? I'd never forgive myself."

I meet her eyes. As worried as she is for me, her naked wrist makes me more afraid for her.

"I'll wait here for you," Ma adds.

"It's not safe. I need you to get out of here." I turn to Cale. "Will you check with Doctor Gregory to make sure it's okay if Ma stays the night at her house, then call her a cab?"

He nods and steps away from us to make the call.

Ma hugs me tight. "Be safe, okay love?"

"You too."

When we've put Ma safely into a cab and she's on her way to Doctor Gregory's, I turn back to Cale.

"Now will you check in with Gareth? Find out if they have a truck?"

Cale calls Gareth, and they have a brief, silent conversation. When he disconnects the call, he says, "They've picked up the truck and they're on their way, but it'll take a while for them to get here. It's going to be tight."

Cale looks truly miserable. If he had a band that would get him into the factory, there's no way he'd let me go in alone. But his floater's band wouldn't make it past the scanners.

"Okay." I drag in a breath. "I'm going in. Wish me luck."

"Wait." He takes hold of my upper arms and frowns at me. "I'm still mad with you for lying to me." His eyes are dark with worry. "But I need you to be careful in there so I can be angry with you a lot more, okay?"

With my bandanna over the lower half of my face, he can't see me smile. "Okay."

He nods. Then he pulls me close and hugs me even tighter than Ma did. "I hate this," he mumbles. "You don't have to do it. We can call it off."

I disentangle myself from his arms. "I'll see you just before the explosion. I promise, everything will be fine." I mean every word of it. No matter what he pretends, I can tell he's mostly forgiven me. There's no way I'm going to let a factory full of stompers and a few explosives keep me from coming back to him now.

At the factory's entrance, I mingle with another group of grunts arriving to start night shift. They're volunteers who are here to avoid raising suspicions before the blast, and I'm impressed by their bravery.

Ma's band gets a green light on the scanner, and I keep my head down to keep from catching the gaze of the stompers who guard the place. Once through the internal doors that lead to the factory floor, the din of the machines gets louder. An enormous conveyor belt snakes around the large room, with various workstations attached for specialized tasks.

One heavily-guarded section is where the knights' weapons are being made. At another, metallic skeletons dangle like nightmare marionettes. At a third, a holo is projecting images of tiny computer chips, magnifying them to a much larger size. A grunt is rotating each image to check every microscopic component is properly in place.

I have no idea what workstation Ma is assigned to, and I don't want to be recognized as an intruder, so I shuffle along slowly, trying to look like I'm ambling toward a workstation at the far end of the factory, near the large roller door. Sure enough, when I get close, I see two completed Skins, ready for shipping. What's even better is that each Skin is standing upright on a wheeled trolley, so the workers can easily transport them.

But like Ma said, there are stompers guarding them. Two men and one woman in black uniforms stand idly chatting, their guns in holsters by their sides.

My plan is simple. As soon as the fire alarm goes off, the stompers will evacuate with everyone else. As soon as they've gone, I'll hit the button to open the roller door, then push one of the Knight Skins out. Gareth and Tori are bringing a truck to load it onto. Hopefully the bomb blast will be enough of a distraction that we'll be able to drive away with the Skin.

Simple.

Okay, so there'll still be lots of stompers around, but Gareth said he and Tori would bring weapons with them, including poppers. We should be able to hold back the stompers for long enough to get away.

Keeping my head down, I walk slowly enough that I can take a look around while I head to the roller door.

"What are you doing?" A harsh voice rings out and I jerk around to see a stomper striding toward me. His eyes narrow at the bandanna over my face. "Why aren't you at your station?"

"Sorry. On my way." I wave an apologetic hand and turn to go, but he grabs my arm with rough fingers.

"Why is your face covered?"

"Allergies."

He snorts. "What workstation are you assigned to?"

"That one." I point to a part of the conveyor belt where small metal rods are spinning.

"Come with me," he snarls, hauling on my arm to drag me in the opposite direction.

"Where are you taking me?"

"Admin. They'll check who you are and where you're supposed to be, and dock your wages while they're at it."

I don't have time for this. If he drags me all the way to Admin, I could be stuck there when the fire alarm goes off. I'll have to get away from him. There are too many people in this part of the factory to try anything, but as soon as we get around the corner, I'll—

An alarm shrieks, so loud it's deafening. The stomper stops dead, looking around. Grunts at every station drop what they're doing and run at full speed toward the exit.

The alarm's gone off early, and I'm nowhere near the roller door.

Wrenching my arm from the stomper's grip, I shove him with all my strength. He falls backward onto the concrete floor. His head cracks against it.

I don't know if anyone saw him fall, but I'm not sticking around to find out. I turn and run toward the roller door. The grunts are all moving the other way, heading toward the main entrance, and I have to dodge through them. Nobody tries to stop me. They're all intent on getting out of the building before it goes ka-boom.

Running up to the roller door, I scan for stompers, but the ones I saw earlier have gone. The door's unguarded, and the button to open it should be on the—

A deafening boom fills my head. Then a shockwave slams into me like something solid and catapults me sideways. I hit the wall, but manage to get my arms around my skull in time to keep my brains from splattering on the concrete.

Dust billows, making it impossible to see, and my ears ring so loudly I can't hear a thing. My bandanna has come loose, and I gasp in dust, then cough and hack, trying to clear my lungs.

The explosives went off too early.

I can't panic. I need to stick with the plan. First, I tighten the bandanna around my nose and mouth so I can breathe without coughing. Then I pull myself to my feet, ignoring the pain in my hip where it hit the wall.

Staggering forward, I feel my way along the wall. Dust fills the air, stinging my eyes and blinding me. The ringing inside my head is gradually replaced by the shriek of the alarm, and I'm not sure which is worse.

Then I hear shouts over the din, faint but unmistakable. Not just shouts, but the barking of orders. *Stompers.* That's definitely worse.

Talking it through with the others, we all assumed the stompers would stay outside. I mean, why come rushing back into a factory that's just been bombed? But the shouts are getting closer and it sounds like they're looking for whoever's responsible. They're probably spreading out, searching the factory, hunting for a target. And I doubt they'll be picky.

Chapter Thirteen

I still can't see a damn thing, but somehow I manage to blunder into one of the Knight Skins. It's been knocked off its trolley and is lying on its side, but doesn't look damaged.

Ma was right; it's heavy. Even with my super strength, straining with everything I've got, I barely manage to lever it back onto the trolley. But finally, it's back in place and ready to wheel out of here.

Now all I have to do is find the button to open the roller door. Not so easy when I'm blind in the swirling dust and the stompers' shouts are getting louder.

I stumble toward where I think the roller door is and slam into the wall again. In all the dust, it's easy to get turned around, so I'm not sure I'm going the right way as I feel along it. I'm trying not to cough in case they hear me, but my throat is burning and each breath is a struggle of will as I drag down more dust.

Then my hand touches cold metal. Success! It can only be the roller door, and the opening mechanism should be on the wall beside it.

Stretching as high as I can reach and then bending low, I run my hand over the wall. My fingers brush against something. A switch. That's got to be it.

Even with my hand on it, I hesitate for a moment. As soon as I open this door, the stompers will be drawn to it. I'll need to quickly take cover somewhere, which would be a lot easier if I weren't blind.

Muscles poised, I jam the switch down. There's a loud clanking noise, then dust swirls violently around me, like a mini tornado has formed. I can't help coughing as I stumble forward. But now I can see a little further. With every step the dust is clearing. It's being sucked out of the factory as the roller door rises.

A sharp crack of gunfire sends me diving forward. A stomper's spotted me. He emerges from the dust, wearing a helmet that must be helping him to see. His weapon is so huge he uses both hands to hold it.

I scramble under a workstation, finding a metal stand to hide behind. It won't protect me for long, though. Judging from his shouts, the stomper's calling the rest of his team over.

The roller door is clattering higher, opening the factory to the street and blowing away the last of the dust just when I could do with the cover. If I try to break out from behind the workstation now, the stompers will have a clear shot.

Glancing outside, my stomach clenches. There are more stompers out there, running toward the open roller door. I can see three of them, their guns already drawn. With stompers both in front of me and behind me, it's only a matter of seconds before one has a clear shot.

What wouldn't I give to be in my Leopard Skin right now, to have some chance of fighting back against their weapons? Instead, I'm pinned. What else can I do but hide?

A horn blasts.

I jerk around to see a truck flying toward the still-opening roller door. The stompers in its path try to leap out of its way, but it strikes two of them, dragging them underneath it. The top of the truck hits the bottom of the roller door with a loud crash that turns into a screech of metal-against-metal as it scrapes through. It skids to a stop inside the factory, next to the Skin I pushed upright.

Tori is in the truck's passenger seat. She leaps out with her gun drawn, firing into the building at the oncoming stompers.

I tug the bandanna from my face. "Tori," I yell, sticking my head out from the workstation so she knows where I am.

She spares me a quick glance, then ducks behind the open door of the truck for cover while she keeps firing.

Gareth jumps out of the driver's seat and throws a popper. "Get down," he yells.

I was pulling myself out from under the workstation, but I dive back under it instead. The explosion isn't nearly as strong as the one that blew up the factory, but it's loud enough to make my ears ring again. A blast of heat hits my face and I suck more hot dust down my already-raw throat.

Cale jumps from the back of the truck, with Keren, Franco, and Spade. They all have guns, and are already firing into the factory. When Gareth said he'd bring weapons, he wasn't messing around.

I crawl out from under the workstation, praying none of the bullets that are flying around the factory find me. Keeping low, I lope over to the Knight Skin and tuck myself behind it as much as I can. The trolley it's on has a remote control unit, but when I push the button that should start it moving under its own power, nothing happens. I need to get the Skin into the back of the truck, but the only way to move it is to shove the trolley along, and that's slow going. There must be some sort of brake mechanism that's keeping the wheels from turning freely.

Cale runs over to me. "You okay?" He throws his weight into trying to shove the Skin as well. "Shit, it weighs a ton."

Though I'm stronger than him, his pushing helps me get some momentum up, so the trolley moves faster to the back of the truck. Bullets ricochet off the Skin, and my adrenaline surges. I give a mighty shove and it rolls into place in front of the truck's open back door.

"Does the hydraulic lift work?" pants Cale.

I shake my head. "Broken in the explosion."

"Then how are we going to lift it into the truck?"

There's only one way I can think of. The Skin's far too heavy, and there's no way for me to lift it off the ground. But I have to.

Getting under it, I drag in my breath.

Be the leopard. I am the leopard.

I grit my teeth and strain every muscle. A scream of pain forces its way up my raw throat, coming out deep and harsh between clenched teeth. Incredibly, I feel the Skin leave the floor. Cale joins me underneath it, letting out a roar of effort as he helps me lift it. Staggering, with my muscles on the point of exploding, we manage to heave it onto the bed of the truck.

Franco was using some packing crates for cover while he shot at the stompers outside the roller door. Now he's looking back over his shoulder at us, the piece of plastic he was chewing on earlier still in his mouth. He stares with wide eyes, shooting forgotten. "How'd you do that?"

My gaze goes past him, first to the fallen stompers he

must have shot, then to the street beyond them. A squad of six knights are jogging down the street toward us.

I suck in a breath, then shout as loud as I can. "Knights are coming!"

As though in slow motion, I see one of the knights raise its weapon. Though it's still a long distance away, my heart contracts. Cale is in front of me, in full view of the knight.

I dive forward, tackling Cale to the ground. He lets out a grunt as he lands heavily on the concrete floor with my weight on top of him. I'm still looking up, at the knight, so I see it adjust its aim downward as Franco starts firing at it.

Scrambling off Cale, I grab his arm and tug him sideways, sliding him over the concrete. I fling him toward the crates that Franco's hiding behind.

Sharp pain sears through my shoulder. I stagger backward, then duck behind the truck, my hand pressed hard against the place that feels like it's on fire. Blood immediately pulses over my hand, but there's no time to worry about it now.

"Everyone in the truck!" I yell.

Tori scrambles into the passenger seat. Keren and Spade run past me, firing at the knights while they leap for the back of the truck. Franco and Cale abandon the packing crates by the roller door, but as they sprint for the back of the truck, Franco stumbles and blood sprays from his neck. The piece of plastic flies out of his mouth. He falls, smacking the ground hard, and lies face down, blood pooling around him.

Cale stops, turning back for Franco.

My stomach clenches.

"He's dead," I yell, breaking cover to grab Cale and yank him to the truck. "Get in!"

Tori's door is still open, and the knights are getting too close to risk running to the back of the truck. I turn to shove Cale in with Tori, but he steps back. "You get in first," he orders, ducking down so he can fire under the truck at the oncoming knights.

I scramble in over Tori. It's going to be a tight squeeze with four of us in the front of the truck, but too bad. Gareth is in the driver's seat, looking into the side mirror at the oncoming knights. His face is pale and his trademark smile seems a long way away.

"We won't get the truck out past the knights," he says. "I've got to scatter them. Milla, can you drive?"

Before I can answer, he jumps out of the truck. He has a satchel slung over his shoulder and he dips his hand into it and throws a popper. When it hits the ground outside the roller door, it explodes.

"Drive," he yells at me. "Go!"

I slide over to the driver's seat and grab hold of the steering wheel with my left hand. Cabs don't have steering wheels, and the only time I've ever seen a car that has one is on the holo. I guess I just turn it to steer, only pain is shooting down my right arm, and that hand doesn't seem able to grip anything.

There's a lever next to the wheel with numbers on it. I guess it should control our speed, but when I push it forward nothing happens.

Tori leans over to stab a button and the truck jolts and starts moving slowly backward.

Cale jumps into the truck, pushing Tori over so she's pressed hard against me. The driver's door is still open, and though I don't have time to look for Gareth, I know he's still okay because explosions keep rocking the truck. He must be keeping the knights back so they don't swarm us.

Problem is, the truck's reversing out past the roller door

so slowly, Gareth's going to run out of poppers before we can get out of here.

"It's on auto-drive." Cale drops the window so he can fire out of it. "Switch it to manual."

"How?"

Tori hits another button on the dashboard, then another one. We lurch backward, then stop.

"Stupid truck." She pounds on all the buttons.

"If we can't get it off auto, it'll drive us to the Meat Locker," says Cale.

I spot a switch that's half-hidden under the steering wheel and flick it. The truck lurches forward, accelerating back into the factory fast enough to press me back in my seat. I yank the wheel hard around with one hand, skidding us in a circle so tight, the truck lurches over onto two wheels before dropping back to all four. We clip the stack of crates, scattering them everywhere, and as we weave out of the roller door, Gareth jumps out of the way.

Keren and Spade are in the back of the truck with the Knight Skin. They'll be getting thrown around, and I just hope the Skin doesn't crush them.

Tori pulls on the lever to kill our speed. We slide to a stop with a knight directly in front of us. "Get in," she yells at Gareth.

The other knights are sprawled on the ground. At first I assume having explosives thrown at them at close range has killed them, until I see them lift their heads and start pulling themselves to their feet.

Gareth throws another popper and it explodes in front of us. The fireball rocks the truck, and the windscreen cracks.

Incredibly, the knight that was standing in front of us staggers forward out of the fireball, like a black demon walking out of hell. It lifts its gun and fires at Gareth.

I shove the speed lever back up to high, and the truck lurches forward. It slams into the knight. For a moment it's stuck on our bonnet, its yellow eyes staring into mine, then it gets whipped underneath us. Our back wheels bump over it.

Staring into the big side mirror, I see Gareth in a heap on the ground. His satchel is open and all his little round poppers are rolling away.

Tori grabs the lever and jams it back to zero, making the truck jerk to a stop. "Wait for Gareth. He's coming."

My heart clenches, but I don't have time to break the truth to her gently because the other knights are getting to their feet. "I'm sorry, Tori. He's dead."

"No!"

Cale sticks his head out of the window to look behind us, but she yanks him aside, fumbling for the door so she can jump out.

"Stop her, Cale." Though I'd give just about anything to be able to go back for Gareth's body, three knights are back on their feet and starting toward us with their weapons raised. I shove the lever back up to full speed and we lurch forward into the street.

"Gareth!" Tearing at Cale, trying to wrench him out of the way so she can open the door, Tori lets out a heart-rending sob. "He might be alive. We have to go back."

"The knights are running after us." Cale puts his arms around her, hugging her tight. "I'm sorry. He's gone."

She tries desperately to shrug him off, grabbing for the speed lever, but he takes her hands. "He wanted you to get away. Don't let it be for nothing, Tori. Give him that much."

I yank the steering wheel one-handed, overcorrecting as I try to steer us down the narrow Old Triton street. We slam into a cab and bounce off it, then hit another cab.

I hang onto the wheel one-handed as the truck skids and rocks, then veers up onto the sidewalk. We narrowly miss the side of a building before I manage to swerve down a side street.

Sirens wail behind us, but by the time the stompers make it through all the carnage we've left in our wake, we'll have a head start.

One problem. I was going to take the Knight Skin to Doctor Gregory, but we won't make it all the way up to New Triton. Not with the stompers so close behind us.

Beside me, Tori is sobbing, her face buried in Cale's shirt. I meet his eyes over her head.

"Why the hell did the bomb go off so early?" Cale demands. "Somebody screwed up."

I shake my head. Whatever the reason, it was my plan that got Gareth and Franco killed. If I hadn't talked them into helping me get a Knight Skin, they'd still be alive. Cale should be raging at me, shouting about how badly I messed up. Instead, he looks pale, and his eyes are dark and full of grief.

"I'm going to drive past the alley that leads to the safe house," I say past the lump in my throat. "We'll stop for long enough to shove the Skin out, and the four of you should be able to get it into the safe house. I'll drive the truck a few blocks further, then dump it and meet you there."

His gaze goes to my shoulder and his eyes widen with shock. "You're hurt."

"I'll be okay."

"Milla, your shirt is dripping blood."

I shake my head and concentrate on driving and not falling apart, which is pretty damn hard when every sob Tori lets out stabs itself directly into my heart.

Chapter Fourteen

I t's early evening and Old Triton has been swallowed by inky blackness by the time I've abandoned the truck and dragged myself back to the safe house. My shoulder is throbbing and I feel weak and dizzy. All I want is to collapse inside and shut my eyes. But at the door to the safe house, I hesitate.

My stomach clenches at the thought of facing Tori. She's going to be sick with grief and she'll never forgive me for getting Gareth and Franco killed.

Instead of facing all the people who'll be here, who loved them both, I could go to Doctor Gregory's. Ma's there, and I'm sure she'll be anxious to get her band back.

But that would be cowardly. I need to face Tori and the others, and at least apologize for dragging them into my plan. Not that I imagine it'll help with their grief.

I take a few deep breaths, bracing myself before I knock. "What's buried will rise," I say through the door.

It opens right away and Cale stands back to let me in, letting out a loud exhale. "You made it. I was so worried."

As I step inside, he takes my arm. "Come and sit down. You look dead on your feet."

I don't think he notices my flinch at his poor choice of words.

They managed to get the Knight Skin inside. It's in the corner, looming over the small room like it's about to come to life and kill us all. The place still stinks as much as it did before. Tori, Keren, and Spade are sitting at the table. There's a bottle on the table that can only be street brew, and they're sipping it out of cups.

"Hey," says Keren. "Glad you're okay."

Tori's eyes are bloodshot and her face is pale, but she gives me a nod. I open my mouth to tell her how sorry I am, but Cale speaks first.

"Milla needs a doctor. She's been shot." He leads me to one of the rickety metal-and-canvas beds pushed against the wall, and I sink down onto it.

Spade drains his cup and gets up from the table. "I'm the doctor. Close enough, anyway."

I look at him doubtfully. He's still covered with dust and dirt from the factory, and his hands are as filthy as the lumpy knitted hat he's wearing. Plus he's been drinking street brew, which is strong enough that a lot of sinkers use it to kill head lice and crabs.

"Don't worry, I've done this before." He gives me a tight, humorless smile, then goes to the makeshift kitchen faucet to wash his hands in the cold water and soak a rag.

"Tori," I say, my voice still raspy from all the dust I inhaled. "I'm so sorry."

She blinks hard, obviously fighting tears, then shakes her head with a scowl. "Gareth should've stayed in the truck. The bastard had to be a hero."

Finished in the kitchen, Spade comes over to me. He's holding a spray can, and his fingernails are still black. He grimaces. "Hate to break it to you, but I've got nothing to dull the pain."

Cale grabs a mug and sloshes in some of the street brew. "Here." He hands it to me. "Drink this."

I've had street brew before, but never developed a taste for it. This stuff smells disturbingly like the lubricant they use on the machines in the factory. The gulp I take incinerates my raw throat before sinking into my stomach like a glowing ember.

Spade motions me to lie down flat, then kneels next to the bed. "Not going to lie to you, this is going to hurt. You ready?" When I nod, he pulls on my T-shirt, easing the cloth out of the dried blood.

I can't help making a keening sound. It feels like he's peeling my skin off.

Cale sits on the bed beside my knees, where he's out of the way. He takes hold of my clenched fist and I grip his hand, squeezing so tightly I'm probably crushing his bones. I clamp my teeth together, willing myself not to cry out again.

Spade pulls a blade out of his boot and cuts my T-shirt right off. I want to tug up a blanket for modesty's sake, but my shoulder throbs so badly I can't move. He dabs gently at my shoulder with his wet rag, wiping it clean.

"You're lucky," he says finally. "A little to the left or right, and you would have bled to death."

I don't feel lucky. I feel heartsick and guilty, and in too much pain to say the things I need to say. My teeth are so tightly clenched together it feels like they've fused shut, and I can't make myself stop crushing Cale's hand.

"The bullet went straight through," he adds. "You couldn't have been shot in a better place if you'd picked it yourself."

He picks up the spray can and coats my skin with an

icy-cold blast. The liquid sticks to the wound, forming a thick coating before it solidifies. It must have a numbing agent in it too, because my pain eases. In spite of my resolve not to make any more sounds, a groan forces its way out of my throat. I release my death-grip on Cale's hand and he lets out a loud, relieved breath.

Spade gets to his feet and looks down into my eyes. His expression is serious and his gaze feels like it has a physical weight. "You did good, Milla. Some would have screamed the place down. One big guy I know took a shot to the leg, and three of us had to tie him to the table so I could get a look at it, while he cried and begged me to stop." He brings two fingers to his forehead in a kind of salute. "You're tough, that's for sure." His salute turns into a pointing finger. "But it's the tough ones who get careless and then regret it. So don't get tempted to use that arm until it's finished healing, okay?" He crosses to one of the other beds, rummages in a box under it, then hands me a T-shirt. "Here."

"Thank you." I pull on his T-shirt gingerly, biting back a cry when I have to ease it over my bad arm. It's too big, but reasonably clean. Cale helps me get it on, then props me up in a sitting position with my back against the wall. My head pounds and I have to swallow down a surge of bile.

"You okay?" He sits next to me on the bed.

"I feel better," I lie.

Spade sits back at the table with Tori and Keren. Tori's finished her mug of street brew, so he pours them all some more.

"I'm sorry, Tori," I say again. Then I sweep my gaze around the rest of them. "I'm sorry, all of you, for dragging you into that fight."

Tori keeps her head down, but Keren and Spade both

meet my gaze. I'm looking for bitterness in their expressions, and dreading finding it. But all I see is sorrow.

"They were fighters." Spade picks up his drink and sloshes the liquid inside. "Eyes wide open and no regrets. That's the way the cards fall."

Karen nods. "We look after each other. Someone dies, it's on all of us." Her gaze shifts to the Knight Skin. "You got that monster in the truck, and I don't know how you did it. Without you, we wouldn't have made it out."

"That's truth." Spade takes a gulp of his drink.

Tori finally lifts her face. Her cheeks are wet. "I can't believe Gareth's gone. He was a great person. The best." Her voice cracks and her shoulders hunch like she's been kicked in the gut. "And Franco was desperate to pay for his kid's schooling, to keep his daughter out of the factories. I don't know how to live like this, Milla. How do we keep going when we have to watch the people we love die?"

My heart stabs with pain. Tori is the strongest person I've ever known, but her expression's so raw, I can't stand it.

Cale speaks up from beside me. "I didn't really know Franco, but Gareth was a good friend to me. He asked me to join the Fist, even though most members didn't want me. They assumed because I come from New Triton, I don't want things to change. Gareth was different. He was willing to give me a chance."

Tori nods at him, then picks up her mug of street brew and gulps it down like she's on a mission to wipe herself out.

"Franco was funny," says Keren. "He cracked me up all the time with stupid puns. I bet he was better at coming up with puns than anyone in Triton."

"Yeah, those puns." Spade snorts. "Franco was a genius with them. And dirty limericks, too." He glances at Keren.

"You ever hear his limericks? He could recite them for hours, and all of them filthy."

"There was a young sinker called Venus," Keren recites haltingly, looking at the ceiling as she searches for the right words. "Who had an eight inch... wait, that's not right."

Spade laughs and takes a gulp of his drink. "He told me hundreds over the years, and I can't remember a single one of them."

"He used to make Gareth laugh all the time," says Keren. "And then Gareth's laugh would crack me up. I don't know what made his laugh so contagious, but it was like Ebola the way it spread. Nobody was immune." She looks at me. "If you heard it, you couldn't not laugh with him. That's just the way it was."

They're all smiling now, even Tori. But I couldn't smile if my life depended on it. They're talking about the men I killed today. Gareth with his contagious laugh, and Franco with his dirty limericks, chewing on a stick of plastic. Both would be sitting here now if it weren't for my stubborn insistence on getting a Knight Skin.

Tori's gaze is on me, and I'm certain she can tell what I'm thinking. It must be written all over my face.

Her expression hardens and she motions to the Knight Skin with her cup. "Gareth and Franco died for that. Now it's up to us to make sure they didn't die for nothing."

I nod, feeling the full weight of her words. "I'll get William out."

"Not just your brother. You have to deal with all the soldiers."

"What do you mean?"

She grabs the bottle of street brew and fills her cup before she answers. "You're going to use the Knight Skin to get into the Meat Locker, right? When you get inside, you need to hit the kill switch on every pod and wipe all the soldiers' chips. As the soldiers operating them start waking up, the Knight Skins will collapse. Then we can put a gun to their ears and blow their murdering metal heads to hell."

I blink at her. I hadn't even thought of doing that. "But how will I get William out if all the soldiers are waking up? There are hundreds of them. What's to stop them climbing out of their pods and stopping me?"

"Good point." She takes a sip of her drink, then points her cup at me. "So instead of wiping their chips, you'll have to kill them in their pods."

My stomach rolls over. "Kill them? But they're *kids*."

"They're the soldiers who murdered Gareth and Franco. Why should we let them live?"

"Not just Gareth and Franco," adds Spade. "Four of our friends were dragged up on stage and shot in front of a cheering crowd. Plenty more have disappeared. And what have we done to deserve it? All the Fist has ever done is broadcast the truth about what was going on in the shelters and factories. For that they get to execute us?"

"It's not the soldiers' fault." Cale pushes one hand into his hair. "They've been in the director's academies being brainwashed for years, and she's using the Skins to change their thought processes. Being in the Skins makes them feel less empathy—"

"All the more reason to kill them if they've been brainwashed against us," Tori interrupts. "They won't stop until they've slaughtered us all."

"I can't kill kids. Especially not teenagers who look like they're sleeping." In spite of the guilt I feel for Gareth and Franco's deaths, there's no way I can do what Tori wants.

She shakes her head, her mouth twisting as though she's disappointed with me. "Then Director Morelle will just make more Knight Skins for them to transfer into, and we'll have to fight them all over again."

"William never asked to be one of her soldiers," I say. "She didn't give him a choice, and when we let her take him, we had no idea what she was planning. How could we? If William knew what he was doing, he'd never fight against the people who raised him. Those soldiers are victims as much as we are."

She studies me for several long, drawn-out seconds, then sighs. "Fine. If you can't kill them, then wipe their chips."

I don't want to do either, but I nod. Though I did all this to get William out, she's right. I can't walk in there without trying to stop the knights. I owe it to Gareth and Franco. Hell, I owe it to all Old Tritoners.

I'll just have to figure out a way to get my brother out as well, even with hundreds of angry soldiers trying to stop me.

Chapter Fifteen

Tori eventually passes out at the table. Cale carries her to one of the beds and pulls a blanket over her. Keren and Spade are almost as drunk as Tori, but they manage to stumble to bed under their own steam.

Cale switches off the main light, leaving a small glowing bulb on so the room's not pitch black. He sits next to me on my bed, careful to choose my uninjured side. "How are you feeling?" He whispers the question, though Tori's already snoring, and the other two won't be far behind.

I consider how to answer. My shoulder still throbs, and so does my head. My throat's sore and my arm feels like a squad of stompers have been jumping on it.

Worse is the tightness in my chest when I try to figure out how I can keep both my promise to Ma and my promise to Tori. The Meat Locker is full of pods. Once I start waking the soldiers and they realize what I'm doing, they'll attack me for sure. How will I wipe all their chips and get William away?

But I'm too exhausted to tell Cale all that. My head is fuzzy. Maybe in the morning I'll be able to come up with a solution.

Instead, when I open my mouth, a question comes out that I've wanted to ask since I saw how worried he was that I'd been shot. "Have you forgiven me?"

Cale's just a dark silhouette on the bed beside me, so I can't see his expression. He lets out a long breath that sounds surprised. "Milla, you saved my life. The only reason you got shot is because you dived on top of me."

"Is that a yes?"

I hear him move before I feel his warm fingers slide over my hand. "Tell me you won't lie to me again."

My heart speeds up at his touch. "Only the truth from now on. I promise."

Maybe it's because sitting in darkness feels like a kind of privacy, and I'm wrung-out and exhausted, but it feels easier to say what I'm thinking than it ever has. Or maybe it's because having to watch your friends die makes everything else seem trivial, and secrets are pointless. Whatever the reason, I feel like I can share anything with him.

"I told you about how I'm stronger now," I add. "Even though I was afraid you'd think I was a freak."

"A freak? Are you kidding? I was jealous." He sighs. "Having super powers would make my life so much easier."

"It's helped, for sure. Without the extra strength, I'd have been carved up in the director's lab. But I don't want to think too hard about it, in case it disappears. Nobody seems to know why my Skin affected me like that in the first place. I could just as easily go back to normal."

"I'm glad it did affect you like that. And thank you for saving my life today."

I shiver at the reminder of how close he came to being

shot. "The only reason I needed to save it was because I put it in danger. I shouldn't have dragged everyone into the fight."

"You didn't drag us anywhere. We're all adults, capable of making our own decisions. Gareth helped because he wanted to get that Skin as much as you did. As soon as he realized you were going to use it to get into the Meat Locker, he was on board. Franco, too."

I let out a long breath and turn my hand over so his isn't just resting on mine, but I'm cradling it. The other three people in the room are all snoring, Tori by far the loudest, so I know nobody else can hear me confess my secrets.

"I feel so guilty," I say softly. "I'm trying not to, but I keep replaying the whole thing in my head."

"Don't." He leans closer. So close that I can almost taste the street brew on his lips. "Blame the knights, not yourself. They're the ones who killed them. Okay?"

"It's hard," I whisper. "I feel responsible."

"You're not." He shifts a little, turning to face me, and lifts the hand that's not holding mine. His fingers find my face in the dark, and run gently over my scarred, hollowed-out cheek.

I try not to flinch back from his touch, but I hate anyone even looking at my scars, let alone feeling how hard and rough they are. How can he want to touch me there? I don't understand.

"Cale…" I hesitate, losing my nerve for just a moment. Then I take a breath and find my courage. "When we were in the Morelle Corporation, you said I was beautiful. Why would you say something like that? I know how I look. My face is the opposite of beautiful."

"Not to me." He squeezes my hand. "Scars are just scars. They don't make you ugly."

I make a noise in the back of my throat. I'm trying to believe him, but surely he sees the same twisted mess everyone else does?

"Your face tells your story," he says. "You're strong, and funny, and brave. And maybe the bad stuff that's happened to you is part of that. Like the way they used to make swords, by burning them and beating them with a hammer to make them strong."

"So I'm a sword?" There's a lightness in my voice I wouldn't have thought I could manage. I like the idea of it.

"The best kind of sword. All your history and strength is right there in your face, and it's made you beautiful."

"I wish I could see what you see. When I look at myself, all I see is my scars."

He lets out a long sigh. "I want to kiss you. But last time, you pulled away."

"If you hold me too tightly, I feel trapped." The words slip out so easily they leave me breathless. Why have I never been able to admit that out loud before?

"What if I don't hold you?" Without waiting for an answer, his lips graze against mine, the lightest of touches. I feel the contact everywhere, as though his lips have brushed my entire body and tickled deep in my belly.

I close my eyes, savouring the sensation, and lean into him, making our next kiss a little less gentle.

"Is this okay?" he asks softly, his lips against mine. Though his body isn't touching mine, he seems rigid, like he's clenching all his muscles.

"It's nice," I murmur.

He lets out a soft sigh that's so full of wanting, it sends a shiver of awareness over me. Warmth uncoils inside me. My body aches, but in a good way.

I want to be closer to him. I'd like to feel his chest press against mine.

Sliding my hand behind his neck, I pull myself so close that our bodies are touching.

He sighs again before his lips claim mine, the kiss so deep I feel like I'm falling into him. His tongue flicks against mine, and every touch sends an electric charge through my body.

Though I let the fingers of my good hand trail across the stubble on his jaw, over his neck, and down his throat, he leaves his own hands at his sides. The more we kiss, the more I want him to touch me. But this feels so good, I don't want to accidentally ruin it. I'd like to do this all night long.

"Lie down with me," I whisper.

"You sure?"

"Do you mind lying against the wall? And don't wrap your arms around me. Is that okay?"

"I wouldn't, anyway. You're injured."

"We'll need to put our heads up that end, because I can't lie on my wounded side."

"You're sure you want to lie so close? I'm afraid I'll hurt you."

"I'm sure."

He lies with his back to the wall, and I lie facing him. There's barely an inch of space between our faces, and our bodies are against each other, thrown together by the sagging mattress. I have to keep my sore arm on my side, because it hurts too much to have it between us. I'm not sure where to put my other hand, so I nestle it in front of me, under my chin.

"Is this okay?" he murmurs.

"It's good."

Kissing him lying down feels different. Our heads can't tilt so much, which makes our noses bump. His jaw is scratchy against my chin. The longing to be able to touch him is even stronger than before. My good hand is tucked awkwardly between us, so all I can do is put my hand on his chest, and with his T-shirt in the way, I can't touch his skin.

"You can put your hand on my hip," I whisper.

He moves slowly, being careful of my sore arm. When his hand finds my hip, his fingers make slow circles. I let out a shuddering breath. I'm in my human body, but right now, I can't imagine anything better. I don't want to be anyone or anything else. I'm *here*, and this stolen night with him feels so good, it makes my pain ebb away.

"Milla," he murmurs, lifting his hand to brush back a lock of hair that's fallen into my face. "I've wanted this for so long."

"I have too."

His fingers run through my hair, then gently over my ruined cheek. I hold completely still, hardly daring to breathe, as his hand traces back over my scars.

I still can't believe he wants to touch me there, but he's kissing me at the same time, his mouth demanding and needy as though he was telling the truth and my scars don't matter.

"Milla," he whispers again. "I like that name. It suits you."

"Better than Rayne?"

"I liked Rayne too."

"I like this. Being here with you."

"I wish we were alone. Does Tori always snore this loudly?"

My snort of laughter feels good. "I can't count the number of nights I lay awake in the shelter, listening to her snore. It's kind of soothing."

"Soothing?" He sounds incredulous. "When I imagined this, there definitely wasn't any snoring."

"You've imagined doing this?"

"Since the first day we met."

I make a scoffing sound. "Not the first day we met. We barely spoke."

He smiles. It's dark enough to make his lips indistinct, but I can hear the smile in his voice. "Since I saw you steal that knife and hide it in your sock. After that, I couldn't stop thinking about you."

"You're weird, Cale. That's not a reason to like someone."

"It was for me."

He kisses me again, softly this time, and warmth spreads through my body. But my exhaustion is coming back, softening my need for him. I still ache for him, but it's not so urgent. I can close my eyes and just enjoy the feeling of his soft lips and his strong body resting against mine.

I could kiss him like this forever. If only my exhaustion wasn't an endless black ocean. I can't fight the wave of tiredness that hits me. All I can do is close my eyes and let myself drift away.

Chapter Sixteen

I wake up with my shoulder throbbing. Cale is fast asleep against me, his breaths long and slow. It's still dark, with the only light coming from the small, weak bulb near the bathroom, but that doesn't mean much in Old Triton. It could be morning already.

Whatever time it is, as much as I enjoyed falling asleep with Cale last night, my wound means I can't roll over, and I'm too uncomfortable to stay put.

Moving slowly, I manage to ease myself off the bed without waking him or any of the others. Tori is still snoring, and the other two are almost as loud.

Before she passed out last night, Tori threw a blanket over the head of the Knight Skin, saying she felt like it was staring at her. Now it's little more than a dark, hulking shadow, but it's still creepy. We should have turned it to face the wall.

I brave the overpowering stench of the bathroom to clean up as best I can under the slow trickle of water that runs from the end of a broken pipe. My arm works a little better today than it did last night, at least.

When I finally emerge and check the window, the gloom outside isn't thick enough for it to still be night. Though I can't check the time on Ma's band, my guess is it's late enough that most day-shifters will be getting ready for work by now.

"What time is it?" mumbles Tori from her bed.

"Not sure. But it's morning."

She groans. "My brain has swelled. It's too big for my head and it's trying to squeeze out of my ears."

I go to the table that serves as a kitchen, rinse a cup that smells like it was used for last night's street brew session, and fill it with water before making my way to her bed in the semi-darkness. "Drink this."

She gulps it down. "Thanks." Then she lies back down and sighs. "I can't believe I'm saying this, but you should turn the main light on. We need to get up and start planning our attack on the soldiers."

"You can't switch it on with your band?"

"This place isn't set up for it. The switch is on the wall."

When I flick it on, the overhead light seems brutally harsh. Cale sits up, blinking. His hair is messy, sticking in all directions, and his jaw has darkened even more overnight. Weirdly, he's even more handsome when he's dishevelled. He flashes me a small smile and his small single dimple appears and is gone again, as though it winked at me.

"Good morning," he says.

My stomach flutters. "Morning." Then I look away. Gareth and Franco died yesterday, and feeling anything but sad is disrespectful to them.

As they wake, Keren and Spade groan even louder than Tori did, and I get mugs of water for them too. When they're all finally up, Cale volunteers to find one of the few street stalls that are still operating, and pick up breakfast. Spade goes with him, and they come back a little while later with steaming coffees and hot noodles coated in sticky sauce.

I sit on the bed to slurp my noodles down. I have to eat awkwardly with one hand because the other arm's still too sore to move, but I'm so hungry I barely chew. Tori focuses on her coffee, cradling her cup in both hands with her elbows resting on the table, and lowering her head to sip it. Her face looks gray, with black rings under her eyes.

She doesn't let me finish eating before she says, "Let's talk about how you're going to get inside the Meat Locker."

"I called Doctor Gregory." Cale pauses eating mid-slurp, and looks at me from his seat at the table. "She said she'll come here to reprogram your chip so you can transfer into the Knight Skin."

"The Meat Locker will be guarded," Keren says through a mouthful of noodles. "Somehow we need to convince all the guards to leave before Milla goes in."

"I'm going to call all of the Fist's section leaders," says Tori. "They don't know about Gareth yet." She blinks hard, then stares down at her untouched bowl of noodles for a long moment before looking back up. "We'll need their help. To make this work, every Fist member should be there."

"A Fist army," agrees Cale.

I frown, sucking up the last of my noodles. This isn't what I expected when I imagined slipping into the Meat Locker to get William. I thought I'd somehow be able to get in and out before anyone could figure out I wasn't supposed to be there. Now it's turning into a full-scale battle, and the chance of me being able to rescue my brother seems slimmer by the minute. Not to mention how dangerous it'll be for Tori and the rest of the Fist to take on the knights.

"An army," Tori repeats with a nod. "And we want as many knights as possible to be there, so we can blow apart their heads when they fall. If they drop in other places, we won't be able to finish them off, and the director will fix their chips."

"Need to make a big noise." Spade wipes his mouth on his sleeve. "Get them to all come running." His grin shows all his missing teeth. "It's going to be fun."

I hold up my good hand, my stomach tight. "Stop. You're talking about fighting all the knights. That's suicide."

"Not if you wipe their chips quickly enough," says Tori.

I shake my head. "There are hundreds of pods in the Meat Locker. It's going to take time for me to wipe every chip."

"I'm going in with you," says Cale.

"In your human body? Are you crazy? It's too danger—"

"That's a good idea." Tori speaks over me. "We'll need to be in communication with you so we know what's going on. But I don't know how to communicate with one of those *things*." She motions at the Knight Skin in the corner, the blanket still over its head. "If Cale's in the building with you, he can keep us updated."

"No way. He won't be able to defend himself."

Keren nods, agreeing with me. "Once you start wiping chips and the knights outside start dropping, they're going to realize what's happening. They'll rush back into the Meat Locker to stop you. Cale won't stand a chance."

"We won't let them go back in," says Tori.

"We'll light them up with so much fire-power, they won't know what hit them." Spade sounds gleeful.

I glare at Tori. "Let's pretend you can really keep the knights out. What about the soldiers inside who'll start waking up when I wipe their chips?"

"You need to kill them," she says flatly. "I know you think I want to kill them as some kind of revenge for Gareth, but if there were another way—"

"There might be an alternative," interrupts Cale. "You think the Fist have any sleeping gas in their weapons cache?"

Tori frowns at him for a long moment, then her expression eases. "I'll find out."

I let out a long breath, shooting Cale a look of relief. Knocking the soldiers out is the perfect solution.

Tori pushes her chair back and stands up. "I'll start calling the other Fist sections. We need to move quickly, before the director figures out we've stolen one of her Knight Skins. If we can—"

There's a sharp rapping on the door.

We all freeze, looking at each other. The knock comes a second time, but whoever it is hasn't said the Fist's slogan to let us know they're one of us. Not that I think a squad of knights would knock, but…

"Anybody in there?" asks a familiar voice from outside.

I puff out a breath, and open the door. Doctor Gregory gives me a smile, then her nose wrinkles and her hand goes up to cover it. The room's stench must have just hit her. I'm so used to it now, I barely notice it.

"Come in," I say. "Ma's not with you? Is she okay?"

The doctor shakes her head as she steps inside. "The poor woman's exhausted. She can't have slept properly in years, and her cortisol levels are off the charts. The stress her heart's under, it's a wonder she hasn't dropped dead."

She puts down the bag she's carrying, glancing around the small room with a look of horror.

My stomach writhes itself into a tight ball. "Where is she?"

"I gave her something to help her rest, and left a note for when she wakes up, asking her to stay put until I get back. She really needs several days of bed rest, and some infusions of—"

"But she's okay for now?" I interrupt.

"If she doesn't exert herself and gets plenty of sleep, she should make a full recovery."

My stomach relaxes a little. The doctor's right, Ma looked haggard and exhausted. It's good she's getting a chance to rest.

Tori introduces herself and the other Fist members, then goes outside. I assume she wants some privacy to call the other Fist units and ask for their help.

The doctor strides over to the covered Knight Skin. "This is it?" She tugs the blanket off.

"You think you can transfer my brain into it?" I ask.

"Your consciousness," she corrects, glancing over her shoulder at me. "I can. But I'm worried about the effect the Skin will have on you, especially with the somatoform injuries you previously sustained, proving you particularly susceptible to—"

"I'll be fine."

She frowns. "I don't have any equipment here to monitor the effect of the transfer. The only tests I'll be able to do are rudimentary oral challenges."

I have no idea what she means, but I nod. "That'll have to do."

"It would be safer to select a different subject. You've already exhibited numerous abnormal effects from a transferral."

Cale stands up and moves next to me. "I'd volunteer," he says. "But even with the weird things that happened to your body, I still think using the Skin will keep you safer than if you were…" He trails off, glancing at the doctor, and I can tell he doesn't want to let her know what we have planned. I'm pretty sure she'd be unhappy at the idea of an army of Fist members fighting an army of knights.

"I imagine you and Milla are the only ones who've had nano transceivers injected?" The doctor glances at Keren and Spade. With a sigh at their blank expressions, she opens the bag she brought with her, and takes out a hand-held scanner.

"Your existing nano transceivers have bonded with your neurons," she says to me. "Which means I can wipe your existing chip and code it with the new Skin's identity markers."

"Wait." I draw back, my chest contracting. "You're going to wipe my chip? I won't be able to transfer into my Leopard Skin again?"

She gives me a puzzled look. "You don't have access to the Leopard Skin, do you?"

"No, but…" I swallow hard. The thought of never getting to be the leopard again makes me feel empty inside. It might not make sense, but I feel like I'm being asked to give up an essential part of myself. Like she's asked me to carve off a limb.

"You don't have to do this," murmurs Cale, his eyes sympathetic. "I like the idea of your human body staying safe and sound in this room. But if keeping your chip means that much to you, I'll transfer into the knight instead."

I bite my lip, then shake my head. "You don't know what William looks like."

"You don't have an image of him?"

142

By way of an answer, I hold up my arm to remind him I have Ma's band around my wrist. She probably has dozens of images, but I can't access them.

Besides, I'm the only one who understands how important it is to get my brother out of the Meat Locker and away from the director. I promised Ma I'd save him, and the only way I can do that is using the Knight Skin.

If I need to give up all hope of ever getting my Leopard Skin back, then it's a price I'll have to pay.

I nod at the doctor, trying to push my anguish deep inside so it doesn't show. "Let's do it."

"Lie down." She indicates the beds. "And please be aware that I have no equipment to monitor your vital signs. The primary danger is if your real body becomes dehydrated or low in nutrients while your consciousness is transferred. Without any way to administer fluids, it's vital you don't stay in the Skin too long."

"Okay." I lie face up on the bed Cale and I slept in last night. It's nothing like the floating-on-air, high-tech pod I used at the Morelle Corporation, but it'll do.

"You're sure about this, Milla?" asks Cale.

I'm anything but sure. It's not just that I hate the thought of letting go of my Leopard Skin. What if using the Knight Skin messes with my head? Or if it does something we don't expect to my human body?

"Ready?" Doctor Morelle holds up her scanner. It must be the thing that's going to wipe my chip.

Folding my hands tightly together, I force myself to nod.

Chapter Seventeen

"You won't feel a thing," says Doctor Gregory.

But I do.

The back of my neck burns as she runs the scanner over it. Maybe it's my imagination. Perhaps it's just like when I became stronger and faster because my mind got used to my body being that way. It probably burns because I believe it should hurt to wipe away my leopard, and remove the best part of who I am.

I let my head fall back on the pillow and stare up at the ceiling, reminding myself why I'm doing this.

"Now, I'll encode the new…" The doctor's words taper off as she goes to the Knight Skin and runs the scanner over the back of its neck, frowning at whatever appears on the screen set into the head of the device. She's obviously concentrating too hard to be able to finish her sentence.

Finally, she comes back to me with the scanner, sliding her hand under the back of my head to lift it before I feel the device on my neck again. "Done." She lets go of my head. "You should be able to transfer into it now. Want to give it a try?"

I rest my head back on the pillow and drag in a deep breath.

Unlike my beautiful leopard, the Knight Skin is a monster. I'm both reluctant to transfer into it, and curious to find out what it'll be like.

When I reach out with my senses, the feeling of finding a destination and falling sideways into it is so gloriously, wonderfully familiar, I want to groan with pleasure. It feels so much like transferring into my Leopard Skin, my heart leaps.

Then color floods my vision. With it comes an awareness of physicality. Of my body, tall and strong.

No, I'm not just strong. My limbs are made of hard muscle interlaced with carbon fiber. My armour can't be pierced, and my bones are unbreakable.

I'm invincible.

I'm hers.

The thought makes me blink. What the hell? I'm hers? Did that really just go through my head?

"What's it like in there, Milla?" Cale is staring at me, at the knight's face rather than my human body. He has to look up because I'm taller than him now.

I turn my armored hands over to stare at my palms, amazed at how huge they are. Then I clench my fists, revelling in the feeling of strength that rushes through me.

"Milla?" he asks again.

"I feel powerful," I say. "The feeling's a lot stronger than the first time I transferred into my leopard."

Keren and Spade both stare at me with wide eyes, like the sound of my voice coming out of the Knight Skin is the weirdest thing ever. Cale is wearing a worried frown. Tori's still outside in the alley, talking to someone on her band. I can pick up what she's saying, though human me couldn't hear her at all.

The doctor tugs a mind pad out of her bag and holds it poised in front of her, ready to record her notes.

"Tell me about your senses, Milla."

"I can hear better." I scan the small room, noticing all the tiny details I couldn't pick up before. "And I can see far better. Even better than I could when I was the leopard. I can't smell like the leopard did though. I can't smell the way you feel, but I can see the skin on your neck pulsing every time your heart beats."

She raises her eyebrows. "And the feeling of power? Can you define it? Is it a physical sensation?"

I look down at my hands again, trying to figure out what sent such a rush of sensation through me when I transferred. "I just know I'm strong. If I wanted to kill you all and break my way out of this room, I could do it easily."

"Kill us and break out of this room," she repeats slowly, as though I've said something fascinating. "Is that something you want to do?"

"No," I say automatically. But it's not quite true. "But I know what I'm *for*," I tell her, a little frustrated because all the things I'm feeling are so hard to describe.

"What do you mean?"

"The reason I was created. Why I exist. It's to serve Director Morelle." I say the name out loud as much to gauge my own reaction to it as anything else. "She owns this Skin. I know that, but I also *feel* it. I feel like I belong to her." I drop my hands to my sides to touch the weapons on my thighs. They're in the perfect position for me to draw and fire as quickly as thinking.

"Loyalty," says the doctor. Her pulse speeds up, the slight quiver of the skin on her neck betraying her excitement. "Just as Sentin said. Director Morelle must have analyzed the chemistry of certain thoughts and implanted modifiers in the Skin's software. What a breakthrough! Think of what would be possible if we can alter—"

"Don't sound so happy about it," growls Cale. "This is a bad thing. Worse than we imagined."

"Much worse," I agree, though I don't feel shocked or dismayed. All I feel is *strong*. I can't wait to get away from them and out of this claustrophobic, stinking room. I want to find my squad and obey whatever orders the director gives me. And as I'm striding down the street, I'm going to enjoy watching lessor beings scuttle to get out of my way.

I cast a glance at the old Milla lying motionless on the bed. How scrawny and weak she looks. She belongs in a pod, shut away where nothing can harm her.

"Is anything else different?" asks the doctor. "Any other idiosyncrasies particular to that Skin?"

Though I don't understand her words, I get what she's asking. "There's a screen in my arm," I say, lifting it and turning my wrist up so they can see the shiny panel embedded there. When I tap it, a six-digit number glows red. It's like the Knights' version of a band.

"That must be your identification number," says Cale. "Better hope they don't scan it, or they'll know you're an imposter."

"And there's this." I concentrate on my hands and make armored claws extend from my fingers. I'm not sure how I know what to do, but it feels natural.

"Hand-to-claw combat," murmurs Cale. "A definite advantage."

As I'm making the claws contract and my hands go back to normal, I hear Tori say goodbye to the person she's talking to. A moment later she comes back in. "It's done. All the Fist sections have agreed."

"Booyah!" Spade pushes his woollen hat back from his

forehead, a toothless grin splitting his face. "We're going to kick some armoured ass."

Doctor Gregory gives Spade a questioning frown.

"It might be better if you don't know what's going on." Cale tells her.

Still frowning, she turns back to me. "I have many more questions to ask you, Milla. Are you able to sit down in that Skin? It would be more comfortable than staring up at you."

"We have planning to do," objects Tori. "We don't have time for a whole lot of pointless questions."

"They're not pointless." Cale narrows his eyes at me. "This loyalty you feel to Director Morelle. What exactly does it mean? Do you think you'll be able to fight against her? Or will the Skin influence you to turn on the Fist when the firing starts?"

All their heads jerk toward me, and it's obvious none of them had considered that possibility. I hadn't thought about it either. And now I'm not sure how to answer.

Closing my eyes, I picture Director Morelle in front of me. For a moment I try to imagine attacking her, but a wave of revulsion turns my stomach.

"I need to protect Director Morelle," I say reluctantly, the words fighting their way out of my mouth. "I can't hurt her."

Tori drags in a shocked gasp of air, and Spade's mouth drops open. Keren sinks slowly onto one of the beds as though her legs have given way.

Doctor Gregory's mind pad is already covered with notes, but more appear, writing themselves onto its surface as fast as she can think them.

"What about your fellow knights?" asks Cale. "Can you fight them? Or do you need to protect them too?"

I imagine drawing my gun and shooting one of my

squad. My body doesn't react, though there's a strong itch in my brain. I should get to my squad and find out what my orders are. My job is to obey. I'm a soldier in the director's army, and it's my duty to…

Clenching my fists, I force myself to cut those thoughts off. "I think I can do it."

"You *think*?" Tori sounds incredulous. "What if you can't? We're all putting our lives on the line." She sweeps her hand around, including Cale, Keren, and Spade in the gesture. "And not just us. All Fist members. The entire organisation. If you get inside the Meat Locker but can't wipe any chips, we'll have no chance."

I nod. Those thoughts weren't mine, and I refuse to let this Skin tell me how to think. I'm Milla, not a mindless robot soldier. I won't let it change my brain.

"I can do it," I say.

"Are you sure? Because if you have any doubts—"

"I'm certain."

She lets out a long breath, staring at me as though she can see what's going on inside my head.

"I'll be with her," murmurs Cale, trying to reassure Tori.

I nod, as though I think Cale's presence will matter. The truth is, compared to the Knight Skin, his human body is so puny that he may as well not be there at all.

Chapter Eighteen

The battle site the Fist has chosen isn't far from the Meat Locker.

Inside the base of a New Triton scraper is an enormous cab manufacturing plant, so huge that it takes up all the available room in the Old Triton section of this building. The New Triton part of the building is probably fancy with big windows. Down here, its raw walls are made of thick, reinforced concrete, with small ventilation holes at regular intervals.

Far above my head, giant machines piece together the cabs' panels in mid air. The panels are held up by claws at the end of long, thin arms that remind me of spider's legs. The arms lower the structures to the ground floor as needed, for those laboring below to do the detail work on the cabs. I'd be constantly terrified one of the metal panels would drop on my head, but I guess the grunts who usually work here are used to it.

Now, however, the factory is silent. The grunts have gone, the huge machines are frozen, and the stompers who were overseeing the workers are lying dead on the floor.

Brilliant lights are set impossibly high in the factory's ceiling. They're strong enough to illuminate the stompers' bodies, though one of the Fist members is currently aiming his weapon to shoot out the lights. Before he squeezes the trigger, I sweep my gaze over the stompers' bodies, trying to figure out why I feel nothing.

The stompers have been murdered, but I don't feel any regret for their deaths. I'm not glad about it either, though I know exactly how cruel some stompers can be.

Is the Knight Skin stopping me from feeling any emotion for them? Or am I still numb from the deaths of Gareth and Franco? Either way, I'm relieved I can look at the bodies without feeling anything. It makes everything a lot easier.

I glance up to the giant mechanical claws that lift and lower the cabs. Almost a hundred Fist members climbed them and are now tethered to the huge concrete wall that faces the street. They made themselves rope slings, and they're dangling in front of the structure's ventilation holes with their weapons trained outside.

Tori, Keren, and Spade are up there with the rest, almost too high for a human to see. But with my enhanced vision, I can make out every strand of Tori's hair as the breeze lifts it, and her intent expression as she peers out through the small hole, waiting for the knights to arrive.

The Fist member aiming at the lights squeezes the trigger. Gunshots echo through the cavernous factory and one by one, the lights explode. It's mid afternoon and New Triton will still be bright, but as the lights go out, the people at the windows become dark shadows in the Old Triton gloom.

Cale is standing next to me. He shifts impatiently, his expression tense with a strain I don't feel. A small pouch under his shirt is stuffed full of poppers, and a few other supplies.

He lifts his hands, showing me his wrists that are bound in front of him with thick cords. "You ready, Milla?" he asks.

I nod, putting my big, armored hand on his shoulder. "Let's go."

We stride out of the factory together. In the middle of the deserted street outside the factory is a huge pile of mattresses. The Fist must have raided a shelter, because there are dozens of them. Walking past them, I push Cale ahead of me as though he's my prisoner. And as we move away from the factory, I can't help but picture all the Fist members peering through the factory's ventilation holes with their weapons trained on me. Maybe I should be afraid that somebody will give in to the temptation to attack a knight, even if I'm on their side. But all I feel is relief that we're finally heading toward the Meat Locker, where the itch in my brain wants me to be.

At the Meat Locker, my squad will be waiting for me and I'll get my orders. At least, that's what the itch is telling me. But I can't let it control me. I refuse to let Director Morelle make me into one of her brainwashed soldiers.

We round the corner. The Meat Locker is at the other end of this street and not far ahead is the spot where Gama was murdered.

We stop beside the remains of the stall where Cale hid last time we were here. It's still standing, though more of its structure has fallen down. Cale ducks inside it like he did last time, managing to hide himself in the ramshackle remains.

"Ready?" he asks.

"Call her," I say with a nod.

Though I don't hear anything, a few moments later he says, "Done."

I stride back toward the factory, but only until I'm just around the corner of the street. Tori was waiting for Cale to give her the signal, so any moment now—

BOOM!

Though I'm expecting it, the explosion still makes me stagger. It's deafeningly loud, and the buildings around me shake. A moment later, I feel the heat from the blast on my sensors, then the glow of a fire lights up the Old Triton gloom. Dozens of mattresses are burning.

I wait, my heart thumping for several endless seconds.

My hand creeps toward the screen on my arm as if it has a mind of its own. I have to fight the overpowering urge to activate it so I can receive my orders.

Finally, I hear the thumping of metal boots coming from the Meat Locker. Still I wait, letting the knights get closer.

Two squads of knights round the corner, and I march toward them as though I'm striding away from the blast.

"Hurry," I shout. "We need backup."

"What's going on?" demands the leader. "Our orders are to investigate and report back."

"We're being attacked. The Fist has formed an army and attacked one of Director Morelle's factories. They're holed up in it, and this is our chance to take them out. You get to lead the attack." I point toward the factory. "But first call in and tell the command center to send all available troops. *Now*." I spin away from them, heading in the direction of the Meat Locker.

"Wait. Where are you going?"

"To mobilize the rest of our forces. This is an emergency. Hurry!"

I jog around the corner, not looking back until I'm out

of sight. I'm banking on the fact the knights are used to taking orders. More than that, they're *programmed* to take orders. Questioning what they're told isn't part of that training.

Sure enough, I hear twelve sets of metal boots moving quickly away, heading toward the huge fire that's lighting up the outside of the cab factory. I walk back to where Cale's hiding in the falling-down stall, hugging the wall so the knights guarding the Meat Locker's entrance can't see me.

"There were two squads," I say quietly.

"How many more do you think are in the Meat Locker?" Cale emerges from his hiding place.

"I guess we'll find out."

Waiting is the hardest part. But only a few seconds later, we hear the cracking of gunfire from the factory, then the blast of another explosion. The ground shakes so hard that more of the ramshackle stall crashes to the ground. If fighting so close to their base doesn't tempt all the knights out of the Meat Locker, nothing will.

Sure enough, more boots thump on the sidewalk, the sound harder to hear over the rising sounds of battle behind us.

"This is it," I mutter.

Cale nods and steps out from behind the stall. I put my hand his shoulder and push him in front of me, steering my prisoner toward the Meat Locker.

Four knights and six stompers jog toward us, weapons drawn.

"Hurry," I shout to them, not slowing. "My squad needs help."

"Status?" asks the leader.

They're probably expecting some kind of soldier-talk in

reply. I hesitate for just a moment while I search for something to say that won't make them suspicious.

"Status critical," I bark. "My orders are to secure this prisoner and return. We need every available soldier to flush out the terrorists who are holed up in there."

Whether that was the right thing to say or not, I have no idea, but a barrage of gunfire from behind me is distracting them anyway. I push Cale forward, urging him to move faster, and we stride past the knights and stompers.

To my relief, they keep going, jogging toward the sounds of battle.

Tori and the other Fist members are now facing at least sixteen knights and six stompers, and it's likely to be a lot more. Every squad patrolling this part of Old Triton will rush to help. They may even have been called in from further away by now.

If I don't manage to get into the Meat Locker and start wiping chips, the Fist won't stand a chance.

The two knights guarding the door of the Meat Locker are just ahead of us. They're the last obstacles to getting inside, and they stare at me as I approach, obviously on high alert.

"What are you doing, soldier?" asks the one on the left. It has a woman's voice, and its tone rings with authority.

"This man is an important prisoner." I shove Cale forward while he drags his feet, making a show of struggling against his bonds. "The director wants him kept safe until backup arrives. He must be alive and unharmed. Those are her direct orders."

The knights barely glance at Cale. "We didn't get those orders," snaps the woman.

"I'm not surprised." I push Cale closer. "It's chaos out there."

"We can hear it," says the knight on the right of the

door. He sounds very young, like he's barely past puberty. "What's going on?"

"Transfer your orders to me," demands the woman. She holds up one arm and the electronic panel above her wrist lights up. She expects me to do a transfer by holding my own wrist close.

"The orders were verbal."

"Then I'll need to confirm them."

As she moves to tap the screen in her arm, I weigh my chances of being able to get Cale safely out of the way and overpower them both. Then Cale yanks his hands free of the bindings around his wrists, and pulls a popper from the pouch under his shirt. He drops it at the knights' feet and ducks to the side.

My heart lurches, before I realize he didn't activate the popper. The knights don't notice it's not live. They jump away, scrambling to get out of range.

As the woman brushes past me, I whip out my gun and grab her neck. Before she has time to jerk away, I press my gun into her bat-like ear. The itch fills my head, and I have to force myself to pull the trigger.

The boy stumbles backward, yanking out his weapon. "What the—?"

I drop the woman's body. As she crumples, six bullets strike my torso, the force of the impacts knocking me backward. When the boy stops firing, I charge him, slamming him against the wall.

He struggles against me, managing to bring the gun up to my head. I ram my shoulder into his chest and grab his arm, bashing it against the concrete. Cale steps in close, shoves a gun into the knight's ear, and puts a bullet in his brain.

I drop the knight's body. It's a good sign that no more knights or stompers rushed out of the Meat Locker to help the guards, but we can't be sure they've all left the building.

"Stay behind me," I order Cale as I go in through the Meat Locker's front door.

Just inside are a couple of meeting rooms with tables and chairs. I can't imagine the knights needing to sit, but maybe stompers use the rooms. Or it could be a planning area where their officers discuss strategy. Right now the rooms are empty, with no knights or stompers to be seen.

Past the meeting rooms is a locked door with a sensor beside it. To get in, I'd need to swipe the panel on my wrist against the sensor, but I doubt my stolen Knight Skin would have clearance to open the door. More likely it would set off the alarms and bring all the knights running back to base.

The door is solid metal set into a concrete wall. I slam my shoulder into it anyway, putting all my strength behind it. Most doors would explode into toothpicks. This one doesn't so much as tremble.

I glance at Cale. Anxiety is written across his face. There's only one way to get through this door, and if it doesn't work, our plan has failed before it started.

Bringing up my wrist, I move to position it against the door sensor.

"Wait!" Cale grabs my arm and pushes it down. "Use one of the knights from outside."

Of course.

I drag in the female knight's body and hold the screen in her arm against the sensor. The door slides open.

Letting out a relieved breath, I step into the massive room I saw on the holo, filled with hundreds of pods. Each pod consists of a narrow, contoured bed with a screen and control panel above it. Inside each, a boy or girl dressed in military fatigues lies with their eyes closed. Tubes snake into each kid. One tube is attached to their arm. Others disappear inside their clothes. It takes me several horrified seconds to realize they're feeding the kids and taking away their waste using the tubes. The director didn't show that on the holo.

Other than the hum of all the equipment, the enormous room is silent and still. Above each pod, the monitors show the soldiers' vital signs. The pods and monitors look just like the one I saw on the holo, which means each should each have a failsafe button that will wipe the chip of the soldier inside.

Cale comes up beside me and gives a low whistle. "So many of them," he murmurs. "Like zombies asleep in their coffins."

"They're not all sleeping." I point to where a woman in her twenties and a young boy are pulling themselves out of their pods. The tubes they've had to yank out of their bodies are lying behind them.

"The knights who were guarding the door." Cale pulls a small mask out of the pouch he has hidden under his shirt, and puts it over his face.

I raise my voice to a shout. "Stop, or I'll shoot."

The young boy raises his arms above his head, fear in his expression.

The woman ducks behind her pod. "You're too late," she yells. "I already called in to base and told them we'd been infiltrated."

Cale throws a small round ball at her. Unlike the last popper, it breaks open when it hits the ground. Instead of an explosion, it lets out a loud hiss.

According to Doctor Gregory, the Knight Skin I'm using won't be affected by the sleeping gas. Something about it having an enhanced respiratory system, but her explanation was longer and more complicated. I just hope she was right.

The woman tries to run, but falls before she gets more than a few steps. Cale throws more poppers and the boy falls too, dropping to his knees and then pitching forward.

"Good thing there are no windows, and the door seems to have a pretty good seal." Cale's voice is slightly muffled behind his gas mask. "The gas is working fast."

I stride to the first pod and find the kill button exactly where it's supposed to be. Funnily enough, the more I ignore the itch in my head, the weaker it seems to get. When I lift my hand to the button, I barely feel it at all.

I punch the button and the pod's monitors go dead, though the soldier inside the pod doesn't stir. The sleeping gas is obviously doing what it's supposed to.

Moving to the next pod, I glance along the row Cale's started on. I haven't spotted William yet, but I can only see into a limited number of pods. The only way to find him is to work our way down the rows and hope we aren't interrupted.

I wipe chip after chip, until all the faces in the pods blur together. All these kids are from the director's military academies. They're Old Tritoners whose parents died or were forced to give them up. A surge of births from the Welcon disaster combined with second-child taxes, and the orphanages were overflowing. An abundance of meat for the director's war machine.

There are no empty pods. Which means these kids don't need to transfer back into their own bodies. Not to eat, sleep, or even use the toilet.

Twenty-four hours a day in their Skins. No wonder they can kill without remorse. They haven't been human in weeks.

I finish the row and start on the next one. There are so

many soldiers. So many kids who never had a choice about where they ended up. The director stole them. Brainwashed them. Used them.

William has to be here somewhere. But what if I can't find him? What if—?

There.

Chest tight, I stride to the pod that holds my long-lost brother.

He was a boy when I last saw him. Now his face has hardened and lost the roundness of youth. He has a jagged, white scar on one side of his chin. My stomach drops to see it. What could have hurt him like that? Whatever it was, I should have been there to stop it.

"I'm sorry," I murmur under my breath. "I'm here now."

I hit his kill switch, then bend to yank all the tubes from his body before I scoop him out of the pod. A seventeen-year-old boy should be heavy, especially because whatever training regime the director put him through has made him wiry and strong-looking. Still, he feels like his bones are full of air, and he looks small in my huge arms. His pasty, sun-starved skin stands out against my black armour. His head lolls back, his eyes still closed.

Iron bands tighten around my chest. "It'll be okay," I whisper. "I've got you." Crossing to the door, I kneel to deposit him gently onto the floor next to it.

When I straighten, a sharp crack of gunfire comes from right outside.

Chapter Nineteen

"**H**urry!" shouts Cale. He's rushing down the row of pods, hitting kill buttons as he goes.

I run back to where I left off, so I can keep going. We've probably wiped a few hundred chips already, but there are still several rows to go.

An explosion from outside shakes the floor. The gunshots are so close, it sounds like the shooters are at the door of the Meat Locker, about to burst inside. I work with one eye on the door, ready to attack if it opens. William's still slumped beside it and I curse myself for putting him in the line of fire. I thought we'd have more time.

The battle noise gets louder and louder, until I'm sure both armies must be in the Meat Locker's lobby, shooting at each other over the meeting tables. Cale and I move as fast as we can, working down the rows.

The firing stops for a moment. Then there's another burst. Then it stops again.

"What do you think the silence means?" pants Cale. Perspiration is dripping inside his gas mask, turning it cloudy.

I don't think he expects an answer, and I don't have one to give him. We only have two rows of soldiers left. Eighty more chips to wipe.

Seventy.

Sixty.

Fifty.

The heavy steel door slides open.

I spin to face it, drawing my gun as I turn.

Five men and three women stand in the entrance. They level their weapons at me.

"Don't shoot!" yells Cale. "We're on your side."

They're Fist members. I lower my gun, hoping they'll do the same. We have less than fifty chips left to wipe, but with the door open, the sleeping gas we filled the room with is escaping.

Sure enough, from his position lying next to the door, my brother lets out a cough. He's closest to the fresh air, which means he'll be the first to wake, but the other soldiers won't be far behind.

"You need to get out." Cale motions them frantically backward. "This room is filled with gas. You'll pass out if you don't…"

One of the intruders falls to their knees. The others stagger back. At least one has the presence of mind to pull his fallen teammate out of the way so the door can slide shut. But now the soldiers in the pods closest to the door are groaning and stirring.

"You have more gas?" I ask Cale.

He shakes his head. "I've used it all."

We hit more kill buttons, but the soldiers are definitely waking up.

William pushes himself up to sitting. "Waz happenin'?" he slurs.

Dammit, if enough soldiers wake up, we may have to

fight our way out of here after all. I can handle it, but what about Cale? Though I'll do my best to protect him, there are over a thousand soldiers in this room. I can't fight off that many.

"We need to go," I tell him.

He keeps moving down the row, pushing more buttons. "We're almost done."

William gets clumsily to his feet, using the wall for support. "Wha' happened?" His voice is getting less slurred.

The soldiers in the front rows are sitting up and tugging the tubes out of their bodies. The entire room's about to come to life. A thousand zombies rising from their coffins.

"Come on." I grab Cale's arm and drag him to the door. There are only thirty or so chips we didn't wipe. Out of a thousand soldiers, that's not many. It's time to cut our losses.

When we reach the door, I pick up William and toss him over my shoulder.

"Hey!" He pounds his hands against my back. "What the hell?"

"Stand down, soldier," I bark. "Your orders are to let me carry you out of here."

To my relief, he goes still.

Beside the door is a control panel, and I grab William's arm and swipe his band against it. The door slides open, and Cale steps through. I tug out my weapon and blast the panel into a smoking wreck before jumping through the door as it slams shut.

The Fist members who tried to come inside are in the meeting room area, just outside the sliding door. Weapons drawn, they're watching the street, alert for more attackers. I must have been wrong about how close the gunfire was, because there's no sign of a battle in here.

"Did you get them all?" demands one of the Fist members, a man with a scrawny beard and blood on his shirt.

"Almost," snaps Cale. He yanks his gas mask off and wipes his face on his sleeve. "We would have if you hadn't opened the door and let the gas out."

I put William down. "Take off your band," I command my brother.

"Why?" He looks a lot more awake now we're in fresh air. "Who are you? What's your rank?"

"Do as I say, soldier. That's an order."

My brother hesitates a moment longer, then presses the release on his band and hands it to me. I pass it to Cale. "Hold onto it for me."

The Fist members are gaping. "He's one of them," says the man with blood on his shirt. "Why are you—?"

"You need to get out of here now." I interrupt the man. "Reinforcements could be on their way."

The man shoots both me and William another suspicious look, then he and his friends go outside onto the street.

I shoot the control panel on this side of the door as well, just to make it more difficult for the soldiers inside to escape. Then I pick up William, throwing him over my shoulder easily in spite of the way he struggles. Cale and I follow the Fist members outside.

Bodies are strewn across the street. Fist members and stompers lie dead. Many more knight bodies lie with them. There's burning debris in the street, but where it came from, I have no idea. The falling-down stall Cale hid in is alight, the flames licking high, and more bodies have fallen near where Gama died.

I draw in a sharp breath.

"Call Tori," I tell Cale. "Make sure she's okay."

"Let's get out of here first."

We jog to the corner. William feels light on my shoulder, like I could carry him all day. But he's squirming around, trying to get free. I have to keep a tight grip on his legs to keep him in place.

"Who are you?" my brother demands, his voice unsteady from being jolted on my shoulder. "Are you working with the terrorists? Are you the reason I was yanked out of my Skin?"

I need to explain everything to him and let him know how the director has been using him all these years. As soon as we get somewhere safe, I'll tell him the truth. But where should we go?

"What are you going to do with him?" pants Cale, obviously wondering the same things I am.

"I'll have to take him to the safe house. I need to get out of this Skin." It seems weird to want to be human again, when I'm so much stronger and more powerful as a knight. But that itch in my brain still has me unsettled. What if I stop fighting it and suddenly find myself calling in to the director's command center for orders? Or if I see Director Morelle on a holo, and can't keep myself from doing whatever she tells me?

"You can't take him to the safe house," Cale says. "You'll compromise it. Besides, I should go to the factory. They might need our help."

"I can't hear any shots. The fighting must be over."

"They could still need help."

"It's too dangerous. We said we'd meet at the safe house." When we arranged it, I didn't remind Tori and the others that I might have my brother with me, because I didn't want to jinx my chances of getting him out.

"What's going on?" William demands. "I need you to tell me who you are."

"Once we're out of here, I'll tell you everything." I turn to Cale. "Let's find a safe place where we can stop and call Tori, to make sure they're okay."

Well clear of the war zone, we find the perfect place. It's a dark and narrow alley that's a dead end, and at the back there's a recess for a stairwell that's been bricked off. Once tucked in the recess, we can't be seen from the road. I put William down, and he glowers at me suspiciously, his eyes narrowed. "You're a traitor, aren't you?" he snarls. "You're working with the terrorists."

I take a breath, bracing myself for his likely reaction to the truth. The director's had him under her control for years. He'll still be loyal to her, and I can't expect him to throw off her conditioning right away.

"I'm your sister." I gentle my tone. "It's Milla."

"Traitor!" He spits the word in my face, his face going red.

I rock back at the force of his vitriol. For years I've been picturing the moment I managed to find my brother. Never in my wildest dreams did I imagine he'd be so furious.

I draw in a breath. "William, listen to me. Ma and I have both been looking for you. I promised her I'd get you back."

"What did you do to my Skin? Why can't I transfer back into it?"

"You couldn't stay in that Skin. The director used it to put thoughts into your head that weren't really yours. I needed to rescue you from it, to stop her from—"

"Rescue me?" His voice rises. "I was in Deiterra. In *combat*. My squad needs me. I have to go back."

"You were in Deiterra?" asks Cale. His tone is calm,

but I can see how shocked he is. "How many soldiers are fighting over there?"

"Why can't I transfer back into my Skin?" He jabs his finger at me. "What did you do?"

"I had to wipe your chip."

"This wiping thing is permanent?" William's face twists with fury. "You bitch!"

"Using the Knight Skin was changing your brain. The director's using a kind of thought control. I'd never lie to you, William. You have to believe me."

"When Director Morelle finds out what you've done, she's going to tear you into—"

"Ma wants to see you," I say desperately. "Will you at least see Ma?"

"The director is my mother."

"What?" I feel like I've been punched in the chest. How badly has the director brainwashed him? "No, I mean your real mother. You have to know how much she misses you."

He lunges sideways, trying to get away. I grab his arm and hold him easily, hating that I need to keep him with us against his will.

"You're talking about the woman who abandoned me." He sounds so furious, a wave of despair crashes over me.

"It wasn't like that. I mean, we needed to send you to the academy. We had no choice. There was no money after Pa died, you know that. We lost our home. And you couldn't move into the shelter with us, they don't take kids younger than—"

"I don't care that you abandoned me. I'm a knight now. The director's knight. And when she finds out what you did, she's going to hunt you down."

"William, please. Ma's been so worried. She needs to see you."

"Let me go." William sets his jaw in a stubborn expression and memories flood back. As a little boy, he'd wear the same expression whenever somebody told him he couldn't have something. He was only two years younger than me, and I thought he was mine to protect.

I loved him more than anything. Hell, I still love him. Even if I've become his enemy.

Chapter Twenty

It breaks my heart to tie William up, but I do it anyway.

Once he's secure, Cale calls Tori. She has a few cuts and bruises, Keren has a broken arm and cracked ribs, and Spade was shot in the leg. They went to a different safe house to get patched up, one closer to the factory, and someone's cleaning Spade's wound when we call. We can hear him cursing in the background.

Tori sounds gleeful. They blasted the brains out of a lot of knights. She's not sure how many, but she thinks there were more than a hundred. If we hadn't been able to wipe so many chips, the Fist would have been crushed.

Reports of knights suddenly falling lifeless are apparently still coming in from all over Old Triton. Fist members have been dispatched to finish those ones off too. And, if what my brother said was true, more knights must have keeled over in Deiterra. I doubt the director will get any of those Skins back in one piece.

By the time we hang up, Cale is jubilant, but the itch in my head is almost unbearable. I have to clench my fists and hold my arms firmly by my sides to keep myself from calling in to base.

"Will you wait here with William?" I thrust my gun at Cale. "I'll get to the safe house faster on my own."

He nods, his smile disappearing as he takes the weapon from me. "You okay?"

"I will be, once I'm human again."

One good thing about this Skin, I'm fast and I don't get tired. My legs eat up the miles, and once I'm back in the safe house, I transfer back into my human body with a sense of relief.

But my relief doesn't last long. It ebbs away as soon as I stand up, when the movement makes my wounded shoulder throb. My human body feels stiff, weak, and painfully slow compared to being the knight. In spite of it messing with my thoughts, I already miss the sense of power it gave me.

It takes forever to get back to the alley where I left Cale and William. It's late at night by the time I arrive, and the alley is pitch black. My eyes are better than Cale's or William's because I see them well before they see me.

"I'm here," I call softly, so I don't startle Cale. I have my bandana tied over my face in case of security cameras or drones, so my voice is muffled.

William peers at me, but with my bandana on, he can't see my scars. I'm glad. I didn't have them the last time I saw him, and I'm not sure I'm ready for his reaction.

Cale calls us a cab and we bundle William into it with his hands tied behind his back and his mouth gagged so he can't give any instructions to the cab's AI system. And when we get to Doctor Gregory's, we hustle him inside, though the doctor doesn't seem happy to let a prisoner into her house. I don't get a chance to explain though, because

Ma is just behind her, and she lets out a cry when she sees William.

"Son!" She pulls off his gag, then throws her arms around him, hugging him tightly. "I was so worried about you. What have they done to you? Are you okay?"

My brother stands sullenly, saying nothing. He looks like he's accepting her hug because he has no choice.

"The director brainwashed him," I tell Ma. "She made him think we're his enemies."

"You *are* my enemies," William snarls.

Ma draws back, looking stricken. "But William, I'm your mother."

My chest tightens at the pain in her expression. "I'm sorry, Ma. It'll take some time, but I'm sure he'll see reason."

"Keep away from me." William's face twists with something that looks like disgust.

Ma's hands flutter helplessly, as though she doesn't know what to do with them. "I missed you so much, love. I didn't know where they'd taken you." She sounds desperate. "I tried calling you hundreds of times."

Cale goes into the kitchen and Doctor Gregory disappears into her bedroom, both obviously trying to give us some privacy. I tug my bandanna off, and William's eyes widen.

"What happened to your face?" he asks. For the first time, he sounds more curious than hostile.

"An accident at the factory."

"I'm glad you're here," says Ma. She tries to wraps me in a hug, but I wince and pull away.

"My shoulder hurts," I tell her, flexing my arm.

"What happened? How bad is it?"

"It's fine. Just a little sore."

She hugs me gingerly on the other side, avoiding my

wound. "Thank you for bringing William back to me. And for coming back yourself. I was afraid for you, sweetheart. I spent the whole time wanting to call you."

She smells just like she always has, an underlying scent that's so familiar it makes my heart ache. But she still looks exhausted and drawn.

"I kept trying to use my band and then realizing it wasn't there," she adds.

"I know how that feels. Here." I offer my wrist so she can take her band back.

When it's safely on her wrist, she puts one arm around me, and takes William's arm with her other hand, like she wants to hug us both at once. "It's like the best kind of dream to have my children with me again. I love you both so much."

"The director's my real mother." William's expression is stony.

"I'm sorry," I tell Ma again, hating to see her face fall. "The director's been filling his head with lies. She's turned him against us, so he'd fight for her."

"But he's not hurt, is he?" Her sunken eyes search mine, desperate for answers.

I can't tell her his brain was altered by his Skin. She'll worry herself sick, and what good will it do? Besides, it's already happened. He's already changed.

"He's not really hurt," I tell her instead. "Hopefully he'll be back to normal soon. The director trained him to be her soldier, but eventually he'll have to remember who he really is." I'm trying to convince myself as much as her.

"Director Morelle will kill you all." William's matter-of-fact tone makes me shudder. "I hope she asks me to do it. I'll enjoy it."

Ma draws in a loud breath, her hand at her mouth,

and I glare at my brother. How can he upset Ma like this, when she's already gone through so much?

Grabbing his gag, I tie it back over his mouth.

"Oh." Ma puts her hand on my arm, trying to stop me. "Must we do that? I mean, I don't like what he's saying, but that can't be comfortable for him. And is it safe? Can he breathe?"

I raise my voice, calling to the doctor who's still in her bedroom. "Doctor Gregory, do you mind if I put my brother in your spare room for now? Then I can take off his gag."

She pokes her head out of her bedroom, her brow furrowed. "How long do you mean to keep him contained?"

"I'm not sure. Don't suppose you have any ideas on how we could undo what the director did to him?"

Doctor Gregory raises her eyebrows and her anxious expression changes into a thoughtful one. She walks closer. "An interesting prospect. I was hoping to have access to the Knight Skin in order to study the neural processes of a subject while their consciousness was transferred. But testing a subject who's undergone a full conditioning treatment could provide valuable insight." She taps her chin, her eyes glazed as though she's looking at something that's not here. "I could devise some tests to measure the extent of the neural changes. It's just a pity we don't have his initial data from before he was exposed to the…"

"I'll put him in the spare bedroom," I murmur to Ma. "He'll be safe in there."

"Do you mind if I take him?" She looks to me for permission, and I feel oddly like we've swapped bodies and I'm now the parent.

"Sure. You can take his gag off, but don't untie him."

"I'm making something to eat," Cale says from the kitchen. "Anyone else hungry?"

"Starving." My stomach grumbles.

Doctor Gregory has already moved to her workbench to make notes on her mind pad. She shakes her head. "I've eaten, thank you."

Ma also refuses, all her attention focused on William. She leads him into the spare room, where she'll no doubt keep trying to convince him that she loves him. That he's refusing to believe her makes me itch to shake some sense into him.

Cale uses the machine in the kitchen to make meat-flavored pancakes, and they're delicious. Much nicer than anything I've ever eaten in a shelter. I call Ma out of the bedroom, trying to convince her to come and eat with us, but she shakes her head.

"William says he's not hungry, but I think he must be," she says, putting a couple of pancakes onto a plate. "I'll take these to him." She disappears again.

After we've stuffed ourselves with pancakes, Cale moves to the living room and flicks on the holo. I sink down on the couch next to him, feeling exhausted. Now my stomach is full, my eyes are closing.

But they snap open again when I hear Director Morelle's voice.

On the holo, two figures are projected, both sitting in chairs. One is a young reporter, and the other is Director Morelle.

"This is shocking news indeed," says the reporter, her expression serious. "In a moment we'll return to the hospital for an update on President's Trask's condition. But first, tell us about today's attack."

I sit up straighter. "Something happened to the president?"

Director Morelle is already answering the reporter. "The Fist's primary objective was the assassination attempt. They attacked a cab factory and used the explosion as a diversion to distract the knights and divide our forces. While many knights were rescuing the innocent civilians caught in the blast, another strike force fired on the president and vice president."

"What?" I meet Cale's gaze. He looks as shocked as I feel. "Did you know they were going to try and kill the president?" I ask, though I can already tell he didn't.

He shakes his head. "Don't fall for her lies. The Fist didn't have anything to do with an assassination attempt."

I let out my breath. "Of course they didn't. Director Morelle probably saw an opportunity and ordered her own soldiers to kill him."

"Why would the Fist do all this?" The reporter uncrosses her slim legs and leans forward. "The vice president's death has been confirmed, and the president is in critical care. But why would the Fist want to destroy our country's leadership and attack our soldiers? Do they want Deiterra to invade us?"

"The sole aim of the Fist is to spread civil unrest and sabotage the fabric of our society. We're closing in on the perpetrators of this heinous act, but until we have them locked up, we're announcing new measures to help the knights track them down and arrest them."

"New measures?" asks the reporter.

"The knights will have full authority to conduct spot checks on all Old Triton citizens. Any citizen found to be a member of the Fist will be dealt with on the spot."

"She means they'll be killed." Anger leaks into my voice.

"She means that even more Old Tritoners will be

killed," Cale corrects. "They're stepping up their murders to a whole new level."

I nod. I only hope that after the fighting today, there are a lot less knights to do the murdering.

"All factory workers will be required to take on extra shifts," adds Director Morelle. "Producing more Knight Skins is our top priority."

The reporter nods, her large eyes earnest. "How many soldiers were injured or killed in today's attack?"

"Very few. And fortunately, only their Skins were harmed, not the soldiers themselves. We're already manufacturing more Skins to replace those which were lost."

The holo switches to show the interior of a factory that looks very much like the one Ma was working in. The machines are active, and the place is full of grunts. The clanking of the conveyor belt is a too-familiar sound.

I catch my breath. "She can't have set her factory up somewhere else already?"

Cale presses his lips together, his expression grim.

I think of all the bodies we saw on the street outside the Meat Locker. Was today's fight for nothing? If the director's already set up a new factory, she'll have new Knight Skins ready for her soldiers in no time. I can't imagine there'll be any way to destroy a second factory. It'll be too well guarded.

The holo goes back to showing the reporter and Director Morelle.

"Surgeons are working around the clock to stabilize President Trask," says the reporter. "First, we'll see if we can get an update, then we'll cross live to Vice President Burn's office, for details of the memorial service that's being organised to honor him."

The director speaks up. "Before your camera switches

back to the hospital, I have a short broadcast that should reassure all Triton citizens."

The camera zooms in close, and suddenly the director's head is all I can see, floating in front of the holo screen, larger than life. "Law-abiding citizens of Triton have nothing to fear," she says in a soothing tone. "As the acting head of Triton's army, President Trask has authorized me to make decisions on his behalf. Until he's made a full recovery, rest assured I'll continue to keep Triton safe."

She nods once, presumably at the person filming, and the projection changes to a street scene. A six-member squad of knights marches down the sidewalk, their metal boots thundering in unison. They're marching through Old Triton. It's the main central street and easily recognizable, but I've never seen it like this.

Neon lights still shine from the storefronts along the street. Above eye level, holograms still show people eating, or trying on clothes, or getting their hair cut. But the stores the holograms advertise are all closed.

Usually the sidewalks are crowded with people. I've bought protein balls and sugar sweets from vendors perched on stools, with their wares displayed on small folding tables that shine under portable lights. They sell everything from street brew to band apps on that street, and music has always blared from dozens of sex clubs and drinking holes tucked away inside the main buildings.

Now, though, it's silent and deserted. There are no sinkers looking for a snack. No kids playing games with their friends, or pickpockets on the prowl. No sex workers propositioning passers-by, trying to drum up trade. No rough sleepers propped up in doorways, hustling for credits. There are no workers hurrying to their jobs.

The busiest street in Triton is even emptier than the streets around the Meat Locker were.

"Where are all the people?" I feel suddenly cold. Are they all cowering in shelters? Have the knights scared them off the streets? Or have they killed them?

"Don't be afraid," says the director's voice. "Your knights are keeping your city safe. The soldiers who patrol Old Triton's streets are ever-vigilant, day and night. They're stamping down terrorism and making sure it can never flourish here again." The scene changes to the breach in the Deiterran wall. Knights are arrayed in a large circle, facing the rubble. They stand motionless, their guns held ready. There's no sign of the bodies, blood, or carnage from the battle we witnessed. "Other squads are deployed across the Deiterran border. Permissiveness has failed. Separation has failed. The wall has failed. It's time to end the fear and finally unite under one rule. The war is almost over, and Triton's knights will secure victory."

The scene changes again. Now a perfectly tweaked New Triton couple are pushing a young child on a swing. The sun is rising behind them, giving the family a golden glow. The well-dressed parents smile at each other, then down at their child. Their eyes shine.

"The Morelle Corporation is bringing you a future that's brighter than ever before. Peace will reign, and your family will prosper. I promise you--"

The holo goes dead.

From the seat next to mine, the doctor lets out a loud breath, her hand at her throat. I was so caught up in the horror of what we were watching, I didn't notice her sitting down with us.

"I had to turn it off," says Cale in a rough voice. "I couldn't stand to watch anymore." He stands up, flexing his fists as though he wants to punch someone. "The Fist didn't shoot either the vice president or the president. We're being set up to take the fall. And the director's brushed off today's attacks like we hardly got rid of any knights at all. Maybe she's been making more in another factory all this time, and we didn't know about it. Perhaps we didn't make as big a dent in her plans as we thought."

I chew my lip, biting so hard it hurts. "She has the money and resources to build as many knights as she wants."

"Even today's fighting played into her hands. An excuse to get rid of the president and tighten her control."

Doctor Gregory is hunched in her chair, deep creases in her brow. "As much as it pains me, I'm starting to believe that you're right. These developments are extremely worrying."

"There must be something we can do," I say. "Some way to stop her."

Cale is silent. He stares at the floor, his fists clenched. His shoulders are slumped.

Doctor Gregory glances at me, then looks away.

I close my eyes, feeling the same despair I can see on their faces. My stomach churns when I think of the deserted street on the holo. Whatever happened to those people – was it our fault? Has the director already taken revenge for our attack?

Chapter Twenty-One

I jolt awake with the cold, stomach-churning certainty that something is terribly wrong.

I'm lying on one of Doctor Gregory's couches, and Cale is on the other. My shoulder is aching, and my internal clock is telling me that it must be almost dawn. The house is dark and quiet.

I pull myself out of bed, wincing at the pain in my shoulder, and creep across to the doctor's spare room. Slowly and silently, I ease open the door. Ma needs her sleep and I don't want to wake her. I just want to check on William.

Ma is lying on the bed, fully clothed and above the covers. There's nobody lying next to her. There's nobody else anywhere in the bedroom. She's alone.

William is gone.

My nostrils fill with the unmistakeable scent of blood when I shake Ma's arm. She doesn't wake up. There's a dark stain on her pillow, and when I touch her hair, my fingers come away sticky. She's bleeding from a cut on the top of her head.

"Ma!" I cradle her face. "Ma, wake up."

She groans a little, but her eyes don't open.

My foot brushes something on the floor. The bindings that were around William's wrists. He probably talked her into taking them off so he could sleep. The window is open, and he must have gone out that way.

"Wake up!" I rush back into the living room and grab Cale's shoulder. "Get up, Cale. William's escaped."

Bleary-eyed, he pulls himself up to sitting. "How long has he been gone?"

"It could have been hours. We need to get out of here. Now." I open the door to Doctor Gregory's room. "Doctor, get up. We have to leave. We're all in danger."

"What?" She gets out of bed, pulling a dressing gown over her pyjamas. "What's going on?"

"Get dressed. Hurry." I turn back to Cale, not caring that he's still doing up his jeans. "We'll take Ma to the hospital—"

Then I hear something that sends a chill down my spine. I spin toward the door.

"Milla? What—?"

"Shhh." I gesture at Cale to be quiet. Metal boots are pounding on the sidewalk outside. "A squad of knights," I hiss.

Doctor Gregory hurries out of her bedroom. "Are they patrolling?"

"They're coming fast. Running." Definitely not just a random patrol. "They're coming for us. We need to get out of here." I rush to the living room window, pushing it open. "This way. Doctor Gregory, quick. We need to get out. They're almost here."

Metal boots pound up the front steps, then somebody kicks the front door. It bursts open so hard, it splinters into pieces.

A knight stands in the doorway, its huge, armored body taking up so much of the frame that it almost blocks it entirely. The knight lets out a satisfied grunt when its eyes lock onto mine.

"Hello again, dear sister," says the knight.

William.

Cale steps in front of me, probably trying to be gallant and protect me. With my increased strength, I should be the one protecting him, but all I can do is gape past him, at the knight standing in the doorway.

William came back. Director Morelle gave him a new Knight Skin and sent him back here to find us. Any faint hope he might not want to hurt us disappears when the rest of his squad crowd into the house behind him.

Six knights. Four humans, including Ma who's still unconscious. The odds don't give me much hope for survival.

"What are you doing here, William?" I ask breathlessly. "Can we talk? Will you listen to—?"

"No." He strides toward me until he gets to the doctor's first workbench, laden with all kinds of electronic gadgets. He flips it over, throwing it sideways. The heavy table slams against the wall, and everything that was on it crashes to the floor.

"I'm not here to talk," he snarls. "As a favor to me, President Morelle allowed me to be the one to come and kill you all."

"*President* Morelle?" asks Cale. He's still standing in front of me, and I elbow him out of the way as William answers.

"Trask died. President Morelle's in charge, as she should be."

I drag in a shaky breath. If only I could transfer back into the Knight Skin. With it, we might have a chance, though it would be six knights against one. In desperation, I reach out with my mind, searching for it. But the safe house is a long way from here. Too far away for me to transfer into it.

"I don't want to fight you." I lift both hands to William, showing him my bare palms. "I love you. I won't hurt you, even though you've injured Ma, and she never did anything to deserve being treated like that."

William gives a laugh filled with such derision, the sound just about rips my heart out. "You don't want to fight me? That's so sweet, dearest sister. But I'd like you to put up a fight. It'll be more fun that way. You might even live a few seconds longer."

He steps closer, his squad moving up behind him.

From the far end of the living room, I hear the doctor make a small, frightened sound. It's so quiet, I only catch it because my hearing is sharper than normal. I should have told the doctor to run into her bedroom and hide under her bed. It might have given her a faint chance of survival.

"William, please," I say, racking my brain for some way to get her and Cale out of the house to safety.

"Please?" He laughs again. "Is that all you can say? I expected better."

"Don't you remember when you were little and I'd sing you to sleep? And when we used to climb onto the fire escape together. Remember how we'd imagine what it might be like if we ever got to live in New Triton?" I take a step forward, my hands still spread. "I dreamed of living in a proper house, but you said all you wanted was for us to always be together. You and Ma and—"

"You really think I care about your stupid memories?" He lunges forward and swipes his hand across another workbench. Equipment crashes to the floor.

The doctor makes another terrified sound, and I

silently will her to start backing up. If she makes it back into her bedroom, maybe they'll take pity on her and let her live.

Cale grabs something from the floor. When he straightens, I see it's the metal bar I bent to show Doctor Gregory how strong I am. He holds it up, and I wish I'd chosen something else to bend, because in a U-shape it doesn't look like a very effective weapon.

"Get out of here," Cale demands in a low, dangerous snarl.

William chuckles. "How sweet, my sister's lover is being brave. Romeo trying to protect his Juliet. It's a very old story, so you might not have heard it. Spoiler alert, both of you are going to die."

On the floor is the doctor's scanner, the one she used to wipe my chip and re-code it. I step to the side to snatch it up. William watches me grab it but makes no move to stop me. He obviously has no idea what it is.

I'm not even sure if it will work on his Skin. The doctor used it to wipe the chip embedded in my human body. But the Skin must have a lot of electronics in its brain stem, and maybe the doctor's device will scramble it enough to kill the Skin's connection to the person using it.

I glance back at the doctor. She's pale and trembling, but when I hold up the scanner and give her a pointed look, she gets what I'm asking and nods.

Okay, good. This weapon will work. And my brother doesn't know how strong I am. Maybe I can wipe one or two chips before he figures it out, but there's no way I can wipe all six, especially with one shoulder not working as well as it should.

"Cale, take the doctor into the bedroom." I pitch my voice low.

He shoots me a frown. "You can't fight them."

"Neither can you."

"So whatever we do, we'll do together."

"Romeo and Juliet," mocks William. "Don't worry, you'll die together." His yellow eyes go to his squad. "I want to be the one who does it," he orders. "Grab them and hold them."

The knights lunge forward, their movements almost too quick to follow. I don't fight, but let one grab me. Cale strikes one with the metal bar, but the knight doesn't so much as flinch. It twists Cale's arms behind his back, forcing him to drop the bar.

With the knight gripping me tightly around my arms, I let my body go limp, as though I've fainted. I let my head drop and loll on my shoulders, though pain shoots through my shoulder.

"What have you done?" snarls William. "You killed her."

"I didn't do anything," protests the knight that's holding me. It has a girl's voice. "I don't think she's dead." It lets go of one of my arms, presumably to check my heart's still beating. I wrench myself free, shooting my hand out to swipe the scanner across the back of its neck.

The knight drops, almost taking me down with it.

I jump back, and in the same movement lunge at one of the knights holding Cale. It lets him go and staggers back, but I don't quite manage to swipe the scanner across its neck before it shoves me away.

"That was a sneaky trick," my brother snarls. He moves quickly, grabbing my arms before I can sidestep him. I use all my strength to tear one arm free, ignoring the pain that sears into my shoulder, and struggling to get the scanner where I want it. He grunts with surprise, but recovers before I can get the scanner in the right place. He hooks his arm around my throat, choking me while he forces the scanner out of my hand.

"One of you keep hold of Romeo," he orders the two knights who've grabbed Cale between them again. "The other come and help me with this one. And keep your grip tight. She's stronger than she should be."

When he releases his arm from my throat, I gasp for breath. With a knight on each side of me, both holding on firmly, there's no way I can get free.

"Why are you so strong?" William snarls in my ear.

I press my lips together and shoot him a glare. My throat feels like it's on fire.

My brother nods at the knight who has hold of Doctor Gregory. "Kill her," he orders. "Not too quickly."

"No!" Cale and I shout in unison.

"Please don't," begs Doctor Gregory. "What do you want? Please take anything you like, but leave us—" Her begging is cut off by the knight's hands around her neck. It lifts her off the ground and her feet flail. She claws at its hands, her face going red and her eyes bulging.

It's Gama all over again.

"Stop. Let her go." I fling myself toward the doctor and feel the knights' grip on me slip before they manage to grab me again.

"Why are you so strong?" snarls William. "Tell me."

"Let her go first, then I'll tell you."

"Tell me now." He nods at the knight holding the doctor. "Finish her."

"No!"

But Doctor Gregory's hands are only moving weakly now, her frantic clawing at the knight's hands turning into a flutter. Her mouth opens and closes as she tries desperately to draw in a breath. Then she goes limp. The knight drops her and she crumples to the floor.

She's not breathing.

I stare at her body, a deep agonising scream ripping its way out of my throat. When I had nothing, Doctor Gregory took me in. Without her, I wouldn't have survived. And William killed her because of me. I did this. I repaid her kindness with death.

My heart is on fire. My throat aches with the need to scream again and again. It can't be real. She can't be dead. Please don't let her be dead.

"Why are you so strong?" demands William in my ear.

"Go to hell," I gasp.

"Tell me, or I'll kill Romeo." He nods at the knight holding Cale, and a black armored hand fastens around Cale's throat.

"A Skin made me strong," I spit at William. "It changed my brain. Just like using that Knight Skin has changed yours."

"Using a Knight Skin made your human body strong?"

"Not a Knight Skin, a Leopard Skin. I was the clouded leopard in the Skin Hunter contest."

He snorts. "You're lying."

"I'm not. Cale was going to use the Saber-toothed Tiger Skin, but he was replaced before the contest. He was on the holo, doing interviews. Do you recognise him?"

William cocks his head in a gesture that reminds me of Sentin. "And after the contest, you were stronger?"

"That's right. My brain got used to me being as strong as the leopard. That was my new normal, and somehow it carried over to my real body."

He considers it for a moment, then nods. "Makes sense." He raises his voice, addressing the knight that's still holding Cale by the throat. "Now I want you to kill Romeo."

"No, you can't," I shout. "I told you what you wanted to know. Let him go."

"I'd rather kill him." He nods at the knight, who lifts Cale off the ground. Cale starts choking and kicking just like the doctor did.

My heart is going to burst out of my chest. This can't be happening. Not to Cale. Not him. Anyone but him.

"I'm going to tear you to pieces," I scream at my brother.

"Sorry sister, but it's going to be the other way around."

Cale kicks harder, and I can't bear to watch. This isn't fair. Cale is the best person I know. All he's ever done is try to help people. He's the last person in the world who deserves to be hurt.

"Kill me," I beg. "Let him go and kill me instead."

My brother chuckles. "Don't worry, it'll be your turn next."

Then he glances down at the panel on his wrist. It's lit up and glowing red. He's getting a communication.

"Stop," he orders the knight who's holding up Cale. "Put him down."

The knight obeys slowly, as though reluctant to let Cale live. As soon as the knight's hand releases Cale's throat, he collapses to the floor, gasping with relief, dragging in air in big, noisy gulps.

"We've been ordered to wait to kill them," says William in a grudging tone.

"Wait for what?" I demand.

"It won't be long." He stares at his screen. "In fact, the person we're waiting for is already here."

The door opens and though there's no noise, I sense another presence in the room. Craning my neck, I see a huge, jewel-green figure moving closer.

Sentin.

My limbs go weak with relief. He's here to save us.

The Reptile Skin stops next to Doctor Gregory's body and stares down at her for a moment. Then he looks at William. "You already killed one." His voice is so cold and emotionless, he may as well be talking about the weather.

"My orders were to bring them in dead or alive, sir." William sounds sullen.

I stare at him in shock. Sentin has authority over the knights? The director—I mean, the president—must have given him that power. She must trust him.

"And you chose dead," says Sentin flatly.

It's not a question, but William nods. "Yes, sir. And we were going to kill the other two."

"Stand down, soldier. President Morelle wants that one alive." He nods at me. "Your orders are to take her into the lab. There's a doctor waiting to run some experiments on her."

I swallow, remembering how the doctor wanted to slice open my Leopard Skin so she could watch wounds appear on my human body.

"Take her back to the Morelle tower," Sentin commands. "Doctor James is waiting for her in the lab on level twenty-six." He frowns. "And don't damage her before you get there or you'll answer to our president."

"You're not taking her anywhere," growls Cale. His voice is raspy and hoarse. "Let her go."

Sentin ignores him, and anger surges through me, giving me the strength to struggle and almost tear myself free again, though my shoulder screams with pain.

"Hold her tighter," snarls William at the knight on my other side. Then he nods at Cale. "What about him, sir?"

"I want to question him before I dispose of him," says Sentin. "Leave him with me."

"Sir, I can help you—"

"I don't need your help. I'm a hundred times stronger than he is, and the girl is more important. Using a Skin altered her physiology, and President Morelle wants to study her. Take the rest of your squad to make sure the girl doesn't get away."

"Yes sir."

"Cale—" I call, but William clamps his hand over my mouth.

As my brother and the other knights drag me away, I can no longer pretend Sentin's on our side, or that he's somehow going to free us, or help us get away.

The way he's giving orders, President Morelle must have given him a senior position in her army. He's on her side, not ours.

He betrayed us, and now Cale's going to die.

Chapter Twenty-Two

Before leaving the doctor's house, my brother binds my wrists and ankles. Then he throws me over his shoulder, carrying me in the same way I carried him. Face down, bumping against his armor with my arms strapped behind my back, the pain in my shoulder is almost unbearable.

Instead of shoving me into a cab and driving to the Morelle Corporation, he strides down the sidewalk with me. Behind him, his squad march in step. It's going be a long walk. I'm jolted with every stride and pain shoots down my arm while his hard armor digs into my flesh.

Every step takes me further from Cale and Ma. I'm leaving them both to die, and I can't do a damn thing to stop it. All I can do is grit my teeth against the pain and try to reason with my brother.

"You hit Ma over the head and she could be dying right now. Do you even care that you might have killed your own mother? The only thing she ever did is love you."

He doesn't reply, so I keep talking.

"Ma and I have been working long hours in factories. I

got my scars on the job. You think I've had an easy few years?" I force myself not to think about what Sentin might be doing to Cale and Ma, or to let my fury, pain, or frustration leak into my voice. I need to sound as reasonable as I can to have any chance of getting William to listen. "Every cent Ma and I earned went into a fund. All these years, our one goal has been to get a place where the three of us can live. Where we can be a family again, and—"

"You two stayed together and sent me away."

He sounds contemptuous, but at least he's listening. That fact alone is enough to light a spark of hope, however faint.

"I was burned right after you went to the academy, and instead of helping out with my treatment, the only thing the company did was transfer me to a different factory. For my own good, they said. But it meant I had to leave Ma. Since then, we've been living in different shelters. I was on my own too, just like you."

The position I'm in, I can't see his face, but his stride seems to hesitate. Could I have finally gotten through to him?

"We both tried contacting you a thousand times after you went to the academy," I add. "We could never get hold of you."

"No, you didn't," He spits the words. "You never called."

"We left hundreds of messages. You didn't get any of them?" I'd suspected he hadn't, but to hear it confirmed is gut wrenching. "When I stayed at the Morelle Corporation, they had a firewall set up to block some functions of our bands. They must have had the same thing at the academy. They made sure you didn't get any of our calls or messages."

"I don't believe you."

"I'm telling the truth, William. President Morelle's the one who's been lying to you."

"Without her, I'd have nothing."

"That's not true. Without her, you'd have me and Ma. We'd never have let her take you if we'd known—"

"Stop talking. Speak again and I'll bash your brains out on the nearest wall."

He sounds furious enough that I clench my jaw shut. How can I change his mind? I'd tell him I love him, but I don't know if it's still true. All I can see is the fear on Doctor Gregory's face before he killed her. Even knowing he's been brainwashed doesn't change my horror over what he's done.

Still, I'd probably say it anyway if I thought it'd help. But he needs time to calm down first, to think about what I've told him, and hopefully start doubting everything that's been drummed into him.

I keep quiet for what seems like a long time. Behind us, his squad are marching in perfect synchronicity, their boots crashing rhythmically on the sidewalk. None of them are talking either, or if they are, I can't hear them.

The sun has risen. It's hot on my back, and when I turn my head up, a blinding glare hits my eyes. The light is shining through the top of the Morelle Building.

It's by far the tallest building in New Triton, and according to legend, Morelle keeps the top two floors for her own private use. Floors one-ninety-seven and one-ninety-eight. The very top of the building is all glass, and when the sun reflects through it, it's too bright to look at. Triton's newest president sleeps up there, with her head in the clouds.

I've never hated her more than I do right now.

We're almost at the building, and William still hasn't

said anything. His armor has been grinding into my torso with every step, and my arm and shoulder are on fire. With unbearable pain shooting through my limbs, wondering if Cale and Ma are already dead, and what's going to happen to me when we get to the building, I'm slowly going crazy.

"Did they treat you well at the academy?" I ask in what I hope is a gentle tone, though I'm speaking through clenched teeth. "We hoped it'd be better than that terrible orphanage, but we worried about you the whole time."

"The academy was my home."

"I'm sure it was nice. Morelle made it that way to turn you and the others against your real families. She's using you, William. Everything she did was so you'd be loyal to her. So you'd fight for—"

"Shut up," he says harshly. "I won't tell you again."

I suck in a breath, wondering whether to keep talking anyway. But I'm afraid to push too hard, and we're both silent when he carries me into the Morelle scraper.

This is the first time I've been back to this building since the Skin Hunter contest. The lobby is huge, with marble floors and walls. Its workers bustle in and out. Most stare curiously, but nobody challenges us.

President Morelle is here somewhere. So is the huge training room on the forth floor where Cale and I trained for the contest, and the laboratory on the twenty-sixth floor, where I was going to be experimented on.

The thought of being so close to that laboratory makes me want to scream. I escaped from it once, and the doctor who wanted to experiment on me won't make the same mistake again. This time, she'll make sure I'm securely tied up before she starts taking me apart piece by piece.

As my brother strides through the lobby, I suck in a breath, searching desperately for something—anything— that might get through to him.

"Do you know what that doctor's going to do to me, William? When she cuts my Skin, my human body bleeds. She's going to slice me into little bits so she can find out how long it takes me to die."

"Hurting your Skin affects your human body?" At least he's decided to respond. He asks the question like he really wants to know.

"That's right. She's determined to figure out why."

"And using a Skin is really how you became so strong?"

"Everything I've told you has been the honest truth."

We stop in front of the elevators and his squad come up behind us. With them so close, we won't be able to speak privately. I've lost my chance to change his mind.

The elevator doors open, and he motions his squad to get in first. In the instant before he steps in, he says, "I can't help you, Milla," in a voice so soft I can barely hear him.

It's the first time he's called me by my name.

As the elevator rises, a pit of despair opens up inside me. With his squad crowded around him, I can't say anything more. But his last words to me sounded almost regretful. If we only had more time, perhaps I could have convinced him I wasn't lying. Maybe I could have saved him from being just another of Morelle's tools.

But it's too late. The elevator doors open, and he marches down the hall then through the door to a small, white room that smells like antiseptic. A room I remember all too well.

His squad stay outside, guarding the exit. Making sure I can't escape.

"It's nice to have you back," says a white-coated woman, as William lifts me off his shoulders. "I'm Doctor James. You remember me?"

One glimpse of her red hair and cold eyes makes my

stomach churn. She's straight from my nightmares. I'd have given anything to never have to see her again.

"I remember tying you up instead of killing you," I growl. "Obviously a mistake, and I won't make it again."

She hands William a pair of scissors. "Cut off her clothes, then strap her to the bed."

"No! William, don't do it."

He dumps me face-up on the bed so I'm lying awkwardly on my hands which are still tied behind my back. Then he takes the scissors. Turning to me, he hesitates for just a moment.

"Please, William. You don't have to do this."

He starts at my ankles and cuts my jeans all the way up. It's an effortless motion, the thick fabric parting easily because the scissors are so sharp.

"You can leave her underwear," says the doctor. "But take off her shoes."

He slices my T-shirt off and slips off my sneakers, leaving me in just my bra and panties. Finally, he passes straps around my knees, thighs, and hips, securing me to the bed before slicing off the ties around my wrists and ankles. Even mostly naked, furious, and terrified, the intense relief I feel when my wounded shoulder releases from its cramped, forced-back position overwhelms everything else for a moment. Shame it doesn't last long.

Working quickly, William loops more straps over my body, forcing my back against the bed and pulling the straps so tight I can't move. He even fastens one across my forehead to hold my head in place.

When he's finished, the doctor tests to make sure the bonds are tight, then nods her approval. "Now fetch the Leopard Skin from Room 419."

William nods and goes out. He and his squad march off together, presumably satisfied that I'm not going anywhere. And I'm not. There are too many thick straps holding me down. When I use all my strength to strain against them, I don't feel any give at all.

I drag in a shuddering breath. "Why are you doing this?" I demand, knowing I won't be able to talk the doctor out of hurting me, but needing to try.

She sticks a couple of small, black electrodes to my forehead above the strap, then lifts my hair to position more on my scalp. "Your idiosyncrasies are unique. You're the only subject so far to exhibit somatoform injuries, let alone the other physiological changes. Do you have any idea why?"

"Go to hell."

She nods as though this were the answer she expected. Against the wall is a small, high table and she tugs it so it glides toward me on wheels. Then she takes her time to position the table beside the bed. Though my head is strapped down so tightly that I can't move, I can still watch from the corner of my eyes.

She picks up a medical scanner from the table and runs it over my body, watching the readout closely and clicking her tongue in disapproval. "Your condition isn't ideal," she says finally, putting it down. "You have several bruises and abrasions, and that's a significant wound on your shoulder. I'd prefer to have a clean slate to work with."

"I'll kill you." I say the words forcefully, making them sound as much of a threat as I can. I only wish I could make good on it.

The door opens, and a knight I assume is William wheels in a gurney. He positions it on the other side of the doctor's table of instruments. My beautiful Leopard Skin is lying on its side with so many thick webbing straps tying it down, only a few tufts of its beautiful fur stick through.

An overwhelming need to transfer into my leopard

surges through me, so strong I can barely fight it. I don't belong in my human body, I never have. My leopard is where I should be.

But my chip was wiped. I can't be the leopard anymore. Maybe I should be grateful for that, but the knowledge fills me with a desolate ache of longing.

When the bed is positioned, the knight stands at attention, and the doctor waves her hand in dismissal. "You may go."

He nods. Is it William? I want my brother to look at me. To do or say *something* that will tell me he feels the slightest bit sorry for leaving me here. Instead he marches out, closing the door behind him.

He and his squad disappear quickly, their black, amored bodies no longer visible through the glass door.

Doctor James studies my face with a little frown, no doubt able to see my anguish. "You're still in your human body?" she asks. "There's the leopard, so close, yet you don't wish to transfer?" She pulls back a little and shakes her head. "No, you do wish it. I can see it in your expression. So perhaps the problem is that you can't."

"Go to hell," I say again, my teeth gritted.

The doctor's expression doesn't change. She loosens the webbing from my forehead so I can move my head, then picks up a chip scanner I recognise because it looks like the one Doctor Gregory used. Forcing my head forward, she runs the scanner across the back of my neck, then raises her eyebrows. "Your chip has been re-coded. Who did that?" She tsks. "Does President Morelle know? I should inform her, yes? If someone outside the corporation was able to re-code your chip, who knows what other trouble they may cause."

When I don't answer, she puts the scanner down. "But

for me, this is fortunate. I can conduct a control experiment before we begin."

She picks something up from her table. A scalpel. My heart speeds up as my gaze fixes on the gleaming blade.

Doctor James turns to my leopard and slices a deep cut into its chest, between the thick straps that are holding it down. The air fills with the scent of blood, and my leopard's beautiful white fur turns red around the wound.

I haul against the restraints, using my horror and outrage to fuel my muscles, tearing and wrenching with everything I've got.

The doctor studies me coolly, then puts down the bloody scalpel and picks up a tablet. "Interesting. There are no signs of corresponding injuries appearing on your own body, though your heart rate is elevated." She tsks at me again. "If you'd stop that pointless struggling, I'd get more accurate baseline data."

I'm glad to mess up her data, but the restraints aren't giving way and there's no point in tiring myself out when I might get a better chance to break free later.

"That's good," says Doctor James when I stop straining. "Just relax." She picks the chip scanner back up, and runs it over the leopard's neck, then over my neck. "Now you can transfer. You can be the leopard again."

I've yearned for those words for so long, I can hardly believe my dearest wish has been granted. But transferring into my Leopard Skin is what the doctor wants me to do, and if I succumb to the urge, she'll be able to run more of her twisted experiments.

Clenching both fists, I fight the need with everything I've got. I don't even dare to blink in case I can't keep my mind from slipping into the leopard in the split second my eyes are closed.

Instead, I stare at my leopard, horrified by how she's

treated it. As well as the deep cut she sliced into my leopard's chest, the wide webbing straps holding it down are so tight, they're digging into its flesh. They cover its snout and its head around both sides of its ears, with barely enough space left to expose one eye. Anger surges through me. How dare she do this to my beautiful Leopard Skin? Has it been secured like this the entire time since I was last here?

"You want to transfer," the doctor murmurs. "Don't fight it."

I glare at her, my jaw clamped so tightly it hurts.

"You keep surprising me, Milla. The leopard is your heart's desire, yes? And it's there." She waves her hand at it. "You won't transfer?"

I narrow my eyes even more, trying to transmit my hatred for her in my gaze.

"Last time you were here, you managed to free yourself from your restraints, because your body was stronger than I expected." The doctor studies my face, her gaze as dispassionately curious as though I were a specimen in a jar. "Why is that, do you think?"

When I don't reply, she sighs. "I've designed several tests to measure your human strength and we'll get to those soon enough. First, I want to know if you still exhibit the same somatoform injuries when the Leopard Skin is wounded. Don't fight it, Milla. You have no choice but to transfer your consciousness into the Leopard Skin."

Like hell. As soon as I transfer, she's going to keep slicing my Skin open with her scalpel.

"If you don't obey, I'll give you a shot which will make you compliant and unable to resist any suggestion I make." She pushes her lips to the side, considering it. "I'd prefer not to take the risk of the drug interfering with this particular experiment, however it will make the process quicker."

Shit.

Which is worse, letting her cut my leopard, or being drugged and then letting her cut my leopard? Not much of a choice.

I screw my eyes shut. Even in this messed-up situation, the feeling of falling sideways fills me with a fierce kind of joy. A joy that intensifies beyond measure when I finally look out once more through my leopard's eyes.

I'm home.

I'm *me*.

This is who I am, who I'll always be. The relief that surges through me at being in my *real* body again is so intense, it makes me wants to roar.

But the strap over my muzzle holds it so tightly to the gurney, even growling is difficult. The webbing's so tight, I'd howl with pain if I could. I can barely flick my ears because of the webbing cutting into my head. The only part I can move freely is my tail, so I swish it violently from side to side.

"Good," says the doctor. I can't smell the faintest hint of pity on her. She reeks of chemicals. The grey webbing is so close to my eyes, it limits my view. But I can see my human body lying on the gurney next to me, and watch the scalpel as she brings it down to my leopard's front leg, just above my paw.

When the blade bites into me, the pain isn't too bad for a moment. It gets more intense as she cuts deeper, until it's searing like fire.

A wound opens on my human arm, just above the wrist. Watching it happen feels surreal, like watching a magic trick. How could skin part like that, all on its own? It shouldn't be possible. Blood trickles from the wound. It doesn't look nearly as deep as the cut she's sliced into my leopard. It's not bleeding as much.

"Incredible," breathes the doctor. She beams at me like

I've done some kind of clever trick. "Even after weeks of being separated from the Skin, you're still exhibiting the same symptoms. Excellent news."

If I could say something I would. If I could do *anything* other than growl, I would. But with my muzzle strapped down so tightly, all I can do is stare at my human body.

Funny to realize it now, but for the first time in my life, I don't hate that body. Sure, it's let me down at a few crucial times, like when I needed the strength to fight off late-night attackers in the shelter. But it's saved me a few times too.

My scars are still difficult to look at. My hollow cheek gives my face a lopsided, sunken look, and the scars twist and pucker my skin. I've always thought of my scars as a burden I've been forced to bear, but Cale was right about them being part of who I am. Why should I hate them?

In my human body, I survived all my years in the shelter, and even managed to escape this place. My body was strong when I needed it most, and now that I'm looking at it with fresh eyes, I can admire its wiry toughness.

I haven't appreciated that body nearly enough. How ironic that now, under the doctor's scalpel, I can finally see how capable that body really is.

I only wish I could save it.

Chapter Twenty-Three

Doctor James slices into me again, the scalpel drawing a painful line into my shoulder. With my mouth bound, unable to curse her, I watch my flesh part. I can't even struggle as I feel warm blood soak my fur and see it trickle down my human arm.

"This is truly remarkable," murmurs the doctor. She picks up her tablet and taps on it, absorbed in whatever data she's collecting.

A knock comes from the door. It opens, and a knight looks in.

Could it be William?

"President Morelle wants to see the subject before you start your experiments," says the knight.

One of my ears is pressed tightly against the gurney, and the other is mostly blocked by the tight webbing. The knight has a male voice, but I can't tell if it's my brother's.

"Her consciousness has already transferred into the leopard," snaps the doctor. "I've begun running my tests." She makes an exasperated sound and picks up a hypodermic needle from her table. "You'll have to wait while I send her consciousness back to origin."

The knight steps forward with a shake of its head. "No need. President Morelle wants both her real body and the leopard. She said she wants to see what happens to one body when she hurts the other."

Doctor James frowns. "But that's absurd. I'm conducting methodical tests and recording the results, just as we discussed. Why would she interrupt my research when it could render the experiment inconclusive?"

"I don't question orders." The knight moves to the gurney that holds my real body. "I'll push this one. You bring the other."

"Where's the rest of your squad?"

"She only sent me."

"I spoke with President Morelle an hour ago, and she was very clear about the tests she wanted me to conduct." The doctor's voice is sharp with suspicion. She touches her band. "You'll have to wait, soldier, while I check your orders."

The knight lunges forward, the movement so fast I might not have been able to follow it with human eyes. It shoves the doctor backward. Her head cracks against the wall, and she crumples to the floor.

Then the knight bends over me. "Milla? You okay? It's Cale."

Bound so tightly, I can't do anything but blink at him as tears fill my eyes. I had no idea leopards could cry, but I'm so glad he's alive, I can't do anything else. How did he escape from Sentin? And how on earth did he find me?

"The doctor strapped you in tight." His tone is grim as he picks up the scalpel and saws through the thick webbing that holds me in place. "I got here as fast as I could, but not fast enough." His voice changes to a growl. "I want to kill her for what she's done to you."

The webbing around my muzzle loosens, and I moan with relief. "You have no idea how glad I am to see you."

"Me too." He starts work on the webbing around my head. "I had to go to the safe house to get the Knight Skin, and I kept picturing the doctor torturing you. Every second felt like an hour."

"I thought you were dead." My voice hitches. "How'd you get away?"

"Get away?"

"From Sentin." The sharp scalpel combined with his knight's super strength means he's cutting through the webbing faster than I'd dared hope. My head's already coming free.

"Sentin's on our side." He frowns. "Why would I need to get away from him?" The head strap parts, and he moves down to my shoulders.

"I thought he was working with Morelle."

"Sentin planned this whole thing. He's the one who reprogrammed my chip so I could transfer into the Knight Skin. Don't tell me you don't trust him?" Cale sounds as confused as if it had never occurred to him to doubt him. But I'm the one who's confused. How could Cale suddenly trust Sentin so completely?

"So he did turn up to save us?"

"Of course he did."

"And what about Ma?"

"She was awake when I left, and I called an ambulance. She took a nasty blow to the head, but she seemed alert and sharp. I'm sure she'll recover."

The wave of relief that rushes through me is strong enough to make me dizzy.

The thick straps around my shoulders part, and I'm

loose enough to work my way out from the last bonds. As I come free, all I want to do is press myself against Cale, to reassure myself that he's really here. But the intense pain of blood flooding back into all four legs keeps me from doing more than trying to straighten them.

Cale picks up some of the webbing he cut free, then bends to the doctor. She groans as he rolls her over and strips off her lab coat.

I sit on my haunches to shake out my front paws while he works the coat free and strips off the doctor's white trousers and shirt, leaving her in her underwear. Then he uses what's left of the webbing to bind the doctor's arms and legs.

"What do we do now?" I ask while he ties her up. "How are we going to escape?"

"We're not escaping. It's the end game, Milla. Our chance to stop President Morelle."

"How will we do that?" My aching limbs are starting to work again, and his words fill me with hope. When I broke out of the Morelle Corporation, this is the moment I dreamed of. I finally have my Leopard Skin back, and I'm strong enough to do anything. "What exactly *is* the end game, Cale? Has Sentin figured out a way we can stop her?"

Cale tests the straps to make sure the doctor's secure, then turns to cut the restraints from my human body.

"I can't hurt President Morelle. Not while I'm in this Skin. But you can." With his hands busy cutting the straps from around my body, Cale nods at Doctor James. "I wasn't supposed to knock her out, but to convince her to help me take you up to the top floor." His armored face shows no emotion. "Instead I bashed her head against the wall, and I had to force myself not to tear her throat open. I'm not sure if this Skin has anything to do with my rage, but I'm having all kinds of terrible thoughts."

"If you hadn't knocked her out, she would have warned Morelle."

"I don't trust myself in this Skin. I can't decide whether I want to kill everyone in the building, or turn us both in to the president."

"Thank you for coming for me." The words aren't enough to express how grateful I am, and I'm not sure if he can read my scent and the flick of my ears as well as he could when he was a tiger. To make it clear, I stumble to him on my still-stiff legs and nuzzle his arm. He smells cold and metallic, nothing like when he's human or the tiger, and I can't get any sense of his emotions.

In contrast, from the gurney, the stench of my human body is pungent. It smells of sweat with a lingering aroma of pain and fear.

He pauses from cutting the straps from my human body for long enough to stroke one armored hand over my leopard head. "We don't have much time. Sentin said we decimated Morelle's army, though she's pretending we didn't. But there's still a squad of knights on duty in this building. If we give ourselves away, they'll be on us in no time."

"Where's Sentin?"

"He's going to meet us upstairs."

"Upstairs?"

"We're going all the way to the top, to Morelle's private apartment. Sentin gave me the code to use her elevator. He said he had a different way to get up there, but it would only work for him." Cale cuts the last strap from my body, pulls the electrodes off my skull, then nods to the gurney my leopard was tied to. "Get back on the bed and transfer into your real body."

"Transfer back?" I flatten my ears back against my head, sitting onto my haunches. "Cale, my human body isn't nearly as strong as my Leopard Skin. I need to be the leopard if we're to have any chance—"

"We don't have time to argue. You need to transfer now, but don't worry, we're taking the leopard with us."

Every cell in my body rebels against the idea of transferring out of my leopard. But I know Cale wouldn't ask me to do it if it weren't necessary, and at the first sign of trouble, I can transfer back. Reluctantly, I lie back down on the hated gurney, roll onto my side, and squeeze my eyes shut. I take a deep breath, trying to force my mind back into my human body. Then I suck in another breath. And another one. My mind refuses to go.

"You need to do this." Cale's voice is gentle. "Trust me, Milla."

I grab hold of his voice, forcing my mind to follow it sideways.

Landing back into my human body fills me with a familiar sense of being *less* than I was before. I don't know which hurts more, the gunshot wound in my shoulder, or the cuts the doctor sliced into me. I'm cold, stiff, sore, and almost naked.

"Here." Cale hands me the clothes he took from Doctor James. "Put these on."

The doctor is taller and stockier than I am. Her trousers are so long, I have to roll them up, and they're loose around my waist. Her lab coat reaches my calves and its sleeves swallow my hands. At least I'm covered, but my feet are still bare. Before I can bend to take the doctor's shoes off, Cale stops me by taking my hand in his. His armor is cold and his hand so big it envelops mine.

"Milla." He lifts my hand and turns it, pushing the sleeve of the lab coat up so he can see the cut above my wrist. "I'm sorry I didn't get here before she hurt you. Are you sure you're okay?"

"It's not bleeding too much." I wriggle both shoulders, testing how painful they are. "I can still move my arms."

"It wasn't just the influence of the Skin that made me want to kill the doctor. Even in my human body, I would have wanted to hurt her." The knight's eyes are bright yellow and chilling, but the way he dips his head to me is familiar, and his tone is soft. The hand that's not holding mine comes up to my face, and he gently touches my chin. "This isn't the form I wanted to be in when I told you this, but I can't help the way I feel about you, Milla. I'd do anything to keep you safe."

I force air into lungs that have forgotten how to breathe. Now isn't the time to tell him that I've never been so terrified in my life as when I thought the knight was going to kill him, or how leaving him with Sentin felt like my heart was being ripped open.

Instead, I squeeze his hard, cold hand. "It never seems to be the right time for us, does it? When this is over, I want us to be together." Though I mean them with all my heart, for some reason the words are so difficult to say, they all but burn my throat.

He nods. "It's a promise."

I drag in a shuddering breath. "Cale…" I stop. My heart is full of words and promises, but now, when there's so much I want to tell him, my tongue feels too thick and clumsy to say anything at all.

Cale nods, like he understands. He gives my hand a final squeeze and lets it go. Then he bends to strip off Doctor James' shoes, and hands them to me. "We're going to take the leopard upstairs." His tone has gone back to being business-like. "If anyone stops us, we're following the president's orders. A knight escorting a doctor, taking a tied-up Skin to the president so she can examine it. No big deal."

While I lace on the doctor's shoes that are a couple of sizes too big, he picks some straps off the floor to tie over my Leopard Skin. Though they look like they're pulled tight, they're only loosely fastened to the gurney. It'll only take one good tug to break them free.

"What about my scars?" I ask. "I look nothing like a New Triton doctor."

He picks up a surgical mask from the doctor's tray of tools. "Put this on." Once it's in place, he fiddles with my hair, pulling it forward over the sides of my face. "Walk with your head down. Here, you can pretend you're reading this." He hands me the tablet from the table. "We only need to get to President Morelle's private elevator. It's down the hall, tucked out of sight behind the public elevators. I took a quick look on my way here, and I didn't pass any knights."

I check my lab coat is on straight. "Okay. I'm ready."

He grabs the gurney with my leopard on it, and pushes it toward the door. "Stay behind me."

Head down, I stride down the hall after him. He sets a fast pace and I concentrate on keeping up. When we pass some people in the hallway, I keep my face angled down and the tablet high. Nobody shouts after us.

Cale pushes the gurney around a corner, down another long hallway, then around another corner. He stops so abruptly I almost run into him, and I risk lowering the tablet for long enough to glance around. In front of us is an elevator door. We've made it.

The door glides open smoothly, but instead of walking in, Cale hesitates.

"What's your business?" A hard, male voice comes

from inside the elevator. It's a knight. Morelle's posted a guard inside it.

"President Morelle wants to see this Skin." Cale motions to my leopard. "She sent me to bring it and the doctor up to the top floor."

The knight draws his weapon. "That's a lie," he snarls. "Nobody's allowed up there."

"I'm following orders she gave me personally," Cale's voice stays calm. "You know how important it is that we obey her without question." The elevator starts to close, and he puts his hand over the door to stop it.

The knight's gun is trained on Cale, but his gaze flicks to me. "Come here, where I can see you," the knight orders. "And both of you put your hands up."

I pretend I'm too engrossed in what I'm reading on the tablet to have heard him, keeping it up to cover my face. Once the knight gets a look at my scars, he'll realize I'm no doctor.

"The president's expecting me." Cale doesn't raise his hands either. If you stop me from following her orders, she'll—"

"Step back and put your hands up." Keeping the gun trained on Cale, the knight activates the screen on his arm. A loud siren screams from the elevator, making me jump.

Cale lunges at the knight and it fires at him, the gunshots blasting over the noise of the siren, deafening inside the small elevator.

I close my eyes and transfer.

The instant my consciousness hits my leopard, I surge up from the gurney, tearing away the restraints. All I can hear is the blasting of the gun. Is Cale hurt? No time to look. I leap at the knight and slam into it, shoving its back against the elevator's far wall. Its gun clatters to the floor. My jaw finds its neck.

As badly as I need to check Cale's okay after being shot at such close range, I can't let the knight go. I tighten my jaws, trying to force my fangs into the knight's armor. There's no way I can pierce it, but I'm bending it, slowly crushing its throat.

The knight wraps its strong hands around my neck, choking me as it tries to shove me away. I clamp my jaws together even harder. The only chance we have is if I don't let go.

Then Cale's voice comes from beside my ear, still perfectly calm in spite of the siren that's still going off. "I'll handle this one, Milla."

He lifts a gun to the knight's pointed ear, positioning it before the knight can jerk away. Then he pulls the trigger. The knight sags. With an effort, I let my jaws relax, and the knight crumples to the floor. I back up, stretching my aching neck.

"You okay?" Cale bends to run his fingers through my fur.

"I'm fine. What about you?"

"The bullets knocked me off my feet." He straightens, jerking his head toward the hallway outside the elevator. "Hear that?"

Through the shriek of the siren, I catch the heavy footfalls of metal boots pounding toward us. More knights are coming.

My human body is lying just outside the elevator, and when the doors start closing, they bump against my feet and slide open again. Cale picks up my body and dumps it on the gurney. He shoves the gurney inside the elevator with me, then steps in to look at the panel beside the door. Instead of buttons to choose a floor, there's a numeric keypad. As the elevator doors shut, he punches in a code. A wall panel slides open and a red display flashes.

With the doors closed and the siren still going off, I can't hear how close the knights are. But I know we don't have much time. If the elevator doesn't start moving soon, we'll be sitting ducks.

"What's that?" I flick my ears at the flashing display.

"Face and voice recognition, and a retinal scan." He activates the screen on the inside of his forearm and a holo image projects from it. It's Morelle's head, replicated in full size, the most lifelike holo I've ever seen. It's like she's in the elevator with us. "Sentin programmed it in." He holds it in front of the screen. "Top floor," the hologram says in Morelle's voice.

The panel goes green, but the elevator still doesn't move.

"What else does it need?" I ask.

Cale shakes his head. "That's all he told me to do."

"We must be missing something. Fingerprints? What's that button below the scanner?"

He stares at the button for a moment, then hits it. There's a jolt, then the elevator starts moving up.

I turn to Cale to ask what will happen when we get to the top floor, but he holds up one hand. "This Skin has communication functions built in, and I can access the main channel. They've figured out where we're going. An alert's just gone out for all the knights in the building to get as high as possible and cut us off."

"At least they can't get to us in here."

The words are barely out of my mouth when the elevator jerks to a stop so suddenly, Cale staggers. On four paws I don't lose my balance, but my stomach takes a second to feel like it's part of my body again.

"As I was saying, they know where we're going. They're on their way to intercept us."

I look up at the ceiling. As strong and capable as my

leopard is, there are some things humanoid hands are better at. "Tear a hole up there. We can climb up the shaft."

Cale's hands transform into claws. He punches through the elevator ceiling, ripping chunks of it away. When the hole is big enough, we both stare up into the endless, unlit shaft. At least neither of us have any problem seeing in the dark.

"We can't go up there without taking your human body with us." Cale nods at the gurney. "But I don't think I can climb and carry it. You'll have to transfer back into it."

"I'll carry it," I bunch the lab coat in my teeth, using it to lift my body so it hangs from my mouth. I'm still much faster and stronger as the leopard than I would be as a human, even with the extra burden.

"You can't climb like that, can you?"

"Watch me," I mutter through a mouthful of cloth. As dangerous as this is, I almost feel like we're practising for the tower again, the two of us racing each other up and down the climbing wall until dawn. This feels like what we were really training for.

Without waiting for him, I leap up to what's left of the elevator's roof. My human body swings from my mouth so I have to make an extra effort to compensate for its weight. Good thing my body's skinny and light.

There are metal struts running up the side of the elevator shaft at regular intervals. Jumping to each one will be easy, even carrying my body between my teeth. I just have to do it without thumping my body against the side of the elevator shaft. Last thing I want is to accidentally bash my own brains out.

"They're going to follow us," warns Cale, hauling himself slowly up the struts.

I want to reply, but if I do, I'll drop my human body.

Instead I leap again, up to the next level. There are doors at every level, and I count them as we go up, calculating which floor we must be on. One-thirty-one. One-thirty-two. One-thirty-three.

Cale is much slower than I am. While my Skin was designed to climb the tower, his is designed for combat. He hauls himself up the shaft with an effort. Every few levels I need to wait for him to catch up.

From below us comes a loud clanking. Three knights are climbing the shaft behind us, but they're several floors below, and as slow as Cale.

"What's that?" Cale points up the shaft. "Some kind of barrier?"

I stare up at it. I can't reply, but he's right. A metal security barrier must have been triggered when the alarm went off. It's blocking the entire shaft, obviously designed to stop intruders from climbing all the way up. Morelle thought of everything.

A gunshot cracks, echoing through the shaft. I duck as it ricochets off the metal barrier above us. The knights are shooting at us.

"Use me as cover," shouts Cale as more shots ring out.

That's right, he's bullet-proof. I jump in front of him, keeping him between me and the knights below us. Bullets hit his legs, making his feet slip off the metal slats, but he keeps dragging himself up while I shelter behind his bulk. I just hope that stopping to fire will slow the knights down even more.

Together we climb all the way to the barrier. Cale slams his armoured fist into the metal. The crash is deafening, but when he draws back, the barrier isn't even dented. He tries again with his claws extended, trying to rip through the metal. His hand bounces off it.

Finally he shakes his head. "There's no way through. We need to get out of this shaft."

With gunfire echoing around us, we move to the nearest door. Cale wrenches it open and we haul ourselves through.

The floor we're on is one huge open office, full of desks with no partitions to separate them. Enormous windows line the far wall, flooding the room with light. But the glass in the windows is opaque. I can't see through it, so there's no way to tell how high up we are.

Surely we must be almost at the top, close to Morelle's private apartment. We need to keep climbing before the knights make it to this floor. There's no cover here, and we're badly outnumbered. If they catch up to us, we'll have no chance.

Cale scans the floor, then moves to a door marked *Stairs*. He tears it open, looks out, then slams it. "More knights are climbing the stairs, and there's another metal barrier blocking us from going up. We can't get out that way."

I drop my human body and allow myself a moment to stretch my aching jaw. "This isn't a good place to stand and fight." I wish I'd left my human body behind in the lab. I can't fight while I'm carrying it, and there's no safe place to leave it here.

The clanking sounds from the elevator shaft are getting louder. The knights climbing behind us are almost here.

We're out of time.

Chapter Twenty-Four

Leaving my body where it is, I cross to the opaque window. "Smash it," I say.

Cale draws back his fist and punches it hard. Cracks splinter through the glass. One more punch and the pane shatters. It falls out of the frame and tumbles away.

Wind rushes in and I poke my head out into what feels like a gale. I'm on top of the world, and the view of Triton makes me dizzy. The city stretches below me, an endless expanse of scrapers, all much smaller than the one I'm in. But there's no time for more than a quick glance down.

Instead, I pull my gaze up and stare toward the top of the scraper, which isn't quite as close as I hoped. There are still several stories to climb. At least the building's exterior is covered with metal sheets and there are small ridges I can use to cling to.

It'll be difficult to make my way up the building's sheer, vertical outer wall, but not impossible. I hope.

"Go," says Cale. "I'll stay here and buy you some time."

"What? No, you're coming with me."

"This Skin wasn't built for climbing. It's too heavy." He flexes his hands as though they ache. "Even scaling the side of the elevator shaft was hard, and that had struts."

"I won't go without you."

"You have to." Though his face doesn't change, there's a weird kind of relish in his voice. "Truth is, I'm done with running. This Skin *wants* to fight. And I need payback for what the knights did to Doctor Gregory."

"But there's a whole squad."

"My real body won't be hurt, remember. I only wish I could say the same for you." He glances down at my human body, sprawled on the floor. "I should have told Sentin that it was too dangerous to bring you up here. I hate that I can't protect you. There are too many of them and I won't be able to kill them all."

"I'll be okay." I pick up my human body by the back of its coat and put my front paws on the lip of the window, ready to spring. The wind buffets me, roaring around my ears and making my human body swing in my teeth.

"Be careful, Milla. Get there in one piece." Cale's hands transform into claws as he turns toward the stairwell.

The stairwell door bursts open and knights pour into the room. At the same time, the first of them emerges from the hallway shaft, hauling themselves up over the edge.

Cale runs at them, claws extended, letting out a blood-curdling war cry.

I leap onto the side of the building, thrusting my front claws into the ridges between the metal sheets. Pushing off with my back claws, I haul myself up to the next ridge.

It's awkward climbing with my human body in my jaws. It thumps against the metal, making it harder to catch the ridges with my claws. I'm trying to be as gentle as I can, and I wince every time my body hits the wall. Hopefully I'm not giving myself anything more serious than a few bruises.

As the top of the building gets closer, a shot rings out, the bullet grazing a furrow in my fur. Knights are leaning out of the window below, firing up at me.

Another gunshot, and pain erupts in my hindquarters. I'm hit.

My claws slip from the ridge I'm clutching, and I scrabble with my back legs, frantic to regain my grip.

Panic and terror lend me extra strength, and when my claws catch, I bound up even faster, ignoring the pain shooting through my flank.

The top floor of the building is just ahead. More shots ricochet off the metal around me, one nicking my paw and another grazing my back.

Three more jumps, then I can scramble onto a small ledge that gives me the purchase I need to propel myself at the top floor window, claws extended at the glass. I have time to realize that if the glass doesn't break, I'm going to bounce right off and fall to my death, leopard and human bodies tumbling together. Then I smash into the glass.

The window crashes out of its frame and I land heavily on the floor in a shower of glass shards.

My human body is torn from my jaws. It lies in a tangled heap, but there's no time to check if it's okay. I leap to my feet, ready to face whatever might be waiting for me in Morelle's private apartment.

The wind blowing through the broken window seems stronger than it was outside, almost storm strength. It lifts and swirls clothes and toys in what's clearly a bedroom. Behind me, the curtains flap and billow. In front of me is a bed with a pink coverlet. My human body has landed on a pink fluffy rug on the floor. Against one wall is a large set of shelves, filled with toys, some of which have fallen onto the floor. Dolls and stuffed animals stare blankly down at me. Is this a little girl's room? As a child, I would have killed for a room like this. Not that I ever had the imagination to dream of something so luxurious.

Morelle has no children. So whose bedroom is this?

Apart from the howling of the wind, the place seems quiet. I can't hear any knights approaching, and the wail of sirens has stopped. Maybe the apartment is empty.

I turn back to my human body. My arm is sticking out at a strange angle and I must have a fresh wound in my upper thigh, because blood is soaking through the white trousers I'm wearing. It takes me a moment to figure out why. The bullet wound. My Leopard Skin was shot, so my human body is bleeding too.

I guess I could try to bandage the wound, but my paws would be clumsy, and it would take too much time. I'm afraid of being ambushed by Morelle or another squad of knights.

Leaving my human body where it is, I limp out of the bedroom. The bullet in my flank makes it painful to walk. Blood is trickling down my fur and the scent of blood is so strong, I can taste it in the back of my throat.

The bedroom opens into another large room filled with more toys. The wind from the broken window isn't as strong in here, but there are still pieces of paper blowing around on the floor. The glimpses I get look like a child's paintings, simple and colorful.

In pride of place in the middle of the room is a giant dollhouse, open at the front and sides, and full of miniature furniture. No, not just furniture. There's a tiny family in there, and they're moving around. The mother is rocking a baby, while the father is in the kitchen, serving a meal to three teeny children.

Next to the dollhouse is a full-sized dog lying curled up

in a basket. It lifts its head to look at me as I walk past, and lets out a mournful whine. But it doesn't smell like a dog. It smells mechanical. A robot dog.

The more I look around, the more wonders I see. Fantastically detailed planets are suspended above head-height, slowly spinning. Ultra-realistic holographs, perhaps? A colorful parrot flies across the room, lands on the hour hand of an ornate clock, then steps into a compartment above the clock face before freezing in place. An inch-high dance recital takes up one long shelf, with tiny mechanical ballerinas leaping and dancing in spectacular unison.

There's too much to take in, and if I had more time I'd stop. Instead, I keep moving into a long hallway. The elevator is at the far end of the hallway, and on either side are several doorways. I limp cautiously to the first open doorway, and stop to peer into the room beyond. It's a large living room with couches. My gaze snaps straight to the large picture window the room is centered around. The window frames an incredible view.

In spite of being worried someone might jump out at me, I stay rooted to the spot, gaping at the window. I've never seen Triton from this height. In fact, I doubt anyone but Morelle has, especially if all the other windows in her building are opaque.

New Triton stretches forever. The view over its buildings is dizzying. Its streets look tiny from up here, and I can see how they're laid out in a grid pattern, with a hole in the center of each square to allow light to filter down to the city below. It looks like a loosely woven fabric, and I get glimpses of Old Triton through the weave. But some parts of New Triton are like a solid square with no hole at all.

Wait. What's over there in the distance? All that green?

A big concrete structure runs in front of the green.

It's the Deiterran wall, so the green must be in Deiterra. This must be the one place in Triton where Deiterra is visible, and I could be the only person apart from Morelle to see what's on the other side of the wall.

Could all that green be...?

I swallow as the realization hits me.

I'm looking at green fields. Miles and miles of green fields. Plants. Trees. *Farms*. I didn't believe it was possible for farms to still exist, but there they are. Are the Deiterrans really growing their own food?

I'm so shocked, it takes me a second to register the noise that comes from behind me.

I spin around too late. Morelle is standing in the hallway a short distance from me. She has a gun pointed at my chest.

"Milla, I presume." Her voice is cold and her mouth drawn down. She looks as immaculately dressed as usual, in a navy suit and high heels. Her silky bob frames her face, not a hair out of place.

"Who else would it be?" I weigh up the distance between us, trying to calculate whether I can leap to the gun before she fires.

"I've always liked that Skin." Her lip curls. "Of all the irritating things you've done, one of the worst will be forcing me to shoot it."

Her finger tightens on the trigger and I spring sideways, trying to dodge in the narrow hallway. The bullet slams into my chest, knocking me backward. Pain sears through me.

She shot me.

Am I dying?

It hurts. Oh god, it hurts.

Forcing myself back onto all four paws, I lurch forward.

I need to get the gun from her before she can shoot me again.

She steps closer, aiming carefully.

My legs are too weak; I can't get to her in time. The next shot will likely kill me.

A dark figure flies out of one of the doorways, moving so fast I can barely see what it is. It leaps at Morelle. She fires at me an instant before the figure hits her, but the bullet blasts through the wall behind me.

The figure slams into her so hard, any other creature on Earth would have been knocked flat. Morelle staggers backward, the gun flying from her grip. It hits the wall and lands on the floor a little way in front of me.

Her attacker grabs hold of her, wrapping his body around her. It's the Reptile Skin, his scales a dull, dark black. Sentin's long fingers dig into her throat while his prehensile toes curl around her arms, holding them down.

She staggers sideways and slams him against the wall. The impact must break his grip, because somehow she manages to wrestle him off and hurl him at me. He hits me hard and I go down. Winded, I gasp for breath.

Sentin gets straight back up, his movements fluid, while I have to force myself onto my paws. I'm swaying, but when I stiffen my legs, they don't feel quite as weak as just after she shot me. My flank and chest both hurt like hell, but now I'm over the shock, I don't think my injuries will kill me. The bullet in my chest feels like it buried itself in muscle. It's painful, and I don't have a full range of movement, but I'm pretty sure I can still fight.

"I'm stronger than both of you." Morelle's tone is surprisingly even. Her gun is between us, but closer to Sentin than to her. She's not looking at it, so I'm pretty sure she's considering lunging for it.

"You are." Standing on two legs in front of me, Sentin

sounds just as calm. He reaches down and pulls a weapon from a holster that's strapped to one of his bent hind legs. It's a weird-looking gun with a cone at the end. "Do you know what this is?" he asks.

She nods. "I think so."

"Then you know I can destroy your Skin with it."

I stare at the gun trying to figure out what it might be. Something more effective than a regular gun, I guess. I've never seen anything like it.

"I'm faster than you know. I can get to you before you can use it."

President Morelle's voice is matter-of-fact, and I believe her. After all, if I were creating a bunch of Skins, I'd give myself the one that could beat all the others.

"Perhaps." Sentin's aim doesn't waver. "Felicity is nearby, isn't she? I can hear her."

I don't understand. Morelle's first name is Felicity. Is he talking about the person operating her Skin?

Now he's brought it to my attention, I *can* hear breathing. It's fast and panicked. Human ears couldn't hear it, much less tell where it's coming from, but I think it's from somewhere inside the next room.

"Ungrateful boy," spits Morelle. "You could have had everything. I gave you the Reptile Skin. I allowed you access to my empire, including my most important research. I did what you asked, and we could have shared it all. This is how you repay me?"

"You made some mistakes," Sentin says, as though he's talking about a chess game.

Her mouth twists. "Surrender now and I'll let you live. If you don't, my knights will kill you."

"You'd allow your knights onto this floor? Even knowing they might uncover your secret?"

She gives a tight smile. "They watched the leopard climb up here. They're bound to follow."

"Not until the elevator is unlocked."

"That won't take long."

"If the knights step foot on this floor, I'll make sure they all see Felicity. You won't be able to explain her away."

Morelle's lip curls. "I'll kill her myself before she's exposed."

I wish someone would explain what Sentin and Morelle are talking about, because I'm not following any of this.

"You'd kill her to save yourself?" Sentin does a slow blink, his eyelid coming up from underneath. The blink is his reptile equivalent of a double-take.

Morelle stiffens, and her fists clench as though he's delivered a major insult. "Even after working with me, you still can't understand what I've achieved. I've built so much already, and now I'm reshaping our entire world. Even if Felicity dies, millions of others will benefit."

Though I don't understand their conversation, her arrogance makes my anger flare. "What good have you done?" The words come out as a growl, more leopard than human. "Your factories are slave pits. You've brainwashed hundreds of children and made them into killing machines. Old Triton is suffering more than ever, thanks to you."

She shoots me a disdainful look. "Old Triton is the engine driving us into the future, and all engines need tuning. I can't achieve great things without sacrifice."

"What sacrifice have you ever made?" I snarl.

"I've lost more than you know."

Sentin nods. Of the three of us, he's easily the calmest. "You're talking about your daughter and granddaughter?"

I have no idea what he means. President Morelle doesn't have a daughter, let alone a granddaughter. If she'd ever been pregnant, it would have been such a big news story, even I wouldn't have been able to miss it. Besides, she's using a *Skin*.

Unless the person using the Skin isn't who I think it is.

Maybe the Skin's operator isn't really President Morelle.

It's my turn to do a double-take as I realize what that means. Somebody's using the Skin to impersonate Morelle, and Sentin knows who it is.

All this time I've assumed Morelle's the one using the Skin, but if somebody's taken her place, then who is it that's been waging war with the Fist and Deiterra?

The elevator at the end of the hallway lets out a loud ding, and the light above the door comes on. Morelle glances toward it and in that instant, Sentin lunges at her. Though his reptile legs don't straighten, he's still taller than she is. He grabs her around the neck and presses his weird gun to her head.

"If they attack, I'll shoot you."

The elevator doors open and five knights spill out. Almost a whole squad of soldiers against the two of us. They stop when they see Sentin holding the gun to the president's head.

"Find cover," Sentin snaps at me. "Come out when I call you."

I hesitate for only a second before doing what he says. Sentin's brain works a hundred times faster than anybody else's. If anyone can get the better of Morelle, it's him.

I limp into the toy room, past the dollhouse and into the bedroom. Wind buffets me as I crouch next to my crumpled human body. Despite the wind, the smell of human blood is even stronger in here now. There's a new bloodstain in the middle of my human chest. So much blood, it shocks me. How much blood can I lose and still survive?

Then I hear something loud and so high-pitched it set my teeth on edge. Wincing, I clap my hands over my ears. A moment later, it stops, and I hear a muffled shout. "Milla!"

I limp as fast as I can back to the hallway, past the toppled dollhouse.

Sentin's weird gun is on the ground, and three knights lie near it, not moving. He's struggling with the two knights he didn't manage to kill, and they already have him on the ground.

I leap onto one of the knights. We tumble across the floor and I manage to sink my teeth into its neck. The back of its neck is where its chip is and all the sensors that keep it going. When we hit the wall, I shift my grip, trying to move my fangs into the right spot.

The knight's claws tear into me, gouging my flesh. I can't bear to think of my human body, what must be happening to it, but instead of letting go, I bite down harder. My fangs can't break through its armour, but I hope I'm doing some damage.

A loud crack of gunshot deafens me. Then more shots ring out. Have more of Morelle's forces come up in the elevator? With my teeth buried in the knight's neck, I can't see what's happening.

The claws that were raking through my flesh turn into fists instead. They pound into me with incredible strength, tearing my jaws off the knight's throat and hurling me across the hallway. I slam against the opposite wall. Dragging myself to my feet, I turn to face the knight. It swings at my head and I dodge, my wounds sending sharp agony searing through me.

Sentin appears behind the knight, holding something awkwardly in his long, reptilian fingers. He presses it to the back of the knight's neck, and it crumples to the ground.

My sides heaving, I scan the hallway. The floor's littered with the five Knight Skins, and the elevator's been destroyed. At least no more knights will be able to come up that way. But where's Morelle?

I turn to Sentin. His Reptile Skin has several deep cuts carved into it from the knights' claws and the scent of his blood is heavy in the air. Morelle's gun is in the holster on his thigh, and the thing in his hand looks like a much smaller version of the hand scanner Doctor Gregory used to reprogram my chip. It's about the size of a plastic, disposable razor.

"Are you okay?" I ask.

Instead of answering, he bends over and picks up his weird gun with the cone on its end. He examines it for a moment, then makes a disappointed sound. "Unfortunately, it's beyond repair. Let's hope no more knights manage to make it up to this floor."

"What is it?"

He turns his hand so I can see it better. "This is a high powered sonic pulse weapon. The Skins' hearing is similar to that of a bat. This weapon is tuned to resonate at that frequency, producing enough feedback to rupture its chip."

"You made that weapon? And the scanner, too? Did you wipe the knight's chip with it?"

He ignores my questions, moving to one of the doorways that come off the hall. He walks slowly, like his wounds hurt as much as mine do. "We need to find President Morelle. I pushed her through here before using the weapon, so her Skin wouldn't be damaged. She can't have gone far. I made sure the elevator is out of commission, so she must still be in the apartment."

"What do you mean, you didn't want her Skin to get damaged?" My voice rises. "What's going on?"

Sentin turns back to me, and studies me for a moment with his head cocked. "I'll show you," he says after a moment.

"Show me what?"

"Her secret. Nobody is allowed onto this level. We'll be the first in many decades to uncover what she's been hiding." He limps through one of the doorways that open from the hallway. Before, I heard breathing. Now it's turned into quiet sobbing.

The room I follow him into has no windows. There's a vReal in the corner, and the largest holo I've ever seen in the middle of the room. There's nobody in here, but the sobbing is louder. Could it be coming from inside the wall?

Sentin runs his long, prehensile lizard fingers over the wall, then glances at me. "There's a hidden door, but the trigger to open it isn't obvious. We'll have to smash our way in."

I give a reluctant nod. Though our Skins are large and strong, we're both badly wounded. Backing up a few steps, I lurch forward and rake the wall with my front paws, punching a hole large enough to see through.

There's a small room inside the wall. Inside are two women, cowering against the back wall.

One of the women takes a sobbing breath. Judging from her wrinkled face and gray hair, she's probably in in her sixties or seventies. She's as pasty as an Old Tritoner, and clearly not tweaked. She's been crying, because her sagging cheeks are wet with tears. Though I've never seen her before, she looks a little familiar. Come to think of it, she has the same eyes as President Morelle. If Morelle had been born in Old Triton, this might be what she'd look like.

The second woman's face is impassive. She's beautiful, with dark skin and blonde hair, and is obviously a tweaked New Tritoner, because her features are doll-like. Her gaze is on us, but her expression is so bland, we might not be here at all.

Wait.

The second woman isn't a woman at all. It doesn't smell human, and its eyes are glassy. It's a robot. Humanoid robots are illegal, but still, there it is.

"Felicity, come out." Sentin's voice is unexpectedly gentle. "We won't hurt you."

The pale, gray-haired woman shakes her head, her eyes wide with fear and brimming with tears. "You're monsters," she says through sobs.

I glance at Sentin. Felicity is acting like a scared child, not a woman. Who is she?

"We're not monsters." Sentin holds his hand out to her. "We're your new friends. Don't you want to pat the big kitty?"

The *kitty*? I'd growl at him for that insult, but it wouldn't help the situation. Instead I lower my head, my eyes narrowed as I study the woman, trying to figure out who she is and how she fits into all this.

"Go away," wails Felicity in a little girl's voice. "Where's my sister? I want my sister."

"Who's her sister?" I ask Sentin.

"She doesn't have one."

His cryptic reply only makes me more confused. Surely the woman knows if she has a sister?

Could President Morelle be her sister? On one hand, it would explain why they have the same eyes. But if Morelle had living relatives, surely everyone would know? As head of the Triton's biggest corporation, everything she does is newsworthy.

"Where's my sister?" demands Felicity again. She leans on the robot, and it staggers a little, but doesn't use the wall for support like a human would. Instead it rebalances by bending its knees in a decidedly non-human way.

"Your sister's hiding," says Sentin. "Do you know where she likes to hide, Felicity? We're playing a game and we need to find her."

The woman bites her lip, looking uncertain. After a moment, she shakes her head.

"What's your friend's name?" Sentin nods at the robot.

Felicity grabs its hand. "Annalisa."

The robot responds by smiling at Felicity. "You're my best friend, Felicity." Its voice sounds surprisingly human. "Shall we play?"

"What's your sister's name?" Sentin asks. "Is it the same as yours? Do you call her Felicity too?"

Felicity shakes her head. "No, silly. Her name is Poppa."

"Where's Poppa hiding? Is there another secret room like this one?"

The woman shrinks behind her robot. She either doesn't know the answer, or doesn't want to tell us.

I turn to Sentin. "Explain," I demand. "What's going on?"

He lowers his voice. "Edward Morelle founded the Morelle Corporation way back in nineteen ninety-one. He was a medical researcher who started out making specialized artificial organs and replacement body parts, but eventually expanded into a lot of other areas. Over the next few decades, he built it into a large and wealthy company."

"Thanks for the history lesson, but everyone knows that."

He continues as though I hadn't interrupted. "Edward had a daughter, but she was a disappointment to him. A hedonist who indulged in risky behaviors. At twenty-two, his daughter gave birth to a child of her own. A daughter she named Felicity." He nods toward the old woman in the hidden room. "Edward's grand-daughter."

"But President Morelle is Edward's granddaughter," I say with a frown. "Edward left his company to her. After he died, she built it up even more, making it the biggest and most powerful corporation in Triton."

"Unfortunately, Felicity was exposed to recreational drugs in the womb, and was born mentally impaired. Her grandfather kept her secluded from an early age so nobody would discover the truth."

I blink at the woman in the hidden room. "If that's Edward's real granddaughter, then who's the Felicity Morelle everyone knows? Who's the woman he left his company to? The one using the Skin, who's been running the Morelle Corporation all this time?"

"Edward Morelle didn't die. He's still running the company he founded."

I gape at Sentin. "That's impossible. He'd be, what? A hundred and twenty? A hundred and thirty? There's no way he's still alive."

"Shortly after his ninety-eighth birthday, Edward Morelle faked his own death. Afterward, he ran his company from this apartment, using an avatar. In the early days, he used a digital simulation of his granddaughter. A synthesized version he wanted the world to see."

"She was just a hologram?"

He nods. "But Edward aimed to make her more than that. The transferal technology was in its infancy, but he could see its potential. He knew he'd eventually be able to manufacture a Skin and appear in public as Felicity." He motions to the woman in front of us. "His version of Felicity, that is. Nobody knows the truth about his real grand-daughter."

"How do you know all this?"

"Around fifteen years ago, Director Morelle emerged from her apartment for short public appearances. The technology wasn't yet perfected, and there were occasional glitches. She collapsed more than once and blamed it on illness. It's only thanks to Edward's dogged determination that the technology's come as far as it has so quickly."

"He's been using a Skin for that long?" I shake my head. "But why fake his death at all? Why not just keep running his own company?"

"He was facing discrimination due to his advanced age, and I suspect his board of directors were pressuring him to find a successor. When we find him, feel free to ask him."

"He's *here*?"

Sentin gives me one of his slow blinks. "Where else would he be?"

I look around, half expecting to see an ancient man stagger out of the nearest doorway. "Then where is he?"

"We need to find him, and his Skin. All communications to this level are blocked, but Edward may have a way to contact his knights from here." Sentin raises his voice, addressing the woman in the hidden room again. "Are you sure you don't want to play hide-and-go-seek, Felicity? Poppa is hiding somewhere, and she wants you to find her."

He turns to me again. "The woman she knows as Poppa—the one she thinks is her sister—is the president's Skin with Edward operating it. Felicity's probably never seen another real person. Her robots take care of her."

The woman steps forward, leaving the robot behind, but still looking wary. "I want to play."

"You want to find your sister?"

She nods and touches a switch. The battered remains of the wall swing out like a door, forcing both Sentin and I to limp out of the way. Felicity edges out of the room, peeking into the hallway. She stops when she sees the armored bodies of the knight soldiers littering the floor, and her eyes widen with shock. "More monsters. Are they broken?"

"They're sleeping. They won't hurt you."

But she's already retreating back into the safety of her secret room. With tears in her eyes, she buries her face in the robot's neck.

"We'll have to find President Morelle on our own," says Sentin. "We'll start at the far end of the building and work down." I follow him through the toy room, into Felicity's bedroom where wind is still howling through the broken window. My human body is lying where I left it, but it looks even worse now. My white clothes are sodden with blood, and so is the rug underneath me. My lips are so pale they're almost blue.

"You need urgent medical attention." Sentin crouches over my body and gently tugs my shirt with his elongated reptile fingers. It's so heavy with blood it barely moves. "Without treatment, you could die."

My stomach clenches. After watching Doctor James slice me up, I swore to take better care of my human body. Now look what I've done to it.

"How long do you think I've got?"

"I'm not a doctor." He stands up. "Let's finish this. The clock is ticking."

I limp after him down the hallway, my heart thumping. I can't stop thinking about my human body, and how I can't even feel myself dying. At any moment, I could just keel over and that would be it for me. It seems so wrong. The first time I transferred into my Leopard Skin, I stopped wanting to be human. But now I'd give anything for my human body to be whole again. I hate having to walk away from it.

A muffled bang echoes from under our feet. "What's that?" Even as I ask, there are more loud thumps.

"I assume another squad of President Morelle's knights are coming up here."

"How?"

"It sounds like they're pulling down the ceiling of the room below us. Then they'll probably blow a hole through the floor."

"How long will that take?"

"Longer than they think. Edward built this apartment specifically to keep Felicity locked away. I'm confident the floor is extra thick, both for sound-proofing and for security."

"Okay," I say, relieved. "That's good."

"But they will certainly manage to get through it," Sentin adds. "It won't withstand a large explosive charge."

I draw in my breath. If they're willing to blow the place up to get in, we'd better hurry. "How big is the apartment?" I ask.

"We'll need to look for more hidden rooms. It'll take time." He glances back at me. "Stay alert. Edward Morelle may intend to ambush us. He wasn't exaggerating when he said his Skin was stronger than ours."

It's weird thinking of President Morelle as male. All this time, he's been using a female Skin. I would never have guessed it.

"His Skin is strong, and we're both already injured," I say. "What's our plan when we find it?"

Sentin holds up the scanner. "We need to wipe Edward Morelle's chip before his Skin can stop us."

Chapter Twenty-Five

The apartment is enormous. Ignoring the muffled thumps and bangs coming from the floor, Sentin and I limp through the living room, then through a dining room and kitchen. We pass a library filled with real, old-fashioned books, a gymnasium, several bathrooms, and a bedroom that contains closets full of Morelle's business suits. We even go past a swimming pool.

We also see several more humanoid robots. In the kitchen is a chef. The gym has its own personal trainer, and two lifeguards stand to attention by the swimming pool, ready to rescue any swimmer who might need saving.

Passing by so many humanoid robots, I find myself agreeing with the reason they were made illegal. They look like real people, only they're not at all surprised to see a giant, blood-covered reptile and leopard padding through their domain. Some greet us with a smile and a cheery 'Hello'. Others ignore us. They're all as creepy as hell.

Felicity's old, and for her entire life, the robots must have been her only companions. It's such a sad thought, I try to push it out of my mind.

On our way past the swimming pool, Sentin asks one of the lifeguard robots if it knows first aid, and when it says yes, he sends it to Felicity's bedroom to patch up my human body and give me plasma. I only hope the robot knows what it's doing and doesn't make things worse.

At the far end of the living room is a staircase that takes us up to a rooftop garden with a glass ceiling and an incredible view of both Triton and Deiterra. In the middle of the room, a giant garden bed is filled with more flowers than I've ever seen, all exploding in a riot of color. I drag in a lungful of perfume, so sweet-smelling it makes me dizzy. I couldn't have imagined a place like this, not in my wildest dreams. It'd be like stepping into heaven, except for the robot gardener on its knees in the corner, tending the plants.

"What now?" I ask Sentin. "He's obviously not up here." I flick my ears toward the glass windows surrounding us.

"I've been looking for walls of sufficient thickness to contain another hidden room. It's impossible to measure the thickness of some, so we may have to start breaking through walls." He sounds annoyed. "That will take time we don't have." He turns, and I follow him back down the stairs and through the long hallway, to the small room where Felicity is still hiding with her robot, sitting on the floor with her arms around her drawn-up knees. Her robot has mimicked her pose and is sitting the same way. In that pose it looks less human because its back is so straight.

"Do you know of any other secret hiding places?" Sentin asks Felicity.

She shakes her head, clutching onto her robot's arm.

"Think hard. Don't you want to find your sister?"

While Sentin questions Felicity, I limp into the next

room. We found Felicity because fear made her breathe loudly, and our Skins have sharp hearing.

Morelle's Skin needs to breathe too. It's made from living tissue, with a heart and lungs. Though I doubt Morelle will pant with fear, I still may be able to hear it.

I start at one end of the house and press my ear against every wall, listening intently. In the library, shelves cover the walls. There are hundreds of books, each probably worth a fortune. Books made from real paper are rare and expensive.

But I can't listen through the books. Wincing at the way the movement hurts my wounds, I swipe them off the shelves and let them crash to the ground. Then I break enough shelves so I can press my ear against the bare wall.

"Sentin."

Though I don't call loudly, his hearing is as sharp as mine, and he comes at once.

"I hear a machine humming." I flick my ears toward the space I've cleared. "Through there."

He bends so his mouth is close to my ear, then whispers. "His Skin will be waiting in there. I need you to keep it busy."

Though he keeps speaking of it as a man, I can't think of the Skin as anything other than the same Director Morelle who wanted to experiment on me, the woman who ordered my brother to kill Doctor Gregory. I can't think of it as Edward Morelle, not yet. That Edward could still be alive, and is the woman I've come to hate, seems too strange to be real.

I let out a low growl. "Keep her busy? What will you be doing?"

Sentin holds the scanner up in his elongated reptile fingers. "Wiping Edward's chip."

I nod, then wince. "I won't be able to put up much of a fight. Don't take too long."

Sentin doesn't respond. He's studying the wall that I've mostly cleared of books. After a moment he moves to a seam between two wall panels. He rips more shelves off the wall, then runs his long fingers along the place the panels join. Eventually, he shakes his head. "I can feel where it opens, but Edward must control it with his band." He glances at me. "Ready to break through?"

I nod.

He steps back a little. "One. Two. Go."

We both stagger to the wall rather than launch ourselves at it. I plow my shoulder into it, and feel the wood splinter and break. It gives way more easily than I'd expected, and I stumble a little, falling forward into the room behind the wall.

Hands land on me, pulling me further in. They yank me across the floor and slam me into the wall. My head hits something hard and pain explodes in my skull. My vision swims, and for a moment I don't know whether I'm upside down or the right way up.

Something crashes. More wood breaking? When my vision clears, Sentin's holding a broken board. President Morelle's shirt is torn and blood is dripping down her side. Behind her is what looks like a giant glass coffin surrounded by monitors and cables.

"Get up," hisses Sentin.

I'm lying in a section of broken wall, where Morelle must have thrown me. I drag myself onto four paws, pulling myself free of the wall. I feel like I've broken every bone in my body.

Morelle launches herself at Sentin, moving faster than I would have guessed possible. She slams into him so hard, he stumbles and falls backward. She lands on his chest and wraps her hands around his throat.

I gather myself, but instead of leaping on her, I stagger, then fall into her. At least I manage to push her off Sentin.

Though she's relatively small and looks deceptively slender, she throws me off as though I weigh nothing. I land heavily, more pain exploding through me than the fall deserves. Scrambling up, I lurch at her again, trying to swipe her with my claws. She's too quick. She dodges to the side, then throws herself onto my back, forcing me to the ground. Hooking her elbow under my throat, she chokes me.

Her feet are braced on either side of me, holding me down, and her grip is like iron. I struggle for breath, fighting to dislodge her, but her hold is too tight.

My strength ebbs, and a stabbing pain intensifies in my lungs. The more I gasp for breath, the more painful it gets. My head feels like it's going to explode.

If I die in my Skin, will my real body die too?

The world darkens and I feel myself slipping away.

Then the pressure around my throat eases, and I manage to drag in a breath that burns going down.

Morelle's weight slides off me as she crumples to the ground. Dragging myself away from her, I brace for her to spring up again and attack me. But she lies still. Her eyes are open, but they're staring up at the ceiling, not looking at me.

Coughing, and sucking in more air through a throat that's on fire, I stretch my nose toward her. I can detect her chest going up and down as she breathes. But now she looks like one of Felicity's robots. Her face is wiped clean of emotion. She's an empty shell with no consciousness.

Sentin is standing next to the glass coffin, the scanner still in his hand. On unsteady paws, I stumble to him.

The lid of the coffin has been thrown back. Inside is a hollow-cheeked, ancient corpse. The dead man's skin is a horrible, greenish shade of gray. His dry skin is puckered over his bones.

Sentin towers over the coffin, but my nose is much closer, and the chemical stench coming from the body is overpowering. So faint that it's almost undetectable underneath the pungent chemicals, I catch a whiff of human sweat.

The corpse stirs.

I jerk back, shocked, as the dead man's breath rasps in through an ancient windpipe, and his scrawny chest lifts. His eyelids flutter, then slowly open. His pupils look milky, but after a moment they seem to focus on Sentin and me.

How is he not dead?

Dozens of tubes feed into the coffin he's lying in. The machines must be feeding him and keeping him alive—though the word doesn't really describe the state he's in.

"Hello, President Morelle," says Sentin.

The old man stares at us for a moment, then tries to speak. What comes out is a phlegmy rattle, so he coughs and tries again.

"You wiped my chip?" His voice is so dry and scratchy it's hard to make out the words.

Sentin holds up the scanner where he can see it. "I did."

"I gave you that Reptile Skin," croaks Edward Morelle.

"You did," agrees Sentin.

"My biggest mistake."

Sentin nods. "One of many."

Edward's filmy white eyes close halfway, as though it's too much effort for him to keep them open. "Should have realized how ambitious you are. How ruthless."

"You're the ruthless one," I interrupt hoarsely, my

throat still throbbing. "You created an army of monsters. You brainwashed my brother and turned him against us. You made William kill Doctor Gregory, and he almost killed Cale and me as well. My own brother!"

The old man draws in a rattling breath that sounds so full of phlegm I'm amazed he's not choking. One of the machines is expelling gas with a long, slow hiss. I guess it must have kept his coffin full of oxygen. Now it's all escaping into the apartment, and he must be finding it hard to breathe.

"You stupid girl." Edward narrows his milky eyes at me. "You have no idea what damage you've done."

My anger surges, strong and deep. I let out a low growl. "What damage *I've* done? I'm keeping you from making the lives of Old Tritoners even more miserable. I'm stopping you from killing us and setting your knights on us. Without you, millions of sinkers might have a chance at a decent life."

He drags in another rattling breath. "I would have made things better..." He breaks off, coughing so hard that his frail body shakes. When he eventually stops coughing, all he manages is one word. "Deiterra."

"Deiterra can't be taken by force. Not the way you tried to do it." Sentin sounds as calm as ever. "A conquered population will never be loyal to a ruler they've been forced to accept."

"Need Deiterra." The old man says. His eyes flutter, then open fully, as though he's gathering all his strength to speak. "Make more Skins." He drags in another breath. "Skins for everybody. Skins to live in. Need less people, but second child taxes don't work. Skins do. No more children."

Shocked, I sit back on my haunches, then wince at the pain of the gunshot wound in my flank. Sentin meets my gaze, and I can see the surprise in his eyes. Guess he doesn't know everything after all. This is something he hadn't realized.

"You think people wouldn't have children if they had Skins?" I ask.

"You were experimenting with influencing thought patterns," says Sentin in a thoughtful tone. "I knew your intention was to control the population, however I hadn't considered you intended to limit procreation."

"A better world." Edward's thin, bloodless lips twitch as though imagining it makes him want to smile.

"And you'd get to run Triton and Deiterra however you wanted, with everyone programmed to do your bidding." I flick my tail angrily from side to side. "And what, nobody would die? All their human bodies would be encased in glass coffins forever." He closes his eyes in weak agreement, and I keep going, the words coming out in a rush. "But who'd make the food to get pumped into the coffins? Who'd manufacture the Skins for their privileged owners to use? Old Tritoners, right? We weren't part of your plan, were we? We're just the grunts who do all the work."

"Don't need human workers. Just machines." He coughs again. They're hacking coughs that shake his whole body and look painful.

"So why use human workers now?" I demand. "In case you hadn't noticed, your factories are full of them."

"You need jobs." What strength he had seems to be draining away, because his voice is becoming so quiet I can barely hear it.

"You think that giving us jobs is some kind of favor you're doing us? You made us into slaves!" I flatten my ears against my head, peeling my lips back in a snarl.

He lets out a soft sigh. "Only want the best for Triton. Old and new."

"No." I glance at President Morelle's Skin, sprawled on the floor. "Whatever lies you tell yourself so you can sleep at night, you have to know that's not true. You never wanted the best for Old Triton. Nobody's hurt us more than you."

He stares at me for a long time, his breath rattling in and out of his lungs. Though his eyes are milky, I can still see the sharp intelligence in them. He called Sentin ruthless and ambitious, but those are exactly the words I'd use to describe him.

"You're a monster," I tell him. "I don't care why you did any of it. You hurt everyone I care about. You deserve to be punished."

Edward's gaze goes to Sentin. "Something I don't understand," he croaks. "Why did you help me if you were going to betray—?"

Sentin puts his hand into the case. He clamps his long reptilian fingers over the old man's nose and mouth, cutting off what the old man's saying.

I jerk around to stare at him. "What are you doing?"

Sentin doesn't look at me or reply. He shifts his weight so he's leaning on Edward's face.

"Stop." I swat him hard with one paw. "You can't kill him. People need to know what he did. They need to hear the truth about the Skins, how they change people's thoughts. There has to be some kind of a trial."

Sentin stands his ground, his hand still clamped over Edward's nose and mouth. "There'll be no trial."

"Don't do it." I shove him with my shoulder, trying to force him away from the coffin. I'm so weak, I can't move him.

"It's done." Sentin takes his hand away. Sure enough, Edward isn't breathing, though Sentin must have had his face covered for less than a minute. Killing him took barely any time at all.

I stare at Edward Morelle's gray, lifeless face. The machines have stopped and the room has fallen silent. All the time I fought and struggled against the director, my hate built with each day. Now, his frail old body looks so small and weak, it's hard to hold onto that hatred.

My throat feels tight. All this time I've wanted Morelle dead, but now he's lying in front of me, I don't feel jubilant or like we've won. My stomach is churning.

"Why'd you do that?" I don't mean the question to come out so quietly, but the words are a whisper.

"Without his Skin, Edward was just a body in a case, unable to move or do anything for himself. When he transferred back into his human body, he must have experienced its pain for the first time in years. His joints were swollen and his organs had long since failed and been bypassed. The machines would never let him die, even if he wanted to. How long would a trial have taken? Did you hate him so much you'd want to see him suffer endlessly?"

I drag in a breath, steadying myself. Maybe Sentin's right and it was better this way, but I'm not sure it was his choice to make.

"Edward said you helped him," I say. "What exactly did you do for him?"

"To quell his suspicions and gain access to his experiments, I assisted his scientists with some mathematical formulas."

Can I believe what he tells me? Sentin seems to be on our side, but I wish I knew for sure. If only he weren't so hard to read.

I shake my head with frustration. "I've had enough mystery and unanswered questions. Please tell me what's really going on here, Sentin. What is it you want?"

"The same thing you wanted. To end his tyranny."

"But you've been planning this a long time. Since well before the contest started. Morelle's dead, so what happens now? Don't tell me you don't have a plan for what comes next, because you always do."

"President Morelle is not dead." His voice is calm. "The Skin is here and I have a scanner."

I gape at him. I must be slow in the uptake because it hadn't occurred to me Sentin might want to take Morelle's place. But of course, it makes perfect sense.

Finally, I understand why he's done all this.

If he transfers into the President's Skin, he'll have absolute power.

President Morelle is running Triton. She has a giant corporation and unlimited funds. The remaining knights are loyal to her. As soon as he transfers into the Skin, they'll be Sentin's army to command.

"Of course, President Morelle will immediately order her knights to stand down," he says. "She'll also order urgent medical treatment for your human body. Using the President's Skin is our only means of escaping this situation, and I believe it's the only way to save your life."

I barely hear him. The full implications are unfolding in my mind, and I'm struggling to catch my breath, feeling like the air has been punched out of my lungs. If Sentin becomes president he can change *everything*. He can make Old Triton safe and give sinkers a better life, providing them with everything Edward denied them. He can stop the war, or decide to take over Deiterra himself. He'll have the entire world in the palm of his hand, and he can decide to either crush it, or transform it and make it better.

If only Sentin weren't so impossible to read, maybe the thought wouldn't make me feel like I was teetering on the edge of a cliff. If only I could trust that he has Triton's best interests at heart.

"That was your plan all along?" I demand. "You did all this so you could become President Morelle?"

"Not me." His silver eyes blink very slowly. "You will."

* * *

Afterword

Dear Wonderful Reader,

Thank you for continuing Milla's journey. I've been writing this story for a very long time, and I'm grateful to finally be able to share it with you.

Milla's story concludes in the final book of the Skin Hunter Trilogy: *Skin Dominion*.

It's time for Milla to wear a new Skin, and this one will be the most challenging by far. She'll face temptations and trials she never expected. Her limits will be tested, friendships and love will be put to the fire, and Milla's actions will decide the fate of both Triton and Deiterra.

Finally she has the kind of power she never dared to dream of. But that kind of power only makes betrayal more certain.

When everything turns against her, Milla must sacrifice everything. But with all of Triton at stake, will it be enough?

- Tania.